Gates of Mars

The Halo Trilogy
Book One

Kathleen McFall

Clark Hays

ISBN: 978-1-7345197-0-9
Copyright © 2020 Kathleen McFall and Clark Hays
All rights reserved.
Library of Congress Control Number: 2020906050
Pumpjack Press
Portland, Oregon
www.pumpjackpress.com

1

"Please state your full name and occupation."

The voice is soft, soothing, with an undercurrent of authority but not threatening. Perfect for me.

I stare into the unblinking eye of the camera and think about the room full of security analysts and intel hacks listening in on the other side of the wall. Or the other side of the ward. Or on the other planet, more likely.

They're watching and listening like they need to be there, but that's really ego on their part. Halo does all the work. It doesn't need them, doesn't need any human at this point. Halo is monitoring everything—the dilation of my eyes, the pace of my breathing, the sweat gathering in the small of my back, the clothes I wore to this little inquest and why. It knows what I had for breakfast—mirror-gin and a squirt of nut protein on a square of kelp cake. It knows my debt (too much), the kind of avatainment I watch (also too much) and the day I will likely die and how.

Halo knows everything about me.

Almost everything.

Halo lives on data, and it's identified a gap in my story. But the biggest, most advanced AI the two planets have ever known can't piece together the missing data.

I need to keep it that way to avoid death. Or worse. Like being sent through a labor-loyalty reconditioning module. But the truth is I don't much care what happens to me right now. What I do care about is keeping Halo guessing about that data gap for at least twelve hours. That should be enough time.

It's going to be a long night. And day.

"My name is Crucial Larsen. I'm an officer in the Law Enforcement Corps, Labor Division, Multnomah Ward."

After a small pause, Halo talks again.

"Thank you, Crucial. May I call you Crucial?"

"Sure," I say. "May I call you Halo?"

"Of course, it's a common nickname."

Another pause, a learned pause.

"Crucial, were you recently on Mars?"

The pause is learned because the q-machines can do everything much better and faster than us, but Halo knows not to rush because speed tends to put humans, slow and sloppy, on the defensive. Sometimes that's a good thing, and Halo knows that too. I guess I should take pride in the fact that it's trying harder with me. Small victories.

Halo already knows ninety-nine percent of everything about my time on Mars. But it wants to know the rest. It's what's in the one percent that counts, what it cares about.

To be accurate, it doesn't care. The Five Families want to know the rest. Halo does their bidding.

From here on out, anything I say will be cross-checked with a million possible answers, correlated with my tone and vitals and eye movements, and compiled into a billion possibilities that can be tested and retested and analyzed for probabilities, and all of that in half a millisecond as it tries to get me to talk too much.

"I was on Mars," I say. "But you know that already. You can only leave Earth on the Dart, and you run the Dart.

Why don't you be direct and ask me what you really want to know?"

"Would you like some water? You are dehydrated."

"Water would be fine," I say. "Or something stronger."

"That's not allowed under the current circumstances."

"Exactly what are the current circumstances?" I ask. "Am I under arrest?"

"Of course not," Halo says.

"I'm free to go?"

"That's not the case either."

I shift in my seat and try to get comfortable. "Then how about a cup of tea?"

Tea, real tea, hasn't grown on this dumpster fire of a planet in gods know how long but they brought it back on Mars. Up there, I had a variety called Irish Breakfast. It knocked my taste buds back to childhood.

"Do you have a preferred flavor profile, Crucial?"

"Something smoky?"

"Irish Breakfast?"

Of course, it knew that's what I drank on Mars. "That'll do."

"Excellent choice."

"I'm glad you approve, since you have no taste buds."

"Sweetener or cream?"

I shake my head.

A square on the silver desk slides back and a steaming mug of tea lifts up on a silent pedestal.

There's a whirring sound as the optics adjust. The room brightens. It's planned of course. To signal that the time for pleasantries has ended.

"Why did you go to Mars, Crucial?"

I didn't want to go to Mars. I spent the first forty-one years of my life trying to avoid that very thing.

"To find my sister, Essential Larsen. She disappeared. I

was asked to help locate her."

"Did you find her?"

"Yes. But I was too late."

"That must have been hard. You spoke to your sister before she disappeared. When was this?"

I sip the tea. It burns the roof of my mouth. Halo can optimize temperature. This is intentional.

"About two weeks ago, give or take," I say.

It's a lie, of course, but it's a half-lie, which is the best kind because I might be able to slip it past Halo. I did talk to Essential two weeks ago, but it certainly wasn't the last time.

Halo knows about that first call she made to me from Mars. It was recorded, like everything else. It was the call that started the whole supernova of events that landed me here in this sterile room being questioned by an all-knowing godsdamned machine.

2

Fifteen nights ago

I like to sleep in the desert at night, without clothes.

The sight of the stars overhead, the sand under me still warm from the sun, the gentle breeze, the red rock cliffs lit by moonlight, the faint howl of distant wolves.

Wolves have been extinct for at least a century. And half the planet is an actual desert now—dusty shadows of dried up oceans and wastelands of plastic.

I'm pretty sure there weren't wolves in the desert, but I'm using a shitty, lo-jack plug-in that was sold to me as what a 20th century desert might look like at night. The creators may have sacrificed accuracy to keep the cost down. It's slowly punching up my debt, but it beats waking up to the dingy mushroom walls of my squat.

An incoming ving interrupts my red-rock desert dreaming. It's a high-end reality feed, with audio. It better be important because I already paid for the desert plug-in.

"Who?"

"Essential Larsen."

It is someone important. "Receive. Neck up only."

The desert falls away from my ceiling and walls into pixelated dust. A new column of data nudges into my scroll, flickers and arranges itself into Essential. She's full-framed and surrounded by grass and trees. I push the other feeds off to the side, even though it'll cost me to keep the ads sidelined. But she's worth it.

"Are you naked?" she asks. "You only headframe when you're naked. You know I hate it when you ving naked."

"Cut me a break. It's early here on Earth."

Essential won the Mars lottery. A few times every year, the Five Families hold a drawing to recruit new people from Earth to fill service jobs on Mars. They don't really need them, the Earthers, I mean. Halo and the robots and the computers can mostly do it all, and they already have an army of permanent-resident employees. But I guess they like the variety of new faces. Or maybe they feel guilty for what they left behind on Earth.

Nah, that's not it.

Whatever the reason, the lottery gives hope to the hopeless that there's a chance they'll get called up to Mars and have their debt cut in half.

Essential tried to get me to come with her on the companion ticket, but I want no part of their little pity zoo. Plus, I can't stand space travel.

She's been gone more than a month. I miss her.

"You'd like it up here," Essential says. "They have animals. Real, wild animals."

"So what? We have wild animals here on Earth."

"Rats and raccoons and pigeons and coyotes don't count," she says. "It's incredible. The stuff Mom used to tell us about. Bears. Wolves. And giraffes. Have you ever seen a giraffe? They are crazy looking. Strange and beautiful."

"They're cloned knockoffs. Not the real thing."

"The real thing is long gone and not coming back. And even if it's one step, or several, removed from bio-reality, it's better than that fake wolf in the desert plug-in you're addicted to." She pulls up a bunch of grass and puts it to her nose. "This is real grass, and it smells good. Like, I don't know, fresh and hopeful."

She is standing in a terrascaped park in one of the domes on Mars. I saw a park like this once during an avatainment special about early efforts to create an atmosphere on Mars. They haven't figured it out yet, so there are domes instead. For now, at least.

"I saw Melinda," Essential says. "She looks great. She said to tell you hello."

"Mel did not say that," I say. "Mars has already turned you into a liar."

Essential laughs. "You're right about Mel, but she didn't say you should drop dead either. I think she misses you."

"Pretty sure she doesn't miss me."

I wave the homecube over. It's an old square on its last roller and twice the size of the sleek new models. I should upgrade, but I'm too cheap. My debt is almost below neutral, and I'd rather spend my credits on mirror-gin and desert sleeping.

I select breakfast-three from the menu of options displayed in my scroll.

The cube rumbles and shakes and prints a rice bagelette, lightly toasted, with greencream spread and strips of smoked sheetmeat. It extends the food out on a degradable tray that immediately goes wobbly because the cut-rate material is never quite strong enough to hold the load. I grab it before my bagelette hits the floor. The cube rumbles back to the wall dock to recharge the food coil. And to subtract credits from my account and tell Halo everything about this latest interaction.

"Well, she should miss you," Essential says. "And you should be here with me. It's … interesting. I could use my big brother."

"Don't get yourself caught up in trouble," I say, taking

a bite. "Serve out your lottery contract and come home. It's just debt relief."

It might be the connection, but it looks like a shadow of worry clouds across her face, and that expression jolts a memory from our childhood.

When we were kids, we had it better than many. Not much, but a little. Essential used to save part of her meals and then slip out at night to share with a beetler. We had pretty good security in the building so she coded a program that fuzzed her location so Mom wouldn't find out. It was good code, but not good enough. The cops came and it took a month to work out from under that flag. Mom wasn't angry, I think she was even proud, but she could never say that out loud.

Just now, Essential's face looked the same as when the cops showed up at the door to talk to Mom more than thirty years ago. It's funny how that turned out, our responses to that interaction. She became even more rebellious; I became a cop.

Better to be on the right side of the badge, the side people are forced to respect—that was my thinking.

"I don't think I'm coming back to Earth," she says.

"Not coming back? Why? Did someone from the Five Families take a shine to you?"

Another ving comes in, this one from work. Tagged high priority, giving me seconds to break the ving with Essential before it overrides.

"I have to go. Priority ving coming in. I want to talk more about this, and soon. Until then, promise me you'll be good. Okay?"

She smiles but doesn't answer. Dammit, she's already up to something.

The priority ving bumps the scroll, pushing off Essential.

"Who?"

"Captain Calvin."

"Headframe and receive."

"Crucial, are you nude? Humans are so puzzling. Get your uniform on and get down to the station fast. This is serious."

3

The lift rattles down to ground level. From the 222nd floor, it takes a while.

One of the neighbors gets on with me. It's awkward because I can't remember his name. Or where he lives. Next door maybe? All I know is he's the guy with the broken sexbot. It's a high-end model, androgynous and very attractive—I saw him bring it home. He probably got it on the black market. He has sex every Sunday at 4 p.m., before the full labor shift starts, and the program gets stuck in the beginning, so it's forever begging him to "put it in me, don't tease, put it in me, don't tease" until he's done and turns it off. At 4:11.

He knows I'm a cop and doesn't meet my eyes.

I don't care. Unlicensed hardware is not my problem.

I call for a Cabarang on the way down and watch the swarm of activity on the map that jostled into my scroll.

At three hundred stories, my building—the Grover—is pretty small, one of the first built after the Fehrven family perfected myco-cement. Mushrooms. The whole damn ward is built out of mushrooms now. Light and cheap and stronger than steel and it grows into place.

The tops of some of the buildings have pretty good views when the wind blows just right and the smoke and noxious clouds move out.

Melinda had a good view. From her window, you could

see all the way to where the ocean once was. The last memory I have of her is standing there, arms crossed, her back to me, looking out the window.

I curse Essential for putting Mel back in my head.

I step out into the gloom and my goggles click into night-vision range. It's shitty outside. It's always shitty outside. The air smells like pickled cabbage and burnt smoke. I up the parameters on the goggles because the smog is so bad even though my scroll says the levels are almost not toxic. A better night than usual.

A hundred years ago, this part of the ward was a city called Portland. I know that because there's a holo-history feed forever shouldering into my scroll. I get debt-free access to this semi-secure feed because I'm a cop. Someone in the Five Families thinks law enforcement can do a better job if we understand the past. I'm not a hundred percent sure they're giving us an accurate history. And I don't really care. The past is only good for burying mistakes. I'd turn it off if I could.

But Mel liked hearing about all that old stuff and anything she liked was good by me. We used to hole up in her squat and I'd read off the scroll stories—it was locked down so I couldn't share it by feed. She loved hearing me describe the river that ran through the city, how people swam in it, and how some people had their own gardens. I skipped over the earthquake, the wildfires and the viral plagues. She didn't want to hear about death, just trees and the sky and free-flowing water.

Now that's what she does on Mars. She recreates all the things she loves.

Damn you, Essential.

The winning Cabarang is waiting at the door. The backup driver on the jump seat is so numbed out in his immersive game and 'tocin juice, he doesn't look up when

I enter. He doesn't need to. The Cabarang already knows where to go based on the ving with Captain Calvin. The driver's job is to take the wheel in the rare case of a software or hardware glitch. He's gigged, so it doesn't matter what job he does, only that he shows up where ever Halo assigns him each night.

From the sounds of it, he's deep in his own historic game immersive. He's a lumberman, cutting trees—he keeps muttering "timber" and talking about his axe—and building a log-cabin empire and sleeping with women and men and probably having a dry-gasm every few hours courtesy of cortical boosts.

A minute later, after the upward thrust, we stop mid-air, an enforced float status, as a VIP motorcade passes above on layer ten. Halo spools off images to everyone within visual range—it's a DuSpoles, a seven-year-old kid on his way to visit the ward's waste plant to give some diligent laborer the news she's been inducted into the membership of the family church, or she's won a trip to Mars or some other equally inane thing. All I know is scrolls across the ward will be cluttered with images from the "surprise" ceremony for days.

Not sure why we have to stop for the motorcade, especially since I'm on police business. No one has clearance for layer ten except the Five Families anyway. They say it's to make sure there are no threats—there are unsubstantiated rumors of a resistance—but Halo can see three moves ahead of everyone. I think it's to reinforce the difference between the royalty from Mars and the rest of us Earthers.

The floor of the Cabarang is clear, and down below I see beetles spitting out people.

Unemployment has been holding steady at about seventy percent for years. If you aren't lucky enough to secure an ongoing gig labor contract with housing, you can get a beetle from the ward—Basic Extreme Environment Transportable Life Support Systems. BEETLSS. Self-contained sleeping units that close up like pill bugs during the day. They keep the inhabitants relatively safe and cool, extrude a pouch of chalky meal slush, and then open up when the sun sets—like clams discharging filthy pearls—and fold into a little backpack. One last little gift of technology to keep the rabble alive after the Five Families pulled out.

By now, Halo has made the allotted gig labor assignments, so these beetlers are shit out of luck. They'll spend the night scavenging for food and handouts trying to supplement their meager lives, the hyper-poor begging from the poor. Or splicing into whatever free games help pass the time while convincing themselves that the ads for oxidized water and body-sheath armor in their scrolls are actually top secret embedded signals from Halo that their lives are about to turn around. Poor shits. Their lives will never be any better, only worse.

There's zero crime on Mars, and not much on Earth. Halo would detect it and then it's easy to track people down through their OCDs. Some of the beetlers break the law anyway—desperate I guess or just stupid.

That's where the labor cops come in. Me, in other words.

Break the law, lose your beetle, or if you're in the higher rank service labor corps—the Five Families' Earth administrators—lose your housing, but there's almost no one at that level who would take that risk. Why would they? The jobs come with pretty much everything they need to survive. And not much else.

But if you do break the law, the only way to get your housing or beetle or whatever back is to earn it, through labor. Free labor. Well, not free, because your debt doesn't stay neutral, it grows like a damn renegade myco-spore.

The tricky part is that laws change every twenty-four hours. Each night at the stroke of six, after gig assignments are made, Halo changes penal codes to meet the labor gap. For the next twenty-four-hour period, begging or loitering—which were perfectly fine the day before—could cost you your beetle. Begging is criminalized that night because the Five Families need more people to break the law so they get the free labor.

The police force, at least the labor division where I work, is basically a conscription force. We don't enforce laws, we harvest free labor after some poor sap breaks a law, knowingly or not.

It leaves a sour taste, but one person can't change Halo. A whole planet full of people can't change Halo. And it's better to be a survivor on the inside than a starving criminal scraping dried rat intestines out of the pest drones in a sheetmeat plant waiting to get their beetle back.

The Cabarang spits me out at the security station. I hear the backup driver whisper "timber" again as the vehicle returns to its thrower.

The station is built on top of one of the holdover cement and stone buildings from the last century. Useless. Doors and windows at awkward places. Made for a time when people worked during the day. Now, our structures are designed for night, when it's cool enough—most of the time—to be outside. Don't know why the Five Families have an attachment to these ancient structures, probably the same reason I have a mandated history plug-in on my scroll.

Opening the door, I nearly trip over an old man—my scroll autoprofiles him: Tippin, 54, in triple debt, cancer and diabetes—sleeping on the station steps. He'll be bounced out soon enough, too weak to work.

I take the lift to the thirtieth floor. The team is assembling in the break room, fifteen cops and a full squad of remote operators who'll run tech. This is a big operation.

Elbowing my way over to Captain Calvin, a next-gen anthrobot, I ask, "What's the emergency?"

"Fire at the central waste treatment plant. Many people were hurt. We need more labor down there immediately."

Robots can do almost everything, but waterproof robots are expensive. It's still cheaper to have humans wading around in the muck unsticking the clogs of fat and plastic that the submersibles can't clear.

"We've got warrants for ninety-three beetlers located in the Fields on various charges related to malfunctioning OCDs. Get geared up for departure in five minutes," Calvin says. "I want everyone to be on alert beyond the usual. We've picked up anomalous readings there in the Fields."

"What kind of anomalous readings?" I ask.

"Unclear," Calvin says. "It doesn't appear related to this labor action but stay alert and investigate on scene. Set weapons to maximum nonlethal."

We adjust our glitter guns and load into a tac-sleigh.

4

The tac-sleigh chugs into the Fields, a housing camp on the edge of what used to be—at least according to my history feed—the river running through Portland. Now it's a canyon filled with huts and shacks and trash and corpses and thousands of beetlers.

And they're the lucky ones, the beetlers, the ones who still stand a chance of being labor-harvested.

The unlucky ones, the ones chased out of the common areas, live on the edges of the dried-up riverbed without beetle packs. Families huddle under cardboard shanties and tents made from discarded drone jackets or temporary shelters coaxed out of stolen myco-cement—without the coding and ultraviolet resin, they'll degrade in weeks. Kids sift through trash, fighting over scraps of waste. They look more like animals than children, covered with scaly, scorched dry-rot skin. Without a beetle, no one lives past thirty.

It's not a pretty sight.

We're rumbling up from the side running perpendicular to the riverbed to cut off escape, locking in on the locations of the ninety-three labor warrants, the tac-sleigh shielded from electronic detection and a swarm of drones patrolling the airspace over us as we make slow but steady progress.

The tac-sleigh is an armored behemoth that could withstand a direct hit from a rocket ship. But we're never attacked—no one so much as throws a rock at us—so the sleigh is more about creating a sense of fear, or resignation, than anything else. The Five Families don't countenance challenges to law enforcement.

It's close quarters inside the sleigh and everyone is a little nervous. It's the anomalous readings. There hasn't been an anomalous reading since ... well, there have never been anomalous readings. Not even during the Consolidation Wars.

I was in the militias during the waning days of the Consolidation, drafted into the Tarteric family, due to Mom's connections. Lucky for me because they were one of the winners.

The story is that when the takeover battles started forty years ago, about the time I was born, a hundred or so global corporations were clawing for dominance. War broke out when profits dried up. When it was all over, five families owned everything.

It was mostly a mop-up operation by the time I was old enough to fight.

Toward the end, some of the actions were ridiculous. One of the biggest tacticals I took part in was the Pilot battle between the Tarterics and the Sounders. It was over a new product, a plug-in for the beetles. Back then, when the families fought, there were surprises because the new tech they developed in secret could be off the charts, but the various AI systems could still predict what was coming, or at least that something was coming. In the Pilot battle, the Sounders used swarms of nano-nukes nobody had seen before. The Tarterics retaliated with forced-air cannons that could punch a hole in a mountain—and did.

The Sounder family surrender included a few key marriages, a polite pretense of maintaining the bloodline, but the Sounders are now a wholly owned subsidiary of the

Tarterics. They're gone.

Everyone on the team tonight is a veteran of the Consolidation Wars, on one side or another. Maybe multiple sides depending on the pay, and so no one would be fazed by a technology surprise, or a new kind of weapon, but what's got us all spooked is there are never anomalous Halo readings. Ever.

It's the first time any of us have ever gone into a labor-harvesting situation without total clarity. I check again and Halo still hasn't told us what's anomalous, and nothing looks off. What the hell was Calvin talking about?

I see the same concern registered on everyone's face. I know most of these people pretty well. Almost everyone goes from a family militia into labor detection and enforcement.

There's Onor. His face is pinched. I once watched him take out fourteen mobile battlefield servers with an organic nuke that he planted under them with a seed rifle.

Two down from him is Brant. Brant is a sharpshooter. One of the best. She has optical implants synched to a rail gun on her exosuit. She brought down three base ships from six miles away without harming a hair on the heads of the crew. At least the human crew. When the robo-attack units came out, she dropped them like pigeons in a brown cloud.

Now that the Consolidation Wars are over, those kinds of battles are a thing of the past. Sure, every now and again, an armed negotiation plays out on Earth, but the Five Families mostly agree to stay within threshold expenditures. In the last few skirmishes, only two people were seriously wounded. Maybe three. And one fatality. He was crushed by a transport truck.

And of course, seriously wounded—at least to a point—means access to upgraded hardware. Medical benefits for the militia are off the charts, even those of us who are now veterans. I was in the Tarteric militia for six years and was lucky, although I saw lots of people get hurt, but that's what bio-enhancements are for. That's how Brant got her special eye.

Brant's looking through the walls of the tac-sleigh and I think she sees something bad because she turns her head a little and starts to say something.

Then there's a flash and the tac-sleigh comes apart.

One second we're sitting there and the next second the vehicle is split in two like one of those pop-top bread balls. The two sides are tumbling end over end and people and gear are being thrown into the sky. Someone is cursing, and I think it might be me.

The half I'm in tumbles off the edge of the Fields into the old riverbed and crashes through the huts and trash and people and shit, finally coming to rest in a cloud of dust and garbage against an old tanker. Pieces of metal are crashing down around us like a steel rain.

My ears are ringing and my vision is blurry from the force of the crash.

My straps hold but others aren't so lucky. Only half of Onor is in the seat. The bottom half.

Next to him, Brant is alive, but her armor got pulled away in the explosion and the force of it ripped the optical jack out—she's moaning and crying blood.

Status report, status report, crackles in my headpiece. But then that goes silent. The steel rain is actually drones dropping out of the sky. We're cut off and isolated, running blind.

I fumble out of my straps and slap the emergency response button. First aid bots, like helpful spiders, start pouring out of the sleigh walls, looking for injuries. One of them is trying to stitch up Onor's waist. It will stop soon because, well, he's only half of himself and what's a bot to do?

We were ambushed. Halo can see everything and it didn't see this coming. How is it possible that we were ambushed?

I hear shouting and see people peering over the edge of the waste river. People with glitter guns. They're not wearing uniforms. I check the charge on my own and flip the selector from trauma to terminal.

Glitter guns grow crystal ammo faster than it can be shot out on streams of compressed air, and it shoots about 2,000 rounds a minute.

"Get the package out of here," I hear someone yell.

I send a long hiss of synthetic diamond microneedles stitching across the skyline. The tiny flechettes are light as a feather and deadly as a saber, piercing through metal and flesh and bone and leaving glittering ends peeking out of the tiny wounds.

There are shouts and screams and I'm happy thinking that at least if I'm going to die upside down in a trash heap in a dry riverbed filled with two-hundred years of shit and body parts, I'm taking some of these colon-plugs with me.

Then I think of Mel. I really fucked up my life.

"That's him, fall back," someone yells. "Withdraw."

I hear more screams. Maybe it's Onor's upper half.

The bad guys—at least the ones that aren't dead from a face full of glitter—pull back. I start making my way up the steep canyon wall with two other cops trailing behind me. We hunch out of sight at the edge, then count to three and pop up, spraying needles at anything that moves. Nothing is moving. They're gone.

Our earpieces crackle back to life. "… the shinks is happening? Report. Report. Backup is on the way."

We make our way to the other half of the tac-sleigh. It's

on its side. I look inside. The first aid bots are massed around one person. They've given up on the rest. Their tiny arms are stained with blood, rising and falling and pinching and stitching and burning as they seal off ruptured veins and cauterize and squirt coagulant foam into a gaping wound.

Brant will live, but she'll need a new stomach. And leg. And hand. She'll be a badass on the other side.

5

Reinforcements—human and synths—arrive fast from the air and drop a containment fence around the ambush site. The fence is made of a razor-sharp lithium lattice with piezoelectric barbs. Until the rotor-birds spool it back up, no living thing bigger than a baby cockroach can get in or out, not in one piece anyway.

It's too late though. There's not a trace left of the people, or machines, that ambushed us. It's like they melted into the ground. I know I hit at least one of them, but there are no bodies, no blood, no bone chips, no parts. There are scorch marks though. Body-sized scorch marks near the edge of the river wall. If someone died there, they kindled their own corpse with a thermite ghost suit.

We heard of them during the Consolidation Wars. Some soldiers were contractors, gigged in with leverage on their families. They couldn't get caught or the debt mitigation policy was rendered null. They wore ghost suits to melt away all traces. I thought it was a legend.

Hard to find any usable evidence in a mound of ash. We'll try though. A rookie tips over a barrel of crime scene investigators. The CSI balls are the size of marbles, and each is packing a tiny lab. In a wave of metal glinting in the glare of floating arc lights, they're rolling and clattering and bouncing and measuring and analyzing every little thing. When they're done, they'll dump the data into Halo and tomorrow we'll know everyone who walked through this little square patch of hell for the last twenty years.

There are at least a hundred cops here now. Some of them are from the Heavy Ordinance Team. They're watching through the scopes of serious firepower. All the frenzied activity has driven the beetlers into hiding. There's one under every rock and trash heap we turn over, but most are just scared and hungry.

The cops on the scene are scared too, even though none will admit it. Outside of militia work, they've never been at the site of a civilian ambush before. If I'm honest, I'm feeling a little rattled. I slip back my visor and drip some booster drops in my eyes—caffeine and taurine and guaranine and all the other "ines"—to help take the edge off.

Whatever hit the tac-sleigh was big, and big things can't hide from Halo. Little things can't hide from Halo. It can detect a power surge in a boilpot left on a second too long when you're making noodle stew, and then charge you for that extra second. Or catch one extra slow down frame as you're blinking through the entertainment news and suddenly a hundred new avatainment stars are generated to crowd through your scroll, begging you to start a new series with them based on whatever you accidentally lingered over.

The fact that an explosive was waiting for us, along with armed criminals in a world in which every gun can be switched off from Mars, means something is seriously wrong.

Captain Calvin is broadcasting to the original arrest team. The deaths of most of that team promotes me to senior officer.

"Crucial, can you tell me what happened?" He sounds bewildered. That's not possible, of course. He's an anthrobot. Bewildered is not a skill it needs. That's my own filter I suppose.

"Negative," I say.

"How did this happen?"

"I don't know," I say. "They were shielded somehow."

"That's not possible."

"Maybe Halo is malfunctioning."

"That's not possible either."

"Maybe I'm dreaming then."

"I'm scanning your brain waves. You are most certainly awake."

"That was a joke, Captain."

"I'm almost certain this is not a time for jokes, Crucial."

An autogurney rolls by, carefully navigating the uneven ground and making its way toward the ambulance. It's got Brant. There's a bloody patch over her eye socket and she's pretty out of it, hopped up on gyth juice, smiling. She waves. "Hey, Crucial. You made it."

I walk along beside her for a little way. "Brant, what did you see? Just before we got lit up, what did you see?"

"I'm pretty tranquil right now and it's all kinda fuzzy but I'm almost sure I saw a guy looking right through the walls at us. Like he was looking for someone. He was looking right through the walls at me, or maybe you," she says. "And he had a rope for a face. It doesn't make any sense."

She starts to laugh and it turns into a rattling cough, and she spits out blood.

"Hang in there," I say.

"I'll be fine. I've already got a new optical jack picked out." She squeezes my hand. "Get this, get this," she says. "I've got my eye on it." She starts to laugh hysterically.

They're holding some beetlers over by a transport bus so I pull my hand free. "Good one, Brant. I'll see you later,

I'm gonna go talk to some of the suspects."

As I approach, they keep their heads down, shuffling around.

"Anybody see what happened?"

Nothing.

"We're taking you all in for questioning and anyone with outstanding warrants will have the privilege of working off your sentence at the waste treatment plant. The first person who tells me what happens, I wipe your record to neutral."

That gets their attention.

They all start screeching at once. Saying all kinds of stuff about coyotes and Mars and high frequency light beams. One of them, an old lady, is glaring at me, but she doesn't say a word.

She's tiny and stooped, as if the weight of even the life support pack is too heavy. I try to get a reading, but she doesn't have a functioning OCD. I point at her. "You. You must know something."

The glare hardens and she spits on the ground. "I know something," she says. "I know it's been a long time since I've seen you and your kind scared. And I know the worst is yet to come, and I'll be cheering when they take you and everyone like you down and jack the shuttle and crash it into the moon and leave those inbred milk thistles on Mars to die. Trapped like the vermin they are."

"Take all of them in for labor sentences," I say. "Except her. Take her in for chemical questioning. She was watching. And she doesn't have a scroll." I look right at her. "That's illegal."

She spits at me this time. It hits my boot with a wet splat. I pull a pair of electromagnetic cuffs out of my pocket—I never leave home without them—and toss them to the uniform. "Cuff her."

I watch as my visual files download to Halo, to see if I missed anything but there's nothing. The Captain waves me off, and I hitch a ride on the backup transport toward home.

I get out at a bar not far from my squat that serves sheetmeat barbecue with veggies if the garden bosses have anything to sell. And salt beer, I need a lot of salt beer right now.

The place is empty. I order a half sheet and three beers, then prioritize the news. My eyes are tired, but the display compensates. A building collapsed on the sixtieth parallel. Some virus in the myco-frame. An earthquake near the Sunbelt ruptured storage tanks filled with radium. A celebrity feud boiled over into the digital death of some three hundred pop-avatars. That's going to piss some people off.

Nothing about the Fields attack. Nothing.

The sheetmeat is good—freshly grown in smoke-infused nutrient jelly, then roasted with injected orange and bourbon barbecue. I savor it, and order more salt beers so by the time I walk home, I'm a little unsteady.

I strip and lie down in the middle of the floor and think about the people who didn't make it back today. The sun will be up soon. Before I can load up the desert sim, a ving bumps through. It's from off-planet.

"Who?"

The properties scroll in: Jynks Martine, deputy chief of security on Mars.

This is weird. And awkward. Jynks Martine is Mel's fiancé.

"Accept."

"Crucial Larsen. I'm calling to inform you of some some difficult news." She's pretty, in an annoying, obvious sort of way. "It seems…" She pauses. "My sensors indicate you're inebriated. And underclothed. Can you flush your toxins and maybe put some pants on?"

"I've got just the right amount of clothes and drunk on. What can I help you with?"

"It's your sister, Essential. She's disappeared. Her OCD blinked out about four hours ago. We can't find her."

That sobers me up quicker than any toxin flush.

"Do you know where she is?" she asks.

"No," I say. "I have no idea."

"She didn't say on her ving with you?"

It's odd that Halo didn't record where Essential was calling from earlier.

"Nope," I say.

"You need to come to Mars and help us find her. Or, in the worst case, find out what happened to her."

6

11:45 a.m., August 31, 2187
Multnomah Ward, DuSpoles CPU, Earth

"So, your sister was missing, Crucial. Is that why you went to Mars?"

The air smells like pine. No, wait, that's not pine. It's the sweet smell of a hot desert night. Fresh, a little metallic, sweaty.

Not a good sign. It means Halo has lapsed into the programmed mode for suspects and catalogued my private holo-preferences. This is no longer a friendly debrief, if it ever was.

"Mind if I smoke?" I ask.

"Smoking is not indicated on your data set," the synthesized machine voice says in the empty room. "Are you seeking to distract from our conversation, Crucial?"

The tone is changed now. More aggressive.

"I'm a little nervous, you know," I say. "Not used to being on this side of a questioning."

"Your bio-signs do not indicate nervousness," Halo says. "But we want you to be comfortable."

"Great. Can you get me a cigarette then?"

The door opens. A delivery-bot rolls in. There's a cigarette on the head tray.

I hate cigarettes. According to my holo-history feed,

28

they used to be filled with shreds of dried tobacco and people actually lit them on fire to inhale the smoke. Now they're atomizers filled with extracts of chamomile, clove and cannabinoids. Mildly addictive, mildly euphoric and worse, they make your lungs feel like numb flowers.

But I have no option. I pick up the cigarette and when I take a drag, it steams out the scented mist. I exhale and think of those old black-and-white movies you can only get in the avatainment archives.

Mel and I used to watch those movies together.

Oh, for fuck's sake, stop thinking about Mel.

"Your heart rate has increased," Halo says.

"Must be the cigarette," I say, exhaling a long stream of vapor and trying to suppress a cough. "Surprising number of people up there smoke. And they guzzle that Martian absinthe like mother's milk. Mostly the lottery winners. Did you know that?"

"People on Mars are happy. We don't see this in a negative light. But it seems you do, Crucial?"

Digging, always digging. Trying to trip me up. I inhale deeply. I need to be sure any anomalies in my bio-signs can be explained.

My training is kicking in. Probably the only good thing to come out of all those years in the Tarteric family militia. The first thing they teach you if you're ever caught is you can't beat Halo. Well, it wasn't just Halo back then. Each family had its own AI system. Sycamore. Angel Lines. Cloudstone. But eventually, the Five Families teamed up and now Halo reigns supreme.

You can't beat Halo but you can slow it down, force it into more computations, and that's what I need to do. Slow this down, stall. The key, the senior opps trainers banged into our heads, is always stick close enough to the truth so you don't trigger a bio-reaction. And always have something in reserve to explain away spikes.

"We are aware of your military background, Crucial," it says. "Do you feel guilt over your role in the Consolidation Wars?"

"I was following orders. Do you have any guilt?"

"I'm an operating system. I can't experience guilt."

"Do you think the Five Families felt any guilt?"

"War is never a preferred outcome," it says. "But sometimes it is unavoidable."

I take another drag. "Do you think that particular war was unavoidable?"

"This history is known to you," Halo says. "And reliving it is an unproductive use of our time together."

"Just to set my mind at ease, that we see history the same way, what led to the Consolidation Wars in the first place?" I ask.

It lets out what to human ears sounds like a sigh. It's all part of its bigger strategy, crafted to match my data.

"Really, I want to know, I mean I was part of it, but only at the end, and I'm not sure I ever really got it from a big-picture perspective," I say.

"Efficiency is essential for a functioning and healthy economy," Halo says, now speaking crisply, like a lecturer. "After global temperatures increased and the oceans rose, and as human populations were diminished during the viral era, an efficient economy required centralized control. The government from this period lost its ability to provide this for the people. It had to be dismantled."

I exhale sweet steam. "When did the Five Families colonize Mars?"

"The development of quantum rocket technology and q-computing allowed the corporate interests to create a habitable situation on Mars. But with thirteen rival organizations, and many more affiliations, there were too many competitors to exist in a stable, collaborative framework."

"And so, the Consolidation Wars?"

"Correct. After the Consolidation Wars ended, Earth was unified under Five Family control."

"Splitting the spoils of war?"

"That is an outdated expression and also inaccurate," Halo says. "Competition between such a large number of corporate interests was not maximally productive. The Consolidation Wars reduced that number to five, a perfectly balanced system. They established wards and the economy has functioned productively on behalf of the people of Earth ever since."

That is not the full story. At least not according to a renegade historian I met while I was on Mars. Her name is Lauren Valentine, and she's part of the resistance.

According to Valentine, long before the Consolidation, when people were worn out from the viral plagues, the big families used that moment to wage a war of words on the government to turn the people against it, to lose trust in governments, then the families used government soldiers to wage war on the people, and about at that time, the whole Earth got hot, oceans rose and clouds disappeared. These families then waged war on each other, which was really an elaborate negotiation over market and territory, until only five were left.

Then the Five Families used the spoils of war to take over the colonization of Mars, building a private utopia for the few. The few and the lucky and the obscenely rich.

But I won't say that out loud, of course. Just need to keep Halo talking and crunching data, that's all I have to do, for another twelve hours or so.

"What was Multnomah Ward before the Consolidation Wars?"

"The ward includes the northwestern coast up to what was once the city of Spokane and south to the Sunbelt frontier, and east to Line 110-A. There are twelve wards across what used to be the United States, and another twenty-eight around the globe. Each is overseen by one of the Five Families, depending on the industry to which its labor pool has been assigned."

I take another puff from the cigarette. "Fascinating. Forty wards, eight for each of the families. And the eight together make up each family consumer protectorate unit, the CPU?"

"Correct, but this is remedial information. Let's return to the topic at hand. Did you find your sister, Crucial?"

"Yeah, I found her. But you know that already."

"Is this why you attacked a giraffe in Baldet Crater?"

"Not really. I mean, I was in a pretty shitty mood."

"You blamed a giraffe for your mood?"

I toss the cigarette down hard enough that it cracks open and the flowery solution leaks out. "She never should have gone to Mars in the first place."

"She? You refer to your sister, Essential. Why did she go?"

"You already know. She's a coder. She was a coder. And a damn good one. A procking brilliant, once-in-a-gen coder. She won the lottery to code, but once she got there and the lottery council saw her in person—"

"She was very beautiful," Halo says.

"So they tell me. Once she got there, they gave her the option to work in the H-suite instead of coding."

While sexbots can perfectly match the needs of anyone, the elites of Mars like the exotic and in this case, exotic means Earthers.

"Did it upset you, Crucial, that your sister opted to take a position in the H-suite?"

Not in the slightest. Better pay, a longer contract, more connections. She would have been stupid not to. Besides, it's only sex. But there's no strategic value in saying that.

"Yeah, it did bother me. All those people using her like a sexbot."

"It appears you're not telling the full truth."

"I'm not lying," I say. I think about my first meeting with Mel on Mars to try to get my heart rate up higher than the smoking took it.

"Crucial, what is your relationship with Senior Scientist Melinda Hopwire?"

What the—?

Halo can't read my thoughts now, can it?

No, it can't. That question is pure coincidence. Halo is doing what it does best. Pulling massive amounts of data and asking questions based on the probable outcomes. Keep going, stay focused, I think. Dribble out a little more of the truth now, control the pace of this interrogation.

"That's a complicated story."

"Did Melinda Hopwire provide your immigration pass to Mars?"

"No. I was invited by Jynks Martine, deputy chief of security for Mars. Like I said, they wanted me to find my sister. But that turned out to be a lie. What they really wanted was for me to infiltrate the resistance."

"They tricked you, Crucial?"

"Yeah, they tricked me. And you helped. And because of all that, that's why I had to kill a giraffe."

Poor godsdamned giraffe. Beautiful thing. Nearly broke my heart.

But that's not all I killed.

"Let's start from the beginning," Halo says, its voice softening again. "What happened when you first arrived on Mars? And would you care for a replacement cigarette?"

7

Thirteen nights ago

The sudden appearance of the planet's arc as the ship breaches the atmosphere is like nothing I've ever seen—or imagined—and it stops my breath for an instant. We've switched to thrust for the final descent and the big ship is thrumming with barely contained power.

As we fly over the curve, my porthole fills with a red landscape dimpled with craters and swirling valleys. I've seen my share of red, given my habit of desert sleeping, but this is red in a way that's brand new. It's like a thousand different shades of red all trying to out-beautify each other.

I momentarily begin to doubt my convictions. Maybe Mars won't be so bad after all.

Esteemed Travelers, we will arrive at Port Zunil in approximately one hour. We expect no turbulence at this time, but please be alert to possible changes in flight conditions. We will keep you informed.

I climb the back stairs up one floor to the deck bar to get a better view of our landing. Deputy Chief of Security Jynks Martine saw to it I had a first-class ride on the Dart shuttle, and while I have no idea why I'm getting the family treatment, I won't waste it.

At the dispenser, I punch in the code for an orange whiskey, neat, and am pleasantly surprised when I realize it's not going to cost me a credit—*A gift from the Dart shuttle for our family passengers*—swipes across my scroll. Let's make it a double, I think. Drink in hand, I slip into a view body-slot. We're getting closer now, and the planet's features come into better focus. Rocky ridges. Crater scars. A circle of white, which I assume is the polar ice cap.

This far up, I can't see the domes yet. But I know what to expect, more or less, from the files Halo gave me, courtesy of Jynks. And everyone on Earth knows what the colonies look like on Mars, at least the scrubbed version of Mars that Halo lets through—live-time vid from the lottery winners hoping to parlay their five minutes of fame into a permanent avatainment feed. Happy people so pleased to clean up after the Five Families members—their smiling, benevolent bosses. In their off-time, the Earthers swim in fake lakes, read actual books in actual libraries, ride horse clones, and a bunch of other crap. All putting on their best face on the off chance they'll win the annual lottery and get to stay, maybe bring up their families, raise their kids on Mars. But that's a chance in a million. More like a chance in sixteen billion.

Still, it's a chance, and so Earthers go to the trades and spend their credits down into the far negatives to become eligible for the Mars lottery labor slots.

Attention, Crucial Larsen, the shift in atmospheric pressure may cause sprits to have an undue effect.

"Thanks, Mom," I say to the steward and code out for a second and third drink.

This is likely to be my only trip to Mars and I intend to

soak whatever I can from the experience until I find Essential. It will be my only trip to Mars because I hate space travel. Even first-class space travel, while it's pleasant enough, is still space travel.

Q-drives power the Dart shuttle from Earth to Mars in about twenty-four hours but because of the entanglement, it feels vaguely like you're in two places at once for the entire trip. It's awful. Most people droop out on pharmachutes for the ride, but that would mess me up for who knows how long. I'll stick with whiskey.

Even worse, q-drives are powered by ambiguity. They're only predictable most of the time. It's rare but every now and again a ship ends up going the other way for some who-knows-why spooky reason and then you have to double the trip. Eventually, one of the Dart shuttles is going to disappear and not come back. I don't want to be on that ship.

When I was in the militia years back, I had to go to the moon. Some crazy guy, like really crazy, was in the lunar asylum, and my orders were to escort him to Earth for dental work. At least that's the story I was told.

It's only a few hours to the moon, but the ship shimmied the wrong way, twice. We ended up way too close to the sun, and three of our solar shields failed. One more jump the wrong way, and we would have melted into little globs of space junk.

That was my first space flight and, until today, my last.

I sip my drink—it's good and smooth, not like that anthracite-filtered crap on Earth—and look out the window. We're coming into orbit and the sun is just visible over the edge of the planet, spilling golden light out across the red landscape.

The sun is really something to behold when it's not scorching out your retinas. On Earth, the sun is a constant threat. People like me, people who don't win lotteries, only ever think of the sun as the enemy.

On Mars, it's the opposite problem. It's too far away to heat things up. Out of the sun, outside of the climate-controlled domes, it's the cold you have to worry about.

I plan on devoting considerable energy to worrying about that.

The ship trembles and then shudders and then out-and-out shakes.

There is no reason for alarm. We are experiencing a normal landing. Please prepare for docking.

We're close enough now that the shuttle-rocket is deploying duality brakes. The domes are coming into view, some big ones and a constellation of smaller domes. There's the faintest glimmer of water, a river maybe, moving through a canyon base.

That must be the terraforming underway, remaking the planet to match human needs. First its water that's expected to take a century or so, then plants and, with enough leafy greens sucking up the carbon dioxide and spitting out oxygen, the goal is to trap a stable atmosphere.

If it all works, the domes will be history and humans can all walk around on a brand-new planet.

Some humans. The rich humans.

The rest of us will be stuck on Earth until it sucks in its last ragged dirty breath. Because Mars is and will always be a gated community.

8

The shuttle lands at Port Zunil, the first crater dome built on Mars because it was deep and small and easy to contain. They put a roof over it, then a roof over that, and then pumped in oxygen. Even though the first few ships lost someone every day, eventually they figured out how to keep the oxygen in and the cold out. Other structures grew up around it.

It's the oldest dome, and it's where the shuttle and other ships tether. Orbit elevators move people back and forth between ships and the surface. Freight drops in gravity pods. Like any port of entry, there's a mix of people. Pilots and crew and shippers arriving and laying over, and hustlers and pimps—for mechanics and sex work—to serve them. There's cheap housing for overnighters and short-timers, even cheaper housing for the service class, and a heavy security presence to make sure none of the undesirables try to leave Port Zunil for the real settlements.

High-speed lev-train rails branch out to the various settlements and you can't get on one of the trains without the right clearance.

Customs is pretty straightforward. Halo knows why I'm here. It knows why everyone is here. It knows what I packed, what I should have packed—the ads have already started choking up my scroll—and what I'll eat for dinner later. Or drink. And it pulled a med-screen minutes before docking to be sure I'm clean.

After I pass through customs, my scroll flashes instructions and I make my way to the lev-train platform.

I'm headed to the Jezero sector, the main settlement on Mars, where most of the Five Families live. According to my scroll, Jezero Crater, small, compact and filled with rich soil, was a perfect staging ground for the original Grande Dome. The Jezero Dome now covers most of the Plains of Isis.

I stop at a window and look out into the red, rocky plains stretching off into the distance. It's a rusty, dusty mess, with a few skimmers hauling workers and equipment to some of the smaller structures not served by the trains. The glare is intense.

I try to imagine where Mel lives.

She works for the DuSpoles family. They own the Intex-ADM companies. They grow the sheetmeat and barrel vegetables that almost feed Earth, and the gardens and game preserves that more than feed Mars. And they run the trains and spaceships and the maxis and pretty much everything else that moves humans around.

Mel is one of the rare ones—she was straight-up recruited to Mars to help grow the plants that will create the atmosphere. It wasn't even a lottery win. She isn't a family member, but she is formally under their protection. Kind of like being adopted, I guess. By the king. Or queen.

Essential's lottery win was for the Tarteric family and the ABC-Royale company. ABC-Royale builds robots and operates Halo. The AI behind Halo is the most powerful force on Earth or Mars. It's connected to everything, runs everything. That's why each of the Five Families has a representative sitting on the Guidance Council to make sure it's working as intended, and to keep it from getting too smart, moving beyond the program parameters and striking off in some strange new direction where humans aren't seen as a necessity. And to keep an eye on each other.

There's a supply shop on the way to the train platform. I get some booster drops to help with the rocket lag, a pair of glare goggles—there's no pollution on Mars, so even though we're farther from the sun, it's twice as bright—three airhoodies, with extra oxygen cartridges for each, and two thermal suits.

There are many, many ways to die on Mars. The top two are the cold and the lack of oxygen. For now, the atmosphere is mostly carbon dioxide. Without a functioning airhoodie, a human won't last more than a few minutes outside of a dome. And without a thermal suit, we'd freeze to death in most places while choking and gasping for air. I check my scroll. It's about minus 70 degrees Celsius out there. Oh, yeah, and there's that whole sizzling out from the radiation. That's the third way to die, I guess, but that takes a while.

I grab another thermal suit.

I'm stuffing them down into my bag when I see a group of people walk up.

"You can always tell Earthers on their first trip," a voice says. "Always so nervous and worried about oxygen."

It's Jynks Martine. She's got three officers with her, two human and one anthrobot.

"If you hadn't lost my sister, I wouldn't be here," I say. "I'm expensing these to ABC-Royale by the way."

"I would expect nothing less," she says. "But the Tarterics are happy to cover your credits."

I straighten up. She's all business in her security forces uniform, a glitter gun in a shoulder holster and sleek glare goggles pinning her hair back. She's even more attractive in person, tall and fit and confident, with clear blue eyes. I don't know what Mel sees in her.

I wonder if Mel told her about us. Probably not. I wouldn't have.

"How exactly do you lose a person when everyone is always accounted for all the time?" I ask.

"Probably the same way a squad gets ambushed in the middle of the Fields," Jynks says.

"You heard about that?" I ask.

She nods. "We all heard about it. Nobody understands how it happened." She catches herself. "Sorry you lost so many people. And sorry your sister is missing. There's not a single trace of her in a dome or out in the Choke."

"The Choke?"

"That's what we call the outside. We've been crisscrossing the entire planet with sniffer drones and nothing. If she's still on the planet, we'll find her. We hope you can help."

Jynks motions toward the platform. "We've got a short trip to Jezero. I've pulled together everything we have on Essential since she got here. I'll send it to your scroll and you can read the details on the way. Sit by the window. The Choke is beautiful."

"Any chance I can get a glitter gun?" I ask. "I'm feeling a little jumpy after what happened on Earth."

"You'll have a babysitter with you at all times, so you'll be plenty safe."

"I had a small army with me in the Fields, and I almost got cut in half."

"I'll ask," Jynks says. "But don't hold your breath." She looks at my gear and the airhoodies. "It would be a shame to waste all that oxygen."

9

We board the lev-train and Jynks steers me to a window seat.

"You're scheduled to meet with a representative of the Tarteric family as soon as we arrive which should be about thirty minutes or so. Want something to eat?"

My stomach is still doing flips from the trip across the universe, and food won't settle it.

"Nope, I think better when I'm hungry."

"Okay, tough guy," Jynks says. "Enjoy the view. I have some business to take care of."

She walks off toward her team.

I size her up with my scroll. She's 1.84 meters tall and 68 kilograms with 12 percent body fat. And she takes long, controlled steps, shoulders back, chin up—she's combat-ready and all in a killer package, a damn near perfect form.

Great, I'm drooling over my ex's fiancé.

I break my gaze away from her retreating form and catch a glimpse of myself reflected in the window. I look like cling-lint from an electrostatic toilet screen, with three-day stubble and dull, hungry eyes.

I focus on the landscape.

We're passing through a dome now, a little one. The ride is smooth as silk, and why wouldn't it be? We're riding on air.

Now we're going through a forest. An actual forest of

living trees. Straight, solid trunks, healthy, bushy leaves—planted in straight lines, a grid. We're sliding past thousands and thousands, hundreds of thousands, of trees—a perfectly symmetrical forest reduced to a flickering blur.

These forests, like the beginnings of the river I saw on the flight in, must be another terraforming tactic. They're engineered specifically for Mars to help reshape the planet to make it habitable for humans.

When they were planning the exodus, there were two camps—should Mars be modified to make it habitable for humans or should humans be modified to make them habituate to Mars. The forest we're passing through answers who won that debate.

The increasing density of the trees throws the car into shadows. I wonder if Mel had anything to do with designing these trees. Plants are her specialty. And living in my head, apparently.

"Mel's team came up with this species," Jynks says, taking the seat facing me. "She's really making a name for herself here."

"No surprise there," I say.

"I'm so proud of her. Nice to see her really bloom—pun intended. After all the years of ratshit she's been through."

"I guess she told you about us?" I say.

"Of course. Don't worry. I'm not the slightest bit threatened." She smiles a dazzling, convincing smile. "I mean, why would I be?"

Jynks turns her hand palm up and touches the subdermal on her wrist. A holo-map mists up between us.

"Let's get you familiar with the basic layout of Mars," she says. "The Five Families live mostly in Jezero under the original dome which, as you can see, is more like a series of smaller interconnected domes. The original dome has a diameter of about fifteen hundred kilometers, and max height of one-and-a-half kilometers. There are a number of other residential domes scattered around, and some smaller, more rustic settlements, but Jezero is the biggest." She zooms in a little. "It's surrounded by twelve smaller domes for the service class …"

"So, people like you and me," I say.

I watch her face. No change of expression. "We're not the same," she says. "I'm the second in command of the Mars security forces. Many service members live outside the dome, but we live in Jezero."

I guess I know where Mel lives now.

She changes the view. "There are two more big domes, one for security and another for science, and ten more on the outermost ring …"

"For manufacturing and agriculture," I say.

"You've done your homework."

She highlights the dome in the inner circle. "We are coming into Jezero from the west side and we'll meet your contact here, in the Tarteric Family Zone."

"Who's my contact?"

"Tarteric Hoost. He's the third-gen cousin of the original lander," she says. "And the sponsor of the lottery Essential won."

"And the one that funneled her into the harem," I say.

"Harem?"

"It's an old Earth term. Means a sex shop, only just for women."

Mom used to have all these crazy ancient books. On actual cellulose. One was a story about a guy who murdered former virgins, and no one seemed to care, until he met one who was good at telling stories with cliffhanger endings. Scheherazade. The ultimate stall, she told the murderer a thousand and one stories, and he didn't kill her because he always wanted to hear the next one.

I don't know how Mom ended up with those books. They were probably illegal.

All I know is I used to read the harem stories to Mel. She liked the idea I was trying to keep her amused so she wouldn't get bored with me. I was a better man in those days. Or at least more willing to try.

I wonder if Jynks reads to Mel.

She continues without acknowledging my response. Pure laced-up tight professional. A strike in her favor.

"Based on my understanding, Essential willingly accepted the offer to spend her lottery days in the H-suite, as it was a significant step up from the code work associated with the original lottery. Erased more debt and in far shorter time."

"I don't care about the sex. I care that she's missing."

"As do her clients. She was very popular and had multiple relations with powerful people. I understand she was talented. By the way, the H-suite is a shared resource across families, but given she was sponsored by the Tarterics, they are taking the lead on investigating her disappearance."

The light slashes through the shadows as we exit the forest, then move out of the dome, and zip back into the dusty desert.

Not for long though. Within minutes, we're entering the massive Jezero dome through a series of air curtains that keep the oxygen in and the carbon monoxide—and the cold—out. The lev-train slides past a succession of low-slung red-orange houses with tiled roofs. I can see a few humans here and there sitting on decks or soaking in steaming pools or stretched out on grass.

I think about life in my ward, the filthy streets and rats,

the flashing signs and eleven layers of fly zones crisscrossing, the beetlers everywhere. It's so damn quiet and peaceful here, it makes me angry.

As we continue moving toward the center of the dome, the houses get bigger and emptier. Space is a luxury.

"Each family zone has a distinctive architectural style, although everything is constructed from materials indigenous to the planet, so the variation is nuanced," Jynks says. "The Tarterics have ancestral roots in the southwest of the Americas continent, long before it was subsumed to the Sunbelt, hence the pueblo look."

"Clever," I say. "Good use of all that red dirt."

The train slides to an effortless stop.

Jynks catches my arm. "Crucial, the Tarterics are worried. That's why you're here. Sorry to have to tell you this, but they fear foul play. I'll let Tarteric Hoost fill you in. But I warn you, Crucial, and I say this as a, well, I guess we're not friends—"

"And never will be."

That was an asshole thing to say. I wish I could retract it. But it doesn't faze Jynks.

"That's probably true. But be wary, this may not turn out well. I hope I'm wrong."

When we get off the train, Jynks's team surrounds me as we walk toward the waiting drone pad. I'm not sure if they are confining me or protecting me. Jynks throws me an enigmatic smile as I slip into a drone jacket.

"Enjoy the crow's eye view. Tarteric Hoost will meet you on the other side of the water park. Coordinates are pre-set. The drone jacket will get you there in time."

10

The drone jacket lifts me up and I look down at Jynks. Her lips are moving and she's half-smiling. She's probably talking to Mel.

Drone jackets are short-range personal fly suits. On Earth, you can get them at rental pads on every corner for next to no credits, but they tend to falter at the worst possible times and often smell like sweat, or worse. Not so on Mars. It's a new, clean, fully charged jacket with plenty of power. It's doing all the work—avoiding other fliers and transport drones and all the various things that buzz around the lower levels.

Like birds.

They've got birds here, all kinds of birds. A brown one, with a wide wingspan and a beak that looks like a deadly hook, flaps by. It's a hawk, according to my scroll. Magnificent. A group of small birds follows, all white. These, apparently, are doves.

Back home, there are only three kinds of birds—crows, pigeons and woodpeckers. The crows and pigeons mostly stay low, looking for food at the surface, but the peckers are small and feisty and survive on 'shroomwood. It's a constant battle between exterma-drones and the flocks of woodpeckers. The peckers swoop in and chip away at buildings and then the exterma-drones spill out and try to zap them with short bursts of freezing nitrogen. The streets are always filled with puffs of shattered feathers.

From the train, it was clear the Choke is cold and desolate. Inside Jezero Dome, it's a different story—cool and shady, the air is fresh and sweet.

I've already climbed to at least thirty meters and I can get a pretty good sense of the place, at least this Tarteric zone. Bubbles of red buildings clustered together, a few tall enough to stand out like guard towers. But nothing more than a dozen stories tall.

I lean forward and drop down into one of the green spaces. There are small shrubs and a stream and more trees. I dip down far enough to touch the grass. A breeze blows—artificial of course—but it feels real and rejuvenating, not like our holo-feeds.

Someone nearby is having a picnic. A man and woman and three kids. Obviously, part of the Tarteric family. They've got a servo-butler hovering nearby, squirting wine into cups and spreading something yellow on little sandwiches.

A picnic. For fuck's sake, a picnic. They're talking and laughing. The little girl is singing. They have a puppy. With floppy ears.

It makes my head hurt.

On Earth, we're constantly buffeted by information, sales pitches and torpedo media and avatainment so there's never any desire for anything other than silence, for a little peace and quiet. For a split second, I envy their pocketed lives.

It passes quickly, though, because I hate them.

The picnicking nobles pay me no mind. I don't belong here, and it shows. My existence barely even makes it onto their scrolls. They probably have OCD filters to block visiting Earthers.

I bend my knees a little and make a motion like jumping

and the drone jacket takes over, lifting me up and away from the park. I look at the houses and the flower-lined paths and underused roadways, then I take it higher, way higher, all the way up to the ceiling of the dome.

I hover there, a half-meter away, and look through the thick sheet of resin. Up close, I can see into the Choke, the expanse of red desert. A lev-train glides by in the distance. A gravel-dredge lumbers across a low hill, paring it down as it gathers raw materials for construction.

I reach out and touch the dome's surface. It's warm, scorched by the sun beating down through the thin atmosphere, but that's deceiving. It's deadly cold on the other side, especially in the shade.

My scroll flashes and the drone jacket takes control again. Apparently, it's time to meet Tarteric Hoost.

It's a short hop to the rendezvous and the suit brings me down to ground level and then skims me across a field of flowers into a lovely park, with water flowing unimpeded through elaborately carved micro-canyons. That much clean water would be worth a fortune on Earth.

Hoost is waiting in a clearing near a waterfall. He's tall and distinguished, wearing an impeccably cut gray suit that sparkles and swirls with hidden accents. He has dazzling aquamarine eyes and a white smile. He offers a fist brush. I swipe my hand near his. My scroll can't pull up his information. I get a "personal content not accessible" message. I'm scroll-blind.

"Tarteric Hoost," he says.

"Crucial Larsen," I say. But he already knows that. Halo is giving him access to everything about me.

"I'm very sorry to bring you to Mars under such troubling circumstances," he says. "I trust the trip was tolerable."

"It was fine," I say. "No quantum sway, so that's a

plus." I wonder if he's ever been to Earth. And even though Halo must have told him I once served in his family's militia, he doesn't mention it and neither do I. "What can you tell me about my sister?"

"Right to business then," he says. "Good." He doesn't mean it. He's not used to hearing Earthers address him as an equal. Or a near-equal. Because we're not, but what do I care.

"As you have heard from Jynks's initial briefing, Essential opted to invoke the pleasure rider and took a short-term posting in the H-suite."

He scans my face and scroll for a reaction.

"You don't seem to be disturbed by this news," Hoost says.

"Why would I care what my sister does with her body?"

"Fair enough," he says. "Some Earthers retain twenty-first century views about sex. At any rate, she seems to have drawn the attention of a young member of our family. Tarteric Lloyds. His unhealthy attention, if you understand my meaning."

"I think I do, but what I don't understand is how my sister could disappear right out from under your monitoring systems, from Halo, on a planet with no place to hide?"

"That's precisely the problem we're trying to solve. Tarteric Lloyds has disappeared as well. We think he may have enlisted help from within, and that they fled to Earth."

"But all interplanetary travel is controlled and logged, there's a record, and any unauthorized craft leaving the planet would be tracked."

"Lloyds has access to a great deal of wealth," Hoost says. "One can do almost anything with enough resources."

"I wouldn't know."

"Please don't begrudge us our wealth."

"Why would I? Some people are born lucky. Very, very few people. The rest of us aren't."

A churning mass of fish gathers in the pool next to us, infinite shades of orange and white and black shimmering in the soft light. It's almost peaceful, except for the rage that now seems to be a constant within me.

I need to find Essential and get off this red rock.

His scroll is probably telling him my vitals are squirming.

"I've arranged a ride to the H-suite with our representative, Sanders. He's been instructed to give you full access and share any information you need."

"Can I have a glitter gun? I feel vulnerable."

Hoost looks at me with something like pity and surprise. "There's no need for you to carry a weapon. There's no criminal activity on Mars."

"Other than the disappearance of my sister and Lloyds."

He is irritated. I don't need my scroll to tell me that. "The actions of Tarteric Lloyds are not in keeping with one of his station, which is why we have asked you here. We need to find him, and your sister of course," he says as an afterthought, "before he irreversibly damages his future."

"Back to my original question, I'd feel more confident if I had a weapon. Just in case I stumble onto something worse than a youthful obsession with a woman below his station."

"I assure you, our security forces are up to the task of keeping you safe."

"Unlike my sister."

Hoost gives me a look that makes it clear we are never going to be friends. He gestures toward the end of the walkway with a sweep of his arm. "It was nice meeting you, Crucial Larsen. I am anxious for you to find your sister. We're all quite upset about this."

I might be more inclined to believe him if he hadn't instructed Halo to block his feed from my scroll.

11

The meeting with Tarteric Hoost leaves a foul taste, and I can't shake the feeling that Essential is in real trouble.

I breathe in hard and shake the dread away. Essential has gotten herself out of bad spots before—maybe not this bad—but still, she's tough and smart and I'm going to find her and give her six kinds of sunny hell for dragging me to Mars.

The ride to the H-suite is only a dozen or so clicks from Jezero, housed under its own dome. Hoost gave me access to his private train car.

The Tarteric family representative is waiting for me inside the train. He's young, probably not more than thirty, and eager, but not too eager.

"It's a pleasure to meet you," he says.

I get his basics on my once-again-active scroll. His name is Sanders Veetoo, his vitals are all perfect and he's calm and exceptionally healthy.

"Nice to meet you, Sanders," I say. "I understand the H-suite was the last monitored location of my sister. I need to understand how she could have gotten out of there unnoticed, either on her own or by force."

"It's not obvious how she could have disappeared," he says. "It seems wholly improbable."

"There's a lot of that going around," I say. "Why don't you explain the setup to me?"

"Of course," he says. "The H-suite is situated inside its own dome. From above the facility resembles a hexagon, with six sides and six separate entrances. Each of the five families has a private entrance. The service entrance on the sixth side is for the use of the people who work there."

"Let's go in that way," I say.

"I'm sorry but that's impossible. We are on the Tarteric lev-bed. This train goes straight through to the private dock located at its designated entrance. As you will shortly see, privacy is essential—"

I raise my eyebrows.

"My apologies. But it is an unusual name."

"My mother had an odd sense of humor."

I was, she would tease me, crucial to the existence of humanity. Essential was, well, essential to interplanetary peace and love, or something like that. Utter bullshit, of course. Mom was an odd bird.

"Privacy is required for discretion," Sanders says. "You can understand."

We're pulling to a stop inside an elaborate docking station with lots of glowing glass and tall plants—ferns, according to my scroll.

"Tell me more about the servant entrance."

"The service entrance, not servant entrance," Sanders says.

"A distinction without a difference here on Mars, I suspect," I say.

Sanders continues talking as if I hadn't said anything, which is what I'd do in his boots.

"The service entrance is accessible only by a custom air transport cube. Nothing else can dock at that port. The cube operates on an independent schedule, ferrying the lottery service Earthers in and out from a central location in Jezero, a non-repeating schedule maintained by Halo to ensure total security through randomness."

"Why so much security?" I ask.

"The Five Families are very wealthy and influential, Crucial, you must realize that. The security is to ensure no people with ill intent infiltrate H-suite."

"I thought there was no crime on Mars?"

"This existence of this system is one factor explaining that phenomenon," Sanders says.

"Is that how Essential would have arrived?"

I notice Sanders has a two-day stubble. A little salt-and-pepper beard. Nothing else about him, from the tri-colored hair down to the white boots, is disorderly. Why the stubble?

"Correct. After she accepted the upgrade employment offered upon her arrival when her exceptional physical appearance was noted, the shuttle moved her to H-suite, where she took up residence. It's luxurious, I'm told, although I've never been in the residential quarters myself. But many of the lottery winners also choose to keep quarters in other domes for the sake of variety."

"So, the cube is the only way in or out for the sex workers," I say.

"Their actual title is hospitality laborer."

"My actual title is accuracy enforcer. What about the trains? Could she have slipped out on one unnoticed, or been taken against her will?"

"The hospitality laborers are not permitted on family trains, unless a specific dispensation has been obtained, which only Halo can grant. There is no record of that happening. She would have been detected immediately through her OCD, and the train would not have been permitted to leave."

"Could a member of the families override the system if her OCD was blocked?"

"In a sense, I suppose. No one has authority to disable the system, but higher-ranking members can request reclassification of monitoring. The system collects the information, but it is stored under Elite Protocols, meaning it is only available upon request, and then only by those of sufficiently superior rank."

"So, Lloyds might have pulled some favors to go dark, and if he did, those files exist."

"It is unlikely Tarteric Lloyds would have that kind of sway," Sanders says.

If what Tarteric Hoost said was true, that an obsessive attachment of a family member to Essential is behind all this, then this tracking system is a slam dunk to solving this case. Why hadn't Hoost told me that himself? Or more to the point, why was he going through the sham of letting it seem like his underling was mistakenly revealing this information?

"I need to chase down every lead," I say.

Sanders looks at me blankly.

"I need access to the Elite Protocols for the time frame after Essential went missing."

"That may not be possible," he says.

"This is Mars. Anything is possible."

The train doors open. "Follow me, please," Sanders says.

We enter a shadowy corridor. Inside, a soft wind blows. It's warm, but not hot. The breeze makes a gentle whistling sound. The smell is something sweet, mild and earthy—I can't place the scent but it's pleasing. In a few feet, we come to a sliding door.

"I've taken the liberty of programming our session," Sanders says.

"Our session?"

"Master Tarteric thought it would be useful for you to

have the entire experience."

"How is it programmed?"

"Every user can program the environment as they wish. But for first-timers like you—"

"But not you? Wait, I thought you said you'd never been here before?"

"I said I had never been to the hospitality laborers' residential quarters. However, on rare occasions, Master Tarteric provides a visit to the common rooms as a gift, a recognition of loyalty and service. It's a useful learning opportunity."

I laugh.

"As I was saying, for first-timers, Halo does a check of your background. Based on this data, it then programs a comfortable environment, adjusting and perfecting this in real time contingent on your biological responses."

"If my heart rate goes up, or I get an erection, then Halo assumes I like it?"

"Crudely put, but yes. With greater familiarity, a visitor can privately input data to develop unique fantasy situations."

"Every sex worker in here is human, right?"

"Correct. As you undoubtedly know, artificial sex can be quite physically satisfying, but there are many emotional and intellectual intangibles inherent in human sex."

That's an odd way to put it.

Pretty sure the only reason wealthy Martians think sex with Earthers is better than sex with robots—or each other—is because Earthers don't all look the same. In a world where perfection—assembled in a factory or shaped under micro-scalpels—is tiredly attainable, there's something exotic about variations and flaws of a natural form. Plus, only Earthers can feel insecure. Sex for the Five Families is about power, control and boredom.

Sanders touches the door and it slides open to a desert on a wide-open moonless night. A spray of stars washes across a dark and tender sky. A night bird is cooing and whistling. A wolf howls in the distance. The environment looks like what I manifest on Earth, where I sleep naked in the desert but about a hundred versions better. The quality, the sense of amplified reality, is stunning. I'm lost in it for a few seconds.

A beautiful woman wearing a loose-fitting dress brings me a whiskey, double, neat.

Not bad, Halo, well-played.

"Where is everyone else?"

"Other visitors are hologrammed into their specified unique experience, but fully masked from one another," Sanders says.

"Can the workers see all the visitors and each of the curated environments?"

"Yes. It's considered appropriate training for each hospitality laborer to understand the desires of any visitor, even if only as an observer."

To my left, two women embrace, one with her back to me. In this light, I can't make out the features, but as I watch, the taller one facing me kisses the breasts of her partner, then moves her mouth down her body, gently separating her legs. Shit, the tall one looks like Jynks.

This just got weird.

I drain the whiskey.

"Turn it off," I say.

"Why?"

"Turn it off. Shut it down. And bring out the one person here who knew Essential best," I say. "Halo knows who that is. Do it now."

The lights flicker and brighten. Without any holograms, the room is a naked series of screens and data-responsive metal, mostly gray. I smell a lemony scent and turn.

There's a girl who doesn't look much older than a teenager, with pink and blue hair. She's mostly naked with the same dye job down below and glittery paint across her breasts with tiny jewels circling her nipples.

I touch her shoulder to see if she's real.

She's warm and soft and trembles at my touch, but her eyes give away an angry kind of boredom. She's real all right.

"This is Tashi," Sanders says.

I try to fist brush, but she leaves me hanging.

"You knew Essential. I'm her brother."

Her eyes narrow and flicker to either side. I've got her vitals on my scroll. Pulse and respiration and blood pressure. It looks like fear, but I can't tell if she's scared of me or something else.

12

"Tashi knew your sister?"

"Do you mind if I stand up and stretch my legs?" I ask.

"Of course, Crucial. As previously noted, we want you to be comfortable."

"Tashi and Essential shared a room," I say. "I think they were friends."

The secret to telling a convincing lie is believing it. Hold fast to that. Always. They were friends. More than friends, it turned out.

"Essential was not in service at H-suite for long. She must make friends very quickly," Halo says.

"She's always been good at that. Me, not so much." I walk over to the window and it lightens as I approach, giving me a view out into the ward. The sky is choked with jump cars and fliers and exterma-drones chasing those damn woodpeckers.

"What's it like out there now?" I ask.

"The toxin level is approaching LD1."

"A lovely night," I say. "I got used to breathing all the clean, pure, synthetic air on Mars."

"Do you feel resentful about that?"

I shrug. "A little. They kind of left us holding the cable

60

here."

"Do you think Tashi shared your negative feelings?"

I sit back down and drum my fingers on the armrest of the chair. "I don't know. She was a good kid. She didn't have much time left on her lottery contract. Did a good job there in H-suite, it seems. She had supporters. Probably could have made a life for herself on Mars. Or merged with an administrator here on Earth and lived in a mushroom penthouse."

"What happened to her was unfortunate."

"You have a way with words."

I'm letting my anger simmer a little, keeping the fires burning. It's good for the dataset Halo is building, but my thoughts are a mystery to Halo. It can make a bunch of educated guesses, of course, but luckily, the human mind remains a shadow inside a question mark.

Advantage humans. Even with all the q-computing and AI technology, no one has ever been able to breach the human mind, just the indirect biological cues correlated to thoughts and emotions. And actions and behaviors that can be predicted with eerie accuracy. But spontaneous, irrational acts are the bane of the Halo system.

Right now, it's good for them to think I'm angry. And after seeing what life on Mars is like, what life on Earth could be like, they're not wrong.

"Tashi said Essential was favored by Tarteric Lloyds," Halo says.

"That's what she said."

"Is this him?" Halo asks.

There's a flicker and an air screen materializes, showing a detailed image of a young man and some vital stats.

Tarteric Lloyds. Age: 24; Height: 170.1 cm; Weight: 72.6 kg.

He's not a bad-looking guy, but he has that scrubbed

clean, slightly overinflated look that makes it clear it took some laser work to get him there.

"You have the same data I have," I say. "But, obviously, I never met him in person."

"Would it cause you distress to watch some video we have of them together?"

"Guess it depends on what they're doing."

The image of Lloyds shimmers away, replaced by a clip of him on top of Essential, humping away, her arms around him.

Apparently, sex used to cause a lot of problems in the old days, what with half the world wanting to fuck all the time, and the other half wanting to fuck all the time while hiding it from everybody else. And there was a whole weird hang-up about same-sex partners and gender.

Sexbots and the eclipse of the judging religions by the prosperity religions mostly put an end to that. Still, it's not great watching some entitled prim squirming around on your sister.

But I know Halo is straight up fishing now. That's probably good.

"That's enough," I say, feigning disgust.

"Sorry, Crucial. But this is Essential, right?"

"Yes. Unless you got some bot gussied up to look like her or faked the imaging."

"This is not a bot nor a fake. And we have her vitals recorded as well. She had multiple orgasms. She seemed to enjoy herself."

"He doesn't exactly look bored."

The image flickers and is replaced by a scene of Essential and Tashi lounging on a couch and holding delicate glasses of pale red liquid—Martian absinthe. A bottle sells for a half-year of credits on Earth.

Essential and Tashi are laughing and intertwined and

relaxed in that way girlfriends have. The image of them together causes my heart to stop a little, thinking about what came next.

Hidden from their view, Lloyds is watching them. He's standing behind a curtain, his face pinched tight like a drone blade, fists clenched.

"The lurking figure is Tarteric Lloyds. His blood pressure is very high in this clip. As if he is angry."

"Or jealous," I say.

Lloyds wasn't jealous.

The key to selling a lie is believing it.

13

Still thirteen nights ago

"Is there someplace we can talk?" I ask.

"Let's walk in the gardens."

Tashi points to a door and starts walking.

I don't budge. She senses that and pauses. "What's the problem?"

"Could you put something on?"

She looks down, then back at me, and shrugs. "You don't like what you see?"

"Oh no, I like it. A lot. But I don't want to spend all my time distracted by your—how shall I put it—your beauty. I'd prefer to have a regular conversation, like regular-clothed humans."

She touches her bracelet and a body sleeve grows around her. It's aquamarine and sheer, with iridescent highlights at her waist and around her breasts that somehow makes her look even more naked.

"Better?"

"Not really. You look like a throwback sexbot in a pawnshop basement."

She shakes her head. "Essential was right. You're boring and a pain in the booster."

"So, you knew her pretty well then."

Tashi laughs, the first real response since we met.

"How old are you?" I ask.

"Older than I look," she says. "The youth thing is valuable in a place like this."

We start moving toward the door and I catch Sanders by the arm. "Give us some privacy."

It's a nonsensical thing to say. The concept of privacy died in 2042 when the International Surveillance Protocols were passed. A lot of people died in those riots. They were the lucky ones.

"What shall I do in the meantime?" Sanders asks.

"In the H-suite with your boss's pass? Use your imagination. That young man over there has been smiling at you ever since we walked in."

Tashi holds the door and we step out into an open space. There's grass up to my knees, and graceful deer grazing by a stream. One of them pauses to look up at me, chewing methodically.

A peacock walks by, its tail fanned out. The colors match Tashi's clothes.

There are rabbits and brightly colored parrots perched in blossoming trees.

"Nice, right?" she says.

I nod, a little breathless. "How do they … all these animals? They don't exist anymore."

"They make them here, from scratch. Geneticists. You'd be amazed at what money can buy."

"No, I wouldn't," I say. "What can you tell me about Essential?"

She takes my hand and squeezes. "I'm so sorry. She's incredible. So smart and kind. And nice to me. We started together, came up on the same rocket."

We sit down on a bench. She's still holding my hand. Still squeezing it.

"So, what can you tell me about this Lloyds character?"

"I never met him," she says, relaxing her grip for a

second, then squeezing again.

"I thought he came around all the time."

"That's what they told me," she says. "But those were always private sessions." She relaxes her grip.

All this hand squeezing—she's trying to tell me something without Halo noticing. It's almost impossible to share information in confidence. Halo passively monitors everything, even the way she's squeezing my hand, so she's being careful.

"She didn't notice him acting, you know, weird or possessive? Did she ever mention that he made her nervous?"

Tashi resumes the pressure. "No, but I heard he was a little obsessed. It's understandable. She is very pretty."

She releases the pressure. She is pretty, not was pretty. I think Tashi is trying to tell me something.

"Got it," I say. She knows the message was received and hopefully Halo is none the wiser. "When was the last time you saw her?"

"Three days ago. She was going into Holden for a liquid symphony concert. We were supposed to have dinner that night. She never came back."

I wonder, is that where Essential was when she vinged me?

She turns to face me. "Crucial, I really liked her. But she's gone." Tears glitter in her eyes. "You have to understand that." She takes my hand again and squeezes so hard my fingers hurt. "You have to let her go. Don't do this, don't torture yourself."

"You've been very helpful," I say. "If you think of anything else, ving me."

She is looking deep into my eyes, searching.

"I'm sorry she's gone too, but I've made my peace with it. It hurts my heart, but things are different on Mars. You'll see. You'll come to accept it," she says.

"People don't disappear on Mars. Or on Earth."

Tashi nods. "I know, but there's a lot of cold, empty space between the two," she says.

A peacock screeches. I realize why this is so unsettling. There's no traffic, no ads, no fliers, no other people. The silence is alarming. My scroll has gone almost quiet. Why?

"Are you saying you think she disappeared in transit? If she got dumped in space, someone is going to pay for it. And I don't care what his family name is."

Tashi shakes her head. "I'm saying we might never know, and that has to be okay."

"She's my sister. I won't give up."

"That's what I'm afraid of."

I stand suddenly and the deer watch me curiously, then continue eating. "Can you show me her room?"

She nods. "We shared a room. Come on."

Tashi leads me back inside and up a set of stairs to a series of residential suites looking out over the Choke. "Essential stayed on this side," Tashi says, pointing at a bed that's bigger than my entire squat. There are clothes and jewelry and instatainment screens scattered across every spare surface, including the bed. Some things never change. Essential has always been a slob. An "Ess-plosion" Mom called it.

"We slept in my bed," Tashi says.

I merge my scroll with the instatainment screens. The first one that slides in is a popular soap opera, an Earth girl living in a beetle meets one of the Singhroys by chance at a church event—the Singhroys own the AmaDis Corporation that runs health and entertainment—romance and happiness ensue and they get trothed and move to Mars and live happily ever after.

It's bullshit. AmaDis churns this stuff out to make it

seem like Earthers have a shot at the good life on Mars.

It's also not something Essential would ever immerse. Tashi is watching me closely. Something is going on here that doesn't add up. And Tashi is in on it.

"How can I get my hands on her list of clients?"

Tashi shrugs. "My guess is not easily. It's the Five Families."

I ving Jynks. She looks relaxed. At home maybe. She's got the feed close-cropped, which means someone is near. Probably Mel.

"What do you want?"

"I need access to Essential's clients the last days she was here."

"They're locked down and encrypted," Jynks says.

"You're the deputy chief of security. Are you saying you can't access those files?"

She furrows her brow. "Of course I can. But only in person."

"Great. See you soon."

"I'm in the middle of something."

"Yeah, me too. Looking for my sister, who disappeared on your watch. I'll wait right here. Don't take too long. The families will be pronked if they can't get their cuddles in."

I disconnect and Tashi is smiling. "You have a special knack for being annoying."

She offers me some Martian absinthe. The red liqueur is beautiful to behold and tastes even better. Smooth and spicy. I'm barely into my third glass when Jynks storms up outside with three officers in tow.

14

I don't need my scroll to tell me Jynks is irritated. She's voice commanding logs to download and tapping her trigger finger on the tabletop. I wonder if she was eating a meal with Mel. Or something else. The thought of interrupting them makes me smile. That, and the Martian absinthe.

"I'm not sure why this is an emergency," Jynks says.

Halo is locked down tight, and the location requirement for access is only one of dozens of security protocols. Jynks has already navigated thirteen hurdle points to get close to the list, and we still aren't done.

"Override, Jynks Martine, Security," she says again.

"Overriding. Please confirm with optical scan," Halo says again.

It's always weirdly interesting to hear the voices Halo selects for various people. The voice for Jynks in this situation is stern but friendly and sounds vaguely like Mel.

We are in the main control room of the H-suite. Jynks leans forward and lets the scan lines sweep her eyes.

"That should do it," she says.

There's a flat beep, another block. No sultry voice this time. Jynks swears under her breath and reads another request on the fixed screen in the room. "Yes, dammit, I want to proceed with the request," she says.

"Please confirm with—"

There's a clunk and a flicker. The lights dim across the H-suite as the screen fades to black. "What in the dark matter is going on?" Jynks accesses the external feeds and shares her scroll, displaying the images for us all to see.

The source of the disruption is clear. There's a hover outside, above H-suite. And it's got a massive air cannon poking from its snout, aimed right at the pleasure dome.

Jynks is shouting for backup and her crew already has their glitter guns out. I'm feeling decidedly unprepared to be stitched up in a needle duel on Mars.

I'm splicing Jynks's scroll, and one of her feeds, flickering with static, is in the garden. The deer are terrified, the peacocks are trying to fly but dragging their tails. Tashi is crouching down by the waterfall, eyes wide. The roof is damaged and dropping bits of debris. The air cannon on the front of the hover shifts and belches out another pulse of concentrated air that shakes the whole building and blows a hole in the dome.

It's chaos in the garden as the thin, cold air rushes in. "They're after Tashi," I say and run toward the garden. She's the one lead I have, and I'll be thundered if these polyps get their hands on her.

Jynks is right behind me, gun up and shouting orders.

We make it downstairs past the workspaces. Sanders is standing by the door, curious about the disturbance and surprisingly unconcerned with his own safety. The young man with him is definitely concerned. He's half in the closet, burrowing into a pile of clothes. There's a bottle of absinthe tipped over, leaking red drips onto the mattress and a tray with cheeses and grapes, a thin knife on the edge. I try to remember if I've ever had a grape, a real grape. Or real cheese, for that matter.

"Crucial, get behind me, quickly!" Jynks yells. "You're unarmed."

She makes a good case.

She's at the door to the garden, looking at the damage on her screen. The dome is self-healing and a swarm of repair bots is already click-clambering up the slick sides, spraying repair foam into the hole. The foam is swelling and hardening and closing the damaged area. The differential is pulling oxygen out though, replacing it with unbreathable air. Birds are dropping, choking. The deer are bug-eyed and panting. Tashi won't last long. Her aquamarine second skin is gleaming in the small hurricane of dust and shreds of plants and peacock feathers.

The hover is still anchored above the apex of the garden dome. I know Jynks is thinking about the precise steps needed to open the door, get into the garden and unleash a volley of diamond flechettes to bring it down before they use the cannon again. It's what I would do, if I had a gun.

I move to the side so the three officers can line up behind her for a hot entry.

Jynks takes a deep breath, throws the door open and steps into the garden, gun raised and finger on the trigger, her people right behind her. Before she can shoot, they hit us again with the air cannon. The force of it shatters the healing foam and sweeps it away, scatters the bots on the outside and blows all five of us back, tumbling like trash leaves into the hallway and across it.

My ears are popping and I'm rattled, but Jynks and her officers take the brunt of it. She's knocked straight into the back wall and is half under a tumbled couch, unconscious with blood trickling from her nose. Her people rattle away like pachinko balls up and down the hall.

I stagger over to Jynks. We're in the same room as Sanders—now he's dazed and slumped across the absinthe-stained mattress, not moving. His partner is pulling the closet door closed to hide. He nods behind me, a warning, as he shuts the door and I turn to see people dropping down into the wreckage of the garden from the hover. They're wearing drone jackets and are packing serious tactical rifles—rail guns from the looks of them, capable of turning an unarmored human into paste with one tiny slug—and glitter guns and thermites. That kind of hardware would cost a small fortune, and the ammo would cost another small fortune. And hiding it from Halo would cost a third small fortune.

But hiding from Halo isn't supposed to be possible.

Tashi is gasping for breath and one of them drops an airhoodie over her, then drapes her with a thermablanket and, holding her close, leaps up into the hover. I can feel the air thinning and my lungs starting to scream.

One of the intruders walks into the hall. I can't tell what's under the gear, but I think it's a man. A man with a very large rail gun. One of Jynks's cops is struggling up and the attacker fires a round. The cop is shielded, but the force is insane, knocking her thirty meters down the hall. She'll live, but she'll need some new ribs. And a new set of lungs.

The intruder turns his attention to Jynks. She's still out of it. He aims at her head. From this range, the slug will vaporize her skull.

He pushes the visor back on his combat helmet so he can be heard. "We're sending a message," he says, finger on the trigger.

Great. I've been on Mars for less than a day, and I'm about to let my ex-girlfriend's fiancé die in a shoot-out.

"Here's your message," I mutter. I've got the cheese knife in my hand and I'm not really thinking. I lunge forward and jam it into his cheek. Today's combat lesson: never raise your combat visor when you're in battle.

He howls and blood sprays out like a ruptured fuel line and he claps his hand on the wound, dropping the rifle. He staggers up into the air, the drone jacket lifting him toward the hover, dripping red as he sputters off and spins around unsteadily.

It's barely a wound, but he's panicked—the blood coursing down his cheek and filling up his airhoodie is freaking him out.

The hover is lifting off as he rises through the hole in the dome. I've got his rail gun now. Been awhile since I shot one of these, but it comes back fast. I let the sight lock on him and then squeeze a shot off and the little slug punches out at about two kilometers per second.

It catches him right in the small of the back and he bends in half the wrong way and then falls like a broken bird, crashing into the red dust outside and bouncing a couple times.

The hover pauses, turns. They know I won't shoot and risk hitting Tashi. But if I can get outside fast enough, maybe I can stop them from rescuing him.

Then I realize they aren't rescuing him. They turn the air cannon around. He's staring up at them with a look that's somewhere between hope and defiance. They blast him into a mist of grimy, crimson molecules, then drop a thermo-bomb in the crater for good measure. All trace of him is obliterated.

I watch helplessly as the hover turns and races out of sight.

The second wave of repair bots are doing their job. The dome seals and extra oxygen is flowing. The deer that made it are wandering up and down the uncloaked hall, dazed, along with one bedraggled peacock and some agitated bunnies that are hop-crawling aimlessly.

Jynks wobbles up to her feet. She's replaying the last few minutes.

"You saved my life," she says.

"Mel would never forgive me if I let anything happen to you."

She looked at me curiously. "What makes you think Mel ever forgave you in the first place?"

"Come on. We need to get you to the hospital," I say. "They do have hospitals on Mars, right?"

15

The hospital is a brushed metal palace. Soft music. Comfortable chairs. Hushed voices. A toast bar. And all for just shy of a dozen people.

Jynks's team whisked her inside the second we arrived and now I'm standing in the waiting room like a backup avatar on one of those shady arcade performances. Pretty sure her injuries aren't lethal—I should leave.

Instead, I look around the room.

This is a far cry from any health portal I've seen on Earth—there, they're filled with the sick and dying, the bloody and the screaming, crying and wailing as their debt load balloons with each passing second.

I chance a look back into the main suite. Four people are receiving treatment. Next to each person is a clinical anthrobot in a crisp, old-fashioned white uniform with a little cap and white shoes. They look ridiculous, almost like animative characters in a historical children's series.

Behind them is a closed slide-door leading into the surgical suite.

An anthrobot approaches.

"Do you have questions, Crucial Larsen?"

"Yes, I have questions. What are you?"

"I'm a medical assistant, Crucial Larsen."

"Even though you are a sack of wires and spinning magnets, drop the Larsen. I don't like it. My name is

Crucial. What's your name?"

"My name is Florence. I'm assigned to you during your wait, in the event you have questions or other needs."

I've got nothing against service bots. They're useful when they're programmed right, but from my experience they usually aren't. A bucketful of broken promises and endless glitches. But maybe that's because on Earth, we only get the rejects and seconds for any use that isn't directly connected to Five Families business. Failed prototypes, or else third-gen bots that have been around for, well, in some cases decades and look less like humans than vaguely human-shaped appliances. But obviously, that's not the case on Mars—why would it be? Florence and the other nurses look as real as high-end sexbots, as real as Captain Calvin.

"Why is this place so empty?" I ask.

"That is an incorrect observation. We are at capacity now. This is a health portal for high-ranking security services, their families and certain other staff dignitary categories."

On Earth, there's a health portal for maybe every couple of hundred thousand people. You only go if you absolutely have no other choice.

"Where's Jynks?"

"Her injuries are moderate. She's recuperating inside the health cradle."

"What's the capability of the cradle?"

"I don't understand the question," Florence asks. "Can you reframe?"

"Can this cradle fix everything, heal any condition?"

"Oh, I understand. You are asking for the technical specifications," Florence says. "The Seventeen-Level Health and Rejuvenation Cradle can detect and repair or mitigate all anomalies within any given human biome, provided a biological baseline has been registered and that funding has been provided to house, and keep at the ready, biological donors."

"Biological donors?"

"Volunteers who provide organs or serve as biological hosts for our patients."

Somehow, I doubt they're volunteers.

"To continue, while certain traumatic injures require time to heal—"

My ribs let out a memory ache from the last time I broke two of them.

"—the cradle can also accelerate that healing. In summary, all known biological anomalies can be reversed or their harmful effects eliminated," Florence says.

"Cancer? Can it cure cancer?"

"Cancer is a legacy disease. We see very few cases on Mars, and they can be easily handled by the cradle."

Cancer's not a legacy disease on Earth. Nearly half the population has it. And the other half has radiation sickness, or the latest virus. Mom always cursed the rich on Mars for keeping the health cradle technology from Earth. Said no one really cared if we lived past prime working years. But I always figured they just want to keep making credits off the treatment. After we can't work anymore, but right before we croak, squeeze out the last of the credits with unaffordable half-cures.

"Please, clarify something for me," Florence says, her voice suddenly not so sweet anymore. "What is the relationship between you and Deputy Chief of Security Jynks Martine? You are not listed on her survivor batch data."

"It's complicated," I say, thinking that Jynks is something between client, boss and source. And rival.

"He's with me," a voice says.

My heart bangs against my chest like I'm doing upside down jumping janes. I turn around.

It's Mel.

She's aged a little, but it makes her even more beautiful. Her eyes are covered with rose-colored glasses, more like goggles, I guess to protect her from all the dust blowing around on this planet. Or maybe it's the fashion. Her jet-black hair is pinned up tight around her head. She used to wear it long and loose, strummed down her shoulders like fine sugar braided into a song. I liked it better long, but I don't mind this look either. Not at all.

Before I'm able to utter even the most meager hello, she leans in to hug me.

"It's good to see you, Crucial. It's been a long time."

She fits against my body like a happy memory, the top of her head resting under my jaw, her arms encircling my ribs. She feels the same and smells the same—the desert wind on an early summer afternoon, when the wildflowers are in full bloom. Or at least the way they smell in my head.

Mel pulls back from the hug, eyes flooded with some emotion. Her expanded specs flash onto my scroll.

Melinda Hopwire, 36 years old. Senior Mars Botanist. Permanent resident status. Reputation level: Six Stars. Under the mentorship of the DuSpoles family. Pending license for nuptials with Jynks Martine. Application for surrogacy parenting submitted.

When I read that last part, my neck gets hot.

Mel lets out a little laugh, a sound that makes everything feel lighter, like the gravity compensators suddenly failed and I'm floating up off the floor. But why is she laughing? She puts three fingers over her mouth, over her beautiful ruby-red mouth. My breath tightens.

"I'm sorry, I don't know what came over me," Mel says. "This is not a laughing matter, but you know it looks like you haven't changed—"

She takes in a breath. And then looks nervously at the ceiling for a few seconds before meeting my eyes again. She seems flustered. Maybe that's a good sign, I think, a sign in my favor.

"I'm sorry about Essential, and I'm glad you're here. If anyone can find her, it's you," she says.

"I hope you're right."

"I know I'm right."

The words come out before I can stop them. "Gods, I miss you, Mel." My brain is shocked at what my mouth just said. She's pre-trothed, and I haven't seen her in damn near eight years.

"I mean, I miss you, you know, like a friend, and Essential mentioned she saw you, which made me think of you …"

I'm blabbering like a lorem ipsum syntax generator stuck in a feedback loop. My brain regains control and stops my mouth from talking.

Mel looks away from me and down at the floor, letting her gaze linger, like there is some puzzle there to be solved.

"May I assist you?" Florence the nurse asks.

"Do you have an update on Jynks Martine?" Mel asks, bringing her eyes up again.

"Your permission level grants you access to her cradle session. Would you like to go back?"

"Yes, I would, thank you," Mel says.

A strand of hair has escaped from the braided ring around her head, drooping down like a brush stroke framing her perfect face. She tucks it behind her ear. "I'll help you any way I can, Crucial, anything you need, I'm there for you. You know I love Essential like a sister."

"I know," I say. "I know, but Mel—"

"I have to go to Jynks now."

She looks at me closely for a long few seconds, her eyes locked on mine. She seems to want to say something, but then shakes her head slightly and turns toward the cradle suite.

I watch her walk toward the main doors. Her body, her gait, bring up a lifetime of good memories—her laughing at my singing, sleeping naked together in the distorted digital desert, reading to her as she fell asleep, sharing noodle bowls and watching rats take shelter from acid rains.

And then another lifetime passes through my mind, the life I might have had if I hadn't fucked it up so completely.

16

My head's a mess after seeing Mel, so I decide to do what any sensible person would do—drink until I almost pass out, take a detox flush and then do it again.

It's been a full day with all the bullshit and violence and emotions, and I've got a bad case of rocket lag. Plus, I'm still getting used to being up in the day. On Earth, it's the opposite. We sleep during the day, work at night. Right now, I feel like I'm running and sleeping at the same time, existing in two separate and opposite states simultaneously.

The Tarterics put me up in a nice place in the heart of Jezero and according to my scroll, it's close enough to the health portal for me to walk.

And why wouldn't I? It's a nice evening under the dome. Perfect, actually. The shielding material turns translucent when the sun sets, and Martian sunsets are blue. Like, corpse-in-a-cryodrawer blue.

Earth, for all its many, many faults, at least has normal sunsets. Glorious, billowing red and orange monstrosities. The more smoke and pollution in the air, the better. That's when the altofumulus clouds, those unholy hybrids of toxins and water and ice, form over the trench dumps and light up the horizon. You can't be outside for long in altofumulus clouds, not without needing new lungs, but at least the sunsets are a treat.

The rocket lag is really hitting me hard. I think I'm being

followed.

Everyone is used to being under constant surveillance, there's a camera feed on the head of every pin, but in my addled brain, I'm convinced I have a good old-fashioned tail on me. A cheerful-looking man with a bald head has been keeping pace with me for the last ten minutes. There's nothing suspicious about him and that makes me suspicious. He's trying hard to not look in my direction and that's a dead giveaway.

Mel would laugh. We used to watch detective movies from the twenty-first century, the old flat-screen classics, where men and women facing great odds would triumph against some fallible enemy. Someone was always being tailed. And someone always wore a trench coat. Must have been hard to be a cop in those days without the Halo data stream.

I set my scroll to search local private feeds, but the man's not broadcasting, just walking and smiling and keeping pace.

I wish I had my glitter gun.

He's getting close.

"You've reached your destination." My scroll lights up.

The man smiles and keeps walking past. "A lovely evening, isn't it?" he says as he passes. "Never tire of these blue sunsets."

Space travel makes me paranoid.

My new accommodations are somewhere between a luxury spotel and a castle. It's made of the same red stone as most of Jezero, with curved roofs and gentle balconies, like bubbles stacked on top of bubbles, and all clustered around a courtyard of cactus and delicate red flowers.

The door slides open when I approach and lights in the floor point toward my room. The door opens to reveal a dream.

Damn.

The view looks out over a garden. I walk out onto the balcony. There are a few lush trees around the edges, and I think I see something furry moving in one of them. Good furry. Cute furry. Not angry, rabid-rat furry. I'm pretty sure I see synthetic clouds drifting through the air.

The quantum lag is really hitting me hard now. I'm feeling thick and itchy.

There's a full bar of bionic-distilled liquors as well as a dispenser for synthetics. I'm used to the replicas, but when on Mars. I'm reaching for a bottle of whiskey when my scroll lights up. Someone I don't know wants to talk to me.

"Send to message."

The ving overrides the deflect.

Someone with a great deal of pull wants to talk to me.

"Ignore."

I get an unwanted geolocate. That someone has a great deal of pull, wants to talk to me and is downstairs right now.

I fill a glass with ice and open the bottle.

There's a knock at the door. A knock. At the door. It's so ludicrous it startles me into action.

A man stands in the hallway. He's tall and dark and has one hand in his pocket.

"Are you Crucial Larsen?"

"Did you knock on my door?" I ask.

"Sorry," he mumbles. "That's not the way we like to do things on Mars. But you wouldn't answer."

"Because I don't want to talk to anyone. And yet that's exactly what I'm doing now."

"We need to speak with you. Downstairs. About your sister."

That gets my attention.

"What's your name?"

"None of your concern."

"That's an odd name."

"No, that's not ... my name is Blevin Flunt."

"That makes more sense."

The Blevin family owns UKD2. They make weapons, as well as cops and soldiers—they're the ones who provide barely enough credits in my account to keep my Earth job.

We walk downstairs. Two others sit at a table with a backgammon board between them. They aren't playing. It's more like a prop. They're attractive. And bored. Hard to say how old any of them are. The Martian lifestyle—good food and health care—is amenable to good looks.

"Let's get this over with," the woman says. "Give him access. Introductions take forever."

I like her. My feed populates with their information.

She's Singhroy Able of the AmaDis Corporation Singhroys. They're responsible for medicine and media, helping us all stay alive long enough to buy the avatainment they're always stuffing into our brains.

According to my scroll, Able is 61, with the body of a 20-year-old. She's 1.62 meters tall, weighs 63.5 kilograms and her heart is beating at 82 reps per minute.

Next to her is Fehrven Modo. The Fehrvens own Thyssen-Bronner. They build, well, everything—from cheese knives to mushroom apartment towers. Modo is younger, at 41, and weighs 77.5 kilograms. He's a little taller, a lot heavier and his breathing is labored.

And my new friend Blevin Flunt rounds out the little trio. He's the youngest, at 35, and in the best shape. His aerobic numbers are off the chart. He broke his ankle a few years back, and his cholesterol is high. He'll need a lipid flush soon.

The access for all three is limited to basic bio data. I can't push past into personal data.

So, what do we have here? We have high-ranking members of three of the Five Families, and not a single DuSpoles or Tarteric in sight.

"To what do I owe this pleasure?" I ask.

"We're temporarily shielded so you can speak freely," Singhroy Able says. "There's more at stake here than you realize."

"The only stake I have is finding my sister."

"We've very sorry about your sister, but you are not getting the full story from our illustrious colleagues."

"I take it you have the full story?"

"Yes," Flunt says. "Well, we have part of it. More of it. Please, sit."

I want to say no, but my legs are rubbery. I think of the bionically crafted whiskey up in my room. I plan on drinking as much of it as my body can handle, but first I have to listen to their pitch. I sit down in a chair that feels like it's trying hard to be a bed.

"Your sister's disappearance may be staged," Able says.

"Are you saying she's in on something?"

"Possibly, but more likely she's being held somewhere against her will until the DuSpoles and Tarterics achieve their goals."

Gentle lights are flickering on in the street outside. It's like a Martian dream of suburbia that died two-hundred years ago. I see the bald man walking back by.

"And what are their goals?"

"We think they might be using this as a chance to tie our families to something unsavory," Modo says. "And the longer this drags on, the more likely it is they will use you to find false information implicating our families in some kind of a cover-up."

"And are you involved?"

"We simply want you to be very cautious and aware of

the possibilities," Flunt says.

"Think of us as allies," Able says. "We can help you with this investigation, help you find your sister and return her safely to Earth. But only if you trust us, and only if you do not become blinded to the motives of the Tarterics and DuSpoles."

"That sounds fine." I know they're reading me, and that they have a dedicated feed into the system monitoring my verbals and biofeedback. They know I don't trust them, and they don't care. "What do you recommend?"

"Don't trust all the Halo data you receive. It might be manipulated."

"How is that even possible?"

"It certainly wouldn't be easy. Or inexpensive. You can see why we're concerned," Flunt says.

I glance past them into the street. The bald man is walking by again in the opposite direction, trying hard to seem nonchalant.

Essential, what have you gotten yourself into?

17

When the morning rolls around, the quantum lag has mostly subsided. I'm in a unified state—even though it's a state of borderline exhaustion.

I'm starving too, so I access breakfast options. There's tea, real tea. I order a pot of Irish Breakfast and a pocket omelet—they have the good stuff: bean protein and extracts of algae, grown around a savory yeast paste—with a side of plantain puffs and a couple of jam sticks. The kitchen cube spits it all out in an instant and I take it out on the balcony as a ving comes through.

It's Jynks.

I headframe.

"Larsen, where were you last night?"

"Wow, you look so much different when you're not passed out and bleeding. I didn't quite catch that. Did you say, 'thanks again for saving my life'?"

"I did not," she says. "You dropped off the grid for almost a half-hour. Where were you?"

I don't want to tell her that I was meeting with some decidedly shady members of the competition who appear to want to keep the DuSpoles and Tarteric factions in the dark, which they seem to have done successfully.

"I was looking for the bottom of a whiskey bottle worth more than my entire life on Earth."

I hold the bottle up. It's half-full. Or half-empty. "I

didn't find that bottom, but there's always tonight. Do you want to come over? I mean, if you're up for it after that brush with death."

"No one disappears from the grid. No one."

"Must have been a glitch."

"There are no glitches," she says.

"Maybe you should try turning Halo off and back on again? Sometimes that clears up my shower hardware."

"Listen to me, you are under scrutiny here. Don't get caught up in something that exceeds your bandwidth. You'll fry like a faulty capacitor on a garbage rocket."

"I appreciate the warning, but all I'm trying to do is find my sister. So far, that's not going well because someone stole Tashi, my only lead. Someone who seems quite comfortable operating outside the grid."

She scowls. "About that, we found the flier out in the Choke. Or what was left of it. No sign of Tashi or the raiders."

"I'd like to look at the crash site myself."

She arches an eyebrow. "I didn't figure you for going into the Choke so quickly. Or ever."

The tea self-steeps and spits out a cube of compressed leaves. "I'm not exactly excited about it, but I would like to see the crash site with my own eyes. You know, from inside an airhoodie or two."

The coordinates pop into my scroll. "You should aim to go around noon. It won't be so blasted cold. When you're ready, connect with Sanders. He'll arrange transport." She pauses, as if deciding. "And here's a link to a cache of files of Essential from the last few days. Some of them are pretty, well, intimate."

There's a pip and a file dump as a terabyte of new data flags on my scroll.

"Thanks," I say.

She looks to the side and her face lights up. "Hey," she says, then, "Oh, nobody. Just work."

She disconnects the ving.

I'm nobody. And that was Mel.

Some mistakes are so great, so massive, that they're more like destiny than a function of poor judgment. Technically, Mel left me. But we both know the truth— there wasn't really a "me" left to leave. She stayed with the withering shadow of me longer than anyone should have, and the whole time it was like I was watching myself do all the things that pushed her away, and was helpless to stop.

Only I wasn't helpless. I was unable. Or unwilling. Or the king of emotional masochists. I was lost and drowning and she was the one person who could have saved me, who wanted to save me, who kept trying to save me, and instead of grabbing on tighter, I kept fighting her and pushing her farther away until she finally believed I really wanted to drown.

I hated her for not knowing me better.

And I hated me for knowing myself too well.

And I hate how much I still miss her.

I take a bite of the pocket omelet and access the files of Essential and promptly lose my appetite. There's a loop of video pieced together from a million cameras capturing the last few days. She had a lot of sex the last few days. Most of it was regular sex with regular rich people during regular sex-business hours. Some of it was special sex with Tashi after the place shut down. They were closer than Tashi led me to believe. A lot closer.

Watching your sister have sex is a major anti-aphrodisiac. At first, I worry I may never want to eat again. Pretty soon I worry I will never want to look at a naked woman again. Or a naked man. Or a naked sexbot.

Spooling out next to the sex clip is a list of destinations

and events and expenses arranged in chronological order. She spent a lot of credit on Martian absinthe. Like way more than any human can drink, and Essential doesn't even like to drink. Why didn't she get it from inside the H-suite where she could have anything she wanted?

And she bought it all from one store.

In central Jezero.

After I finish my breakfast, I slip into a drone jacket and hop downtown. The business sector in Jezero is like nothing on Earth. There, stores and restaurants and bars are crowded with kiosks overflowing with cheap shit no one wants and people shoulder to shoulder buying it anyway, or haggling for lower prices or trying to steal something or wanting to stand in the middle of the chaos and scream because it's better than sitting in your squat alone watching the short clips of the same movie interspersed with immersion ads, each with different avatars doing endless variations of the same things slightly differently.

But in Jezero, here on Mars, there are only a handful of stores—one for wine, one for drugs, one for bio-enhancements, one for produce and flowers, another for toys. They exist in case a family member of the space-ocracy, by some chance, decides they want to drop in and have an old-fashioned shopping experience and pick up something special. A new arrangement of flowers. Some perfume.

There's one staff person, a real human, in each store, all Earth lottery winners, standing at attention whenever their door opens or a ving comes through to drone something.

Right now, the stores are empty, the sidewalks are empty, even the skies are empty.

That's the only good thing money can buy—quiet. No billboards shouting deals, no holocoupons following you around like starving rats, no competition in the scroll with ad space going to the highest bidder, no jostling and jockeying with other people, no stepping over passed-out beetlers and piles of human waste and garbage fires, no people talking endlessly to others and no one listening.

Just quiet.

Quiet like an absinthe store on Mars.

I'm standing in front of Trouvelot Distilling. It's open, and like all the stores, empty except for one person in the back.

Nothing is ostentatious on Mars. There's no gaudy sign in front of the store, no giant three-dee blinking, throbbing bottle towering above it—just a modest sign curved in the middle like the unique, machine-blown bottle, a stylized image of the crater and sparkling font the exact color red of the absinthe.

That's because there's no competition here. That's reserved for Earth.

I read the information that's popped onto my scroll about Martian absinthe. The ingredients, including the wormwood, are raised in the Trouvelot Crater, a farm dome. It's machine-distilled in Jezero and then aged in solar barrels out in the Choke.

I open the door and the man in the back says, "Welcome," and turns with a smile that dies quickly on his face.

It's the bald man from the night before. He does not look happy to see me.

18

For just a microsecond, I think this may go okay. He looks like he has something useful to say, and that he is rational, but then I see the confidence leak out of his eyes until only fear remains.

"Don't do it," I say, but he bolts out the back door, still holding a bottle of absinthe in one hand.

I'm no expert on escape and evasion, but it doesn't seem like there are too many places to hide inside a dome. I connect to the security scroll and find a dozen cameras outside, but there's no sign of him.

This can't be right.

I bust through the door and he's right there looming above me and I realize with a sinking feeling that I can't trust my scroll anymore. Only my own eyes. And then only in some situations. Halo's reality can be faked. Just like Singhroy Able tried to warn me.

He's swinging something—the bottle—and I try to block it and mostly succeed, but it still clips me on the side of the head and cracks open and splashes absinthe in my eyes. The liqueur goes down smooth, but in my eyes, it stings like fire.

He shrugs into a drone jacket, hops up into the air and zips off. Mine is slow to start, trying to understand why my feed is blurry and registering all kinds of alcohol. I stagger up and hit the manual override and leap up after him.

He's headed toward a construction site maybe 600

meters away. It's quiet and contained, unlike anything on Earth, and awkward—top-heavy builders are clomping around on their tiny legs and smoothing rough edges off myco-forms with their great, whirring sandpaper arms.

As I get closer, I can see a giant vacuum tube capturing the dust and venting it into a reclamation box, but the particle count is still thick. It sets off alarms in my already beleaguered scroll, along with the general alarm associated with breaching a building site. The builders, two stories tall, have stopped working and are stomping around aimlessly and waving their gritty arms, not used to having humans disobey the keep-out border and programmed to avoid causing any bio-injury.

The bald man goes low and shoots under a new arch.

I'm getting nothing on my scroll, but it's clear my quarry is an Earther. No member of the Five Families would have anything other than thick, perfect genetically luxurious hair.

I'm gaining on him. Manual override gives you more speed, up to a point, and I'm reaching out to grab the back of his coat when he cuts power and drops straight down. I'm going too fast and swerve and try to adjust but everything is all gummed up with booze and mushroom dust and the drone jacket fails. I skid off a wall and careen into a builder.

It catches me like a baby and cradles me in its sandpaper arms and even though the blades are no longer turning, I feel the back of my shirt and some of the skin on my hands and legs scrape away when it arrests my fall.

"You should not be here, Crucial Larsen. Danger, Crucial Larsen. This is a construction zone, Crucial Larsen. You should not be here, Crucial Larsen."

The builder is looking down at me with its flat face, like an oversized shovel with one red ocular lens.

"Put me down, you big idiot," I say, trying to spot the bald man.

There's no sign of him.

The builder lowers me gently to the ground and then returns to its post, dragging its arms across the wall but with a human in harm's way the sandpaper isn't turning.

My clothes are shredded, my hands and elbows are raw, and my eyes are still blurry from the red booze.

I stagger back to where he dropped down and I first overshot him. The myco-dust is thick, halfway up my ankles, so I can see where he landed. And I can see his tracks. They end at a half-finished wall.

I'm scanning my scroll and see a few fliers, but not him. But by now, I know it doesn't mean much. Somehow, he's manipulating Halo. If he hopped again, he's long gone by now. But there's something about the tracks. They literally end at the wall. Not near it. There's not enough room to hop up from there, unless he jumped backward.

I adjust my scroll and scan the content of the ground down to ten feet. Myco-dust, then volcanic basalt, then some heavy concentration of hematite.

I switch to ground penetrating radar. It's faint, but there's space below us. Lots of space. How the hell did that fat little bastard get underground?

I don't have time to figure it out. I ving Jynks. She's surprised.

"I don't have time to chat," I say. "I'm at a build site on the edge of downtown Jezero. Can you geolock?"

"Yeah, I've got it."

"I need control of the builders. I'm in pursuit of a suspect and he's gone underground."

"I can't—"

"Do it! I'm not kidding around. I've been assaulted and sandpapered."

She breaks the connection and leaves me fuming. Three minutes later, the builders shuffle over, all six of them towering above me like two-story skyscrapers.

I point at the end of the tracks. "There's a tunnel here. I need in. Get to stomping."

The robots probably weigh a couple of tonnes each, and even though they have chicken legs, those chicken legs can deliver a lot of impact. They form a circle and lock arms for support and then in sync, begin pneumatically driving their legs into the dirt. Dust billows up around them and the ground shakes—the force is impressive.

There's a cracking sound and the ground falls away, revealing a narrow tunnel lined with metal handholds stretching down into the darkness. One of the builders topples in, flailing its sandpaper arms helplessly. The others let it go and step back, watching me impassively for my next instruction—they're programed to prioritize humans. I look down at their companion. It's twisted up and sparking at the bottom of a deep cavern twenty meters below us.

"Get back to work," I say to the others, and start down, hand over hand.

It's dark, but my scroll clicks through to enhance my sight. The wall of the chute is smooth Martian stone, the rungs bolted deep into the rock. Near the bottom, it opens into a large room.

I make my way down and stand near the fallen builder. It won't be shaping any myco-structures anytime soon.

"Do you have any lights on board?"

"Yes, Crucial Larsen. I am equipped for nighttime and underground work."

"Light up then."

I'm nearly blinded as the builder turns on all its lights. We're at the edge of a huge cavern. The walls are crystalline and gleaming white, dazzling in the harsh lights generated by the robot. I touch my hand to the surface. It's cool and smooth. I lick my thumb and swipe it across the crystal, then taste it. Salt. I'm in an ancient salt cave. There used to be water on Mars. This must be a remnant from those days.

I stand there for a long minute.

My scroll blinkers and then goes silent. I'm cut off from everything. Just me and a dying robot in a cave full of salt crystals deep under the surface of the red planet. I've never felt so, I don't know, content, I guess. Unsettled and content. Alone and almost happy.

"Do you have anything on board that could be used as a weapon?"

"Please reframe the question."

Fucking builders are dense like the myco-bricks they shape.

"Do you have any tools, any detachable tools, that are small enough for me to carry that I could use to, you know, pry open a door or puncture a bladder of oil?"

The builder is all twisted, but manages to open a door on its back and extrude a tool. It's half screwdriver, half wrench, with a built-in light. Better than the nothing I have.

To my right is the mouth of a tunnel. I walk toward it under a heaven of salt crystals glittering in the fading light of the builder-bot.

I switch on the light in the tool and duck into the tunnel. It's big enough that I almost don't need to bend down, barely, and only crack my head on salt layers about every fourth step.

There's light ahead and I switch off my tool and grip it in both hands. I hear voices. I step into a room, but it's empty save for a screen. There's an avatainment movie running on a loop. Some sexy-alien-meets-naïve-Earth-boy number with lots of soft dialogue, juicy breasts and waggling erections. I switch it off permanently with my half screwdriver, half wrench.

There are two beds, a food cube, a rechargeable shower and a vaporizing toilet. People were living down here in the salt caverns.

On one wall, polished smooth, is a glowing sign in neon bioluminescent algae growing right off the calcite minerals.

We are the Variance. Change is inevitable.

19

"Crucial, was the salt cave the first time you learned of the resistance?"

"Yeah," I say. "First time."

That's not exactly true. We've all heard rumors about the resistance. But I never believed them. And I've never seen any official reports, never heard of any arrests, never saw a shred of evidence that there was any organized resistance to the Five Families.

I look out the window. The day has turned darker. I imagine the ward waking up, getting ready for the labor shifts. There's a storm coming, a wall of altofumulus clouds welling up out of the Pacific desert. It's going to sweep over the ward like a brown fog. If it starts raining, the burning kind of rain, I'll be glad I'm inside being interrogated by an unwavering lens linked to a relentless AI named Halo.

"I pay attention to the news and I'm in law enforcement, so I have access to data," I say. "But there's never been mention of a group trying to take on the Five Families."

"Providing coverage to a small group of malcontents would provide unwarranted legitimacy."

"I can see that. But it should be pretty clear by now that

it's not exactly a small group. It's a large group. Large enough to pose a threat, no matter how unlikely, to the status quo."

"Do you share their beliefs, Crucial?"

"I don't waste my time thinking about a different kind of world. I've never seen the point. But maybe I should have. I mean, the Five Families have everything."

"Some might say wanting others to fail comes from a sense of jealousy or insecurity."

"Yeah, the people who already have everything might say that," I say. "The ones who are born with everything and make sure no one else can get a fair shake would say that."

"Your words border on treason, Crucial, but your bio-signs are not elevated. It seems you do not attach much emotion to these beliefs. That's good, because most people would be required to register for historical reeducation by now."

"My Mom always said I wasn't like most people."

I have a newfound respect for the countless people I've interrogated during the last few years. This whole thing blows like a supernova.

The only thing that really matters is Halo still thinks I have useful intel, otherwise my memories would be chemically flushed already. That means everything is going to plan, and there's a possibility I can still make a difference.

I tap the teacup, long ignored, and it heats up to steaming in seconds.

"The man I chased, the bald man, he was part of the resistance. What do you have on him?"

"He had a false identity. On Mars, he was Sigi Franks, an expert absinthe distiller. His real name was Omor Denuble. He was in the militias, like you. He fought for the

AmaDis group, which as you know is the Singhroy family. Believed killed in combat during the last days of Consolidation Wars."

"Obviously, an error of corpse counting."

"Obviously."

"Ships are monitored. How did he get to Mars?" I ask.

"There are several possibilities. Thirteen, to be precise. They will be mitigated."

"And the salt caverns? How many more of those are under Jezero? And all the cities?"

"The Mars security forces are investigating. They've found seven tunnels and two living quarters."

"Any arrests? It would be great to interrogate a few members of the Variance."

"Your word choice now indicates you are supportive of the Five Families. Is this correct?"

"I'm supportive of my life on Earth."

"There have been two fatalities so far, but no arrests."

"How did he avoid your notice, how did he disappear from my scroll?" I ask.

"Members of the Variance have been found with illegal coding that allows them to create a temporary digital clone presence based on common routines in expected places. To the authorities, it appeared that he was sleeping or moving about his shop, when in reality he was underground, or elsewhere."

"So, you're not infallible."

"We are reexamining data and eliminating flaws."

The rain breaks and starts lashing the windows with the rusty sludge that leaks from trash clouds. Dark rivulets twist and twine and splash off the sill. It's a far cry from Mars, with its parks and botanical domes and habitats.

Mel had this dream of helping regenerate Earth. Using what she knows about intero-botany to reclaim the wastelands, to clean the air and eventually refill the oceans. She thought the Five Families could be convinced to drop the credits, they just needed to realize it was possible, needed to see the business case.

They didn't care. They knew a talent when they saw it and they pulled her into their orbit, put her in charge of designing and building entire ecosystems on Mars. She may still have that dream, I don't know. Maybe she tells herself she still has the dream. Now, she's growing gardens with orchids and synthetic microcumulus clouds for rich people.

And Earth is still broken. The Five Families are in no rush to spend money down here until they have Mars fixed up exactly the way they want it.

And why would they?

We can't go anywhere. We can't not work, we can't not do their bidding, we can't tell them to go to hell. They make or grow everything. All the food, all the tech, all the medicine. We rely on them for everything. How do you stand up to petty gods who hold life and death in their hands and use Halo to tip everything in their favor?

Mel always believed things could get better. She wanted me to believe too, but I'm a realist. A pragmatist. You can't change the system. All you can do is make the best of things from inside it.

It took her years to come to the realization that she was never going to change Earth, to accept the disappointment, and finally give up and go to Mars. Me, I was born disappointed, and I think she always begrudged me that a little, knowing I was right all along and that I'd made my peace with it.

But if you can't accept reality, if you can't lower your expectations to things that are achievable—a decent job, food, a home, access to poverty-inducing health care—life is a never-ending series of disappointments. Save your dreams for sleeping, because you need to be wide awake in the real world.

Otherwise you go crazy with sadness.

Or join the resistance. Or the Variance or whatever the prock it calls itself.

"When was the next time you crossed paths with the Variance, Crucial?"

"I guess it was when I finally made it outside the dome to investigate the crash site."

"Things did not go smoothly for you in the Choke?"

The rain is falling harder and starting to overwhelm the filters. I can smell it, the sharp, yeasty smell of high acid content. This will eat away building exteriors and those godsdamn woodpeckers will be out in full force tomorrow.

"That's one way of putting it," I say.

20

Eleven nights ago

Every minute I'm on this planet, the more pissed off I get. This time it's because of the tech. It's amazing, like it's from 150 years in the future.

I'm in the head of some sleek mechanical beast, vaguely human-shaped but with six springy, spidery legs. It's scurrying across the Choke, the Martian desert, carrying us to the crash site of the flier that snatched Tashi. The legs scramble over rocks and across canyons with ease and, with its gyroscopic cockpit, it's a surprisingly smooth ride. Sanders and I are side by side in ergo seats looking out through the oval transparencies that would be its eyes.

Damn, this thing is fast. The landscape is passing by in a blur and when the beast clambers up sheer walls, my stomach does barrel rolls.

"How...much...farther?" I ask, trying to keep my breakfast of whiskey and protein paste down.

"We're getting close," Sanders says. "But I'm still unclear on why we're doing this. It seems pointless, a waste of time and resources, and potentially dangerous for you."

Sanders is handling the trip better than I am. He's relaxed into the foamy chair and is rolling and rocking with the motion.

"Well it's a good thing you aren't—"

I fight back a wave of nausea as the beast launches over

the edge of a crater and uses rockets to drive back toward the surface.

"—making the decisions," I finish.

"What can you possibly expect to find?" Sanders asks. "The cleaners are thorough to a fault."

Truth is, I'm not sure I'll find anything. But I'm desperate. "I'll know it when I see it," I say.

"Be sure to point it out to me as well," Sanders says. "I am curious."

I look down. We're about forty meters up from the surface and dropping fast. A dust devil swirls across the barren landscape. Hard to tell its size with nothing for perspective, but it leaves a new set of ridges across the soil in its wake.

"What's that?" I ask, looking the other direction at a group of lights reflecting off metal in the distance, flickering in the afternoon sun.

"Terraformers," Sanders says.

"Human?"

"Machines. Very few humans willingly go into the Choke."

"What are they doing?"

"Planting a cross between trees and moss. They were designed by Melinda Hopwire. Have you heard of her?"

I nod.

"She's brilliant. In another half-century, they'll be enough plants to tip the atmosphere from carbon dioxide to oxygen. Humans, or any oxygen-breathing creature, will no longer asphyxiate on the surface."

He seems almost cheerful.

"But this little contraption will let me breathe now?" I ask. "I'm used to airhoodies."

I'm dolled up in a silver one-piece jumpsuit, which fits as tight as a glove up to the neck, and then balloons into a triangular-shaped helmet covering my head. It's hot and moist and clingy inside.

"The Stern suit is far more stable than an airhoodie," Sanders says. "The suit takes in your carbon and extrudes oxygen, generating a mini-atmosphere. Once activated, it will basically last indefinitely."

The beast lands with a graceless jolt and starts scrambling forward.

"This thing I'm wearing right now is alive?"

"Not alive as you think of it. However, the fabric is engineered to generate respiration."

"The wind looks pretty brutal out there," I say. Small waves of sand are whipping by the oval eye windows.

"This conveyance, known as a Blackwall, is designed for these conditions. Once you drop out, the Blackwall will tip over and its legs will oscillate at high speed, generating an opposing force vector to keep the wind at bay in an area of approximately …" He checks his scroll. "… a forty-five-meter radius."

"Why forty-five?"

"The approximate size of the crash site with some room to spare along its circumference," Sanders says. "It will also provide enough energy to give you a gravitational field, not as strong as Earth, but you won't accidentally bound away, and it will provide a temporary radiation shield as well."

"Great. Helluva a multi-tasker. Sounds perfect," I say, with more confidence than I feel.

"Ten minutes until you descend."

I gaze out again through the eyeballs of the Blackwall, again struck by how desolate and beautiful the planet is— no people, no buildings, no smoldering waste. I wonder if it's like this in the Sunbelt on Earth? I magnify my scroll until I can make out the blackened rock swirls in the distance. Using geolocation, my scroll provides the answer to the question I was about to ask.

These features are ancient lava flows. Current evidence suggests Mars has no, or only a limited, molten core. Geologists believe Mars is either tectonically dead, or dying, although landforms such as these provide evidence that the planet was once very active in this regard, with continuous eruptive events and mountain-building. The majority of current geological activity is non-constructive, meaning the planet is in erosive mode.

The Blackwall beast slides and shudders to a standstill.

"Crucial, I'm instructed to require you to say out loud, for the liability waiver, that you understand how the suit works."

"I got it, I got it. Click the head piece closed and away we go."

"I'm also instructed to advise you that you have twenty-four minutes on the surface—"

"That's not very long."

"The forecast has shifted. We will not have enough fuel to generate the gravity and anti-wind field beyond that. We do not want to be stranded in the Choke. I fear our rescue would not be prioritized."

That's comforting. Twenty-four minutes. I've had shorter times at crime scenes, although not by much, and definitely not in the Choke on Mars.

"We'll be in contact while you're on the surface through the audio," Sanders says. "Please click it for confirmation."

I click the headpiece into place. A layer of warmth floods the inside of the suit, like I wet my pants, only slower and across my entire body.

"I hate this suit," I say.

"It's very useful for staying alive though," Sanders says.

"That remains to be seen," I say. "Let's go, before I

smarten up."

My words reverberate like an echo chamber, but Sanders understands just fine.

"Lucky for you, the temperature is ideal. A balmy twenty-three, but this won't last long. As the orbit turns us away from the sun, the temperature will drop significantly and rather quickly," Sanders says. "It's imperative you don't loiter. The suit offers some protection, but it's not infallible."

"So, I might freeze to death before I suffocate," I say. "Fun planet."

"I'm activating the exit sequence," Sanders says.

A circular panel on the floor whirrs to life and slides open. There's a tube down to the surface that looks like a do-or-die avatainment fun ride.

"A fucking slide?" I say through the helmet. "You're sending me to my death on an inhospitable planet in a soggy space suit on a children's slide?"

Sanders gives me an encouraging thumbs-up.

I sit on the edge and dangle my legs, trying to work up the nerve to jump out.

"You shouldn't waste the wind break," Sanders says and then the little shit gives me a nudge.

I slip down the silver tube, bumping and bouncing against the walls, and land with a thump, feet first, and fall back onto my ass. Cursing, I stand and brush the soil from the suit.

Up close, the dirt isn't really red, more like rust.

I turn slowly around in a circle. Even in the blowing wind and cold, it's magnificent, but I'm not sure why.

Then it hits me.

The silence. Only the very small whispers of blowing sand. I've never heard nothing, or almost-nothing before. I'm mesmerized, and stand still in the emptiness, feeling a wholly unfamiliar sense of peace as rusty dust motes swirl around me.

"Is everything okay, Crucial?" Sanders asks, ruining everything.

"All good."

My scroll says I'm at just two degrees left of center of the crash site. I plot out the grid in my head and impose it on my scroll, setting up the parameters so I can work my way up, then back, then across.

One column of my scroll is on maximum magnification, another is running a soil spectrograph, another is looking for signs of hidden salt caverns. So far, there's not one godsdamn grain of soil out of place.

Fourteen minutes remaining.

It's too damn perfect. Someone wanted to cover this up and executed on that with expert precision, but I already suspected that would be the case.

Twelve minutes to go.

I expand my perimeter to the full circumference. On the edge, I notice a craggy outcrop of black rock. Getting closer, I see it's the opening to a small cave. My scroll tells me it's a basalt tube where lava once flowed a zillion years ago. Well, my scroll doesn't say zillion but it's too many zeros for me to care.

Ten minutes to go.

All very interesting, but entirely unhelpful. I turn away from the tube to resume the grid search when Sanders screeches in my ear.

"Crucial, the weather is deteriorating. A tornado-level vector is passing through with a wind force that cannot be mitigated, even by the Blackwall."

"That sounds bad," I say. I knew I was going to die out here. I hate it when I'm right.

"I have to re-vertical the ship. Can you make it to the

Blackwall in thirty seconds?"

"No, I cannot." I can do a lot of things when I'm scared. Breaking the laws of physics is not one of those things.

"Then you must take cover until the tornado passes."

That I can do. I scramble into the basalt tube and shimmy deep inside just as a gust of wind hits. I feel the sand and grit scouring me like a blast from a glitter gun.

Inside, it's big enough to almost stand and I try to slow my heart rate.

"How long will this last?" I shout.

A jolt of red dust and grit blasts through the opening. I move back another meter into the tube. I can hear the wind howling, and pebbles banging around against the tube's opening.

"Sanders!" I shout.

The audio is out. My scroll is dead. What the prock, how is that possible?

Okay, the last time I checked, I had ten minutes to keep fueled up, and no more than two have passed—still plenty of time left. I fire up a light on my suit sleeve and look around the lava tube. There's little concave area ahead, a dead end, and I shuffle into that space to hole up.

I hear the wind whipping by and gravel and sand banging against the outside of the tube. The force could easily rip my suit open.

Eight minutes until we're stuck out here in the Choke, and then Jynks and her security forces will have to rescue us. It would suck to overnight it with Sanders—he has the personality of a rice milk latte—but it beats the alternative. At least I have plenty of oxygen thanks to this living suit.

An alarm starts clanging and a warning beacon flashes on my scroll.

Danger. Oxygen depletion. The suit has sustained irreparable damage. Return to habitable conditions immediately.

I really am starting to hate Mars. I am going to suffocate and freeze at the same time, double die, and for nothing. There was literally nothing at the crash site.

Nothing, absolutely nothing. The flier was reduced to microparticles that blew away in this insane storm, and how is it possible in the course of under five nights I've gone from sleeping naked in the fake desert thinking about Mel to being trapped in a volcanic lava straw on Mars searching for my sister and about to die?

Six minutes.

Suffocate here or maybe make it to the Blackwall. Not much of a choice.

I squirm around and position myself by the head of the tube and look out across the crash site to the distant Blackwall, crouching there like a mechanical spider.

What the hell was I expecting to find at the site? The weapons up here are state of the art. There was never going to be any evidence to find, not after a blast of that magnitude.

A blast from an air cannon as big—or bigger—than anything the Mars security force has.

An air cannon the resistance should not have access to.

An air cannon that couldn't have come from Earth.

That's it. My next play. Track the weapon. It had to come from Mars. It's a slim clue, a ghost of a clue, but it beats going home to Earth with my tail between my legs. Or dying like a sausage pop in a silver bio-pastry sleeve.

Three minutes of air left and falling fast.

There's a break in the wind—it drops from insane to just angry—and with a curse, I bolt out of the lava tube and aim toward the Blackwall.

The audio comes back on and Sanders is talking to me.

"… suit is damaged. Crucial, you must hurry," Sanders

says. "Please, hurry."

"Roger that," I say.

Yeah, the Choke, it's a good name for this godsforsaken place. Beautiful sure, but it'll kill you. With the gravity dampers offline, I'm covering ground a lot faster than expected, bounding twice as far between each step. For once, Mars is doing me a favor.

I'm getting close. The wind is picking up again. The Blackwall is shuddering. I see the door and I'm running toward it, all the while watching my oxygen level drop into the red. The suit is cold. I can feel the liquid starting to frost and harden.

I'm out of air, which makes running a challenge, even in the lighter gravity. I can feel my lungs fighting against this new deadly reality, and I aim for the door and jump hard, even as darkness is edging in around my eyes.

I'm going to make it. Dammit, I'm going to make it.

My foot catches on a little outcrop and I stumble and clang into the side of the Blackwall.

Damn you, Mars. Then the red turns to black.

21

"We'll be arriving at Holden Crater in a few minutes," Sanders says. "Are you absolutely sure you need another whiskey?"

"That was a traumatic time out there," I say, watching the dispenser vend another shot-cup. "I almost died."

"Technically, that's not true," Sanders says. "You were briefly unconscious, but you were never seriously at risk."

"I still don't know how you got me inside."

"I'm stronger than I look," he says. "Plus, I had access to a manual forklift used for moving rock samples."

If Sanders hadn't shimmied down the slide and hoisted me up into the belly of the beast, I'd be a frozen corpse in the Choke.

"Well, thanks for not letting me die."

"I was happy to help, and you obtained what you think is a useful clue, so this is a good outcome," he says.

Sanders might be a little on the boring side, but he's been mostly reliable so far.

We're approaching Holden Crater by lev-train. Holden is the biggest industrial center on Mars, and the closest thing the red planet has to an Earth-style city. It takes humans to manage the code for the assembly lines and oversee the robots in the warren of factories and assembly facilities, so there are 30,000-plus lottery workers in Holden, living in stacked-up high-rises in the residential section, and a few thousand members of the Five Families living nearby—the ones who like to pretend to get their hands dirty.

The lottery workers on Mars aren't the only ones who got lucky. Being born into one of the Five Families is like winning the lottery, only for life, and for the life of your heirs in perpetuity—and you don't have to work, or ever worry about anything.

I guess the people in the resistance, or the Variance, would like to see that changed. And I suppose they have a point. It doesn't seem fair that the random good fortune of being born into the economic plutocracy should offer every advantage over those who had the misfortune of being born to regular parents. Like mine.

But life isn't fair. That simple truth keeps proving itself over and over. Some are born rats and others are born feral cats. And I don't think humans, on Earth or on Mars or anywhere, have it in us to come up with a system that can offset that truth.

The lev-train slips into the airlock and some workers disembark. Sanders and I stay on the train, and then off we go again, not as fast this time, sliding past the gleaming buildings that house the weapons assembly facilities.

It's a big city. Data on my scroll put the crater at about a kilometer deep and the dome rises almost half that again, and it's 140 kilometers across. But it's function over form. No parks, no circular rivers, none of the good Mars stuff. Just industry. And housing. A few communal dining centers.

Still, it's clean and well-organized and not smash-crowded with teeming masses of people like I'm used to. Holden looks like Earth with a tenth of the people and none of the perpetual trash fires. Or beetlers. Or beggars. Or toxic air. Well, it's not so much like Earth, I guess.

"That's where they put together quantum drive ships,"

Sanders says, pointing to a huge hangar. "The parts are made on Earth, where the environment is more suitable to the associated waste. And then the ships themselves are assembled on Mars."

"More suitable to the associated waste?"

"I'm told the externalities associated with these fabrication processes can be quite damaging. Mars would be ruined," he says matter-of-factly.

I should shout and rage at the unfairness of his casual statement, but I don't have the energy. Instead I say, "Sanders, that's my home."

"Of course, how thoughtless of me," he says. "Then you may be pleased to learn there are efforts to locate some of these manufacturing facilities in free-floating orbital stations or on meteors, but without success thus far."

"Yeah, that's a lie," I say.

In the hangar, a small army of robots is carefully wheeling a new ship toward the launch pad, leading it like a newborn pet tethered to them with thick steel cables.

"Right past this area is where they assemble energy weapons," Sanders says.

"That's our first stop, then."

We get off at the next platform and take the travellator, along with a dozen or so workers, to the entrance of the facility.

The Holden Arms Research and Manufacturing facility is a joint venture between the Fehrven and Blevin families. It's highly secure, but not when you have a special pass from the Five Families. They really want me to find Essential and so far, nothing is off-limits. We'll see how long that lasts.

We're scanned and ushered inside by a young man with acne, which means he is most definitely a lottery-Earther. He seems to be expecting us.

He leads us to a well-appointed waiting room that looks down over the factory floor. It's a blur of activity and flashes of sparks and electricity as robotic arms weld and rivet and grind and polish and push and pull. Not a single wasted motion, except for the few humans who are following mobile managerbots, taking performance readings and entering data about the robots as they trundle around taking performance readings and entering data. That's what it's come to—humans are the backup monitoring system for a monitoring system that never makes mistakes.

Except one—not detecting the theft of heavy ordinance subsequently used in an attack on the H-suite. Or being blind to that cannon theft.

"Please wait here," our guide tells us. "Blevin Crease will be joining you."

Five minutes later, a man in a pale green suit enters. He has smooth, dark skin and a touch of gray at his temples. Gray hair, for the wealthy, is a choice.

We brush fists, and Crease nods at Sanders.

"Sanders, nice to see you again. Crucial Larsen, I understand you are here investigating a somewhat personal matter. Sorry you are visiting our little red planet under such difficult circumstances. How can I be of service?"

"We have reason to believe that whoever attacked the H-suite and snatched the person best able to help find my sister was using a highly-advanced air cannon. Of the type that could only be fabricated here at your HARM facility. We think someone may be diverting some of your products."

"I assure you that is simply not possible. Every unit produced, every scrap of metal, every motion of every robotic arm is tracked and cataloged by Halo."

"Then maybe you sold the air cannon to the Variance."

Blevin Crease looks at me like I'm something he just tracked out of a bathroom bio-atomizer.

Sanders clears his throat. "Crucial Larsen did not mean to imply that you are actively funding the resistance," he says. "Perhaps if you gave us access to processing and shipping data, we could sort this out and be on our way."

"I wouldn't mind a peek at the production sector for air cannons too," I say.

I think Crease is having a conversation with someone else, blinking responses into his scroll. The rapid eye movement gives it away. Either that or he's got some neuro-tick, but nobody has neuro-ticks on Mars. Unless it's a visiting Earther.

"Your scroll is synced," he says at last. "Follow me."

I get a huge shipping and processing data dump and start sorting through it as we take a waterfall lift down to the fabrication and assembly floor.

It's orchestrated chaos, with arms and pincers quietly doing their work in a fidgety sequence—braiding wires and affixing circuits like buttons and threading in screws that expand instantly, permanently bending metal shapes to guns.

We're at the edge of the glitter gun unit. They've been churning them out by the millions to ship down to law enforcement on Earth as the population, and discontent, begins to rebound from the last virus outbreak.

These are personal size, fitting snugly into a pocket. Beyond them are the side arms, and beyond that the rifle sized. And past that, the kind they mount on fliers. A flier-mounted glitter gun can bring down thousands of people in a few seconds. I should know—I operated one during the Consolidation Wars.

"I wouldn't mind slipping one of these into my pocket," I say, pointing at the small personal size glitter guns. "I've been feeling a little unprepared ever since I got to Mars."

"It wouldn't do you any good," Crease says. "Our weapons are linked to Halo, every single one. Until it's paired to the owner, it won't work."

"Someone forgot to tell that to the people who attacked my squad on Earth. And the ones who attacked the H-suite. They didn't have any trouble firing their weapons."

"We're looking into that," Crease says. "And when we find out who is responsible, they will be punished to the fullest extent of the law."

"Here's a thought. What if it's a member of the Five Families?" I ask.

"Impossible. But if by some unforeseen circumstance, it was a member of one of the families, they would undoubtedly be excommunicated from Mars."

Three clear balls, each slightly taller than a person, roll to a stop in front of us.

"The ACU is on the far north corner of this facility. We'll take rollers."

Rollers are gyroscopic conveyance devices, a ball within a ball, well-suited for industrial settings. Crease leads the way, the rollers propelled by hidden magnetic stripes under the floor.

It's an education on weaponry as we roll past guns and rifles and cannons and missiles and bombs of all types.

According to the schematics I'm reviewing as we roll, the air cannon unit is the largest. They are expensive to produce but cheap to operate since air is the ammunition. And the damage is extreme. I segment the data by output and look for anomalies. There's nothing there.

But nothing isn't an option. Essential is counting on me, and I'm starting to get genuinely worried.

We arrive at the edge of a restless sea of mechanical

arms that rise and fall in waves as air cannons are fashioned from scratch.

"Let's take a look at your most powerful," I say.

"This way," Crease says and walks off through the chattering machinery.

"Any chance of getting hurt by this equipment?" I ask.

"Zero," he says. "These machines are programmed to exacting specifications and cannot deviate. And they are also programmed to protect all humans." To prove his point, he stands next to an arm swinging a welder, the tip glowing red hot. It misses his face by inches, touches a trigger mechanism lightly to bond the metal, then swings back past. He moves closer, into its path, and the arm freezes.

"Impressive," I say, still scrolling through the logs, looking for any missing equipment or any idled robots.

There's nothing. Every air cannon assembled is accounted for in every bill of lading. And every bill of lading was officially signed off by ... Tarteric Lloyds.

That's interesting. And interesting means potentially anomalous. Essential's secret, creepy admirer-stalker, Tarteric Lloyds, was in charge of shipping out the final product.

"How about we take a look at wherever it that the cannons ship out?"

"Very well," Crease says.

The dock is a busy place, with lev-barges wobbling under heavy loads as shiftbots trundle injection-molded myco-crates cradling new cannons from the production floor to the shipping nexus.

There's an elevated panoptical control tower in the center, and two workers inside monitoring display screens appear to be tracking surveillance streams for anomalies.

"Can we talk to them?" I ask.

The two lottery workers are surprised to see us when we enter; they aren't used to seeing humans on the dock.

"This man is conducting an official investigation for the Five Families," Crease says. "Please answer his questions."

I sync my scroll. One of them seems nervous. Her name is Drell. She's from the Everglades Ward on Earth. Been on Mars about a year. The other is Loop. He's been here almost five years. Nearing the end of a rotation that was twice renewed due to excellent work. I can't get a fix on where he's from.

"Do either of you know Tarteric Lloyds?"

"Of course," Loop says. "He's the unit boss. I mean, I've never met him, but he clicks off on every piece that shuffles out of here." His bio-stats seem relaxed.

"An air cannon may have gone missing. A big one. How could that happen without his click-off?"

"It couldn't," Loop says.

"What about you?" I ask Drell. "Have you seen him recently? He seems to have disappeared." Her numbers are spiking. It doesn't necessarily mean anything. Any conversation with the police is usually a bad thing and can end in a labor sentence. And usually does. At least on Earth.

Drell shakes her head. "Never met him. But I noticed his click was missing these last few days."

"But he left something," Loop says. "Something curious." He presses a button and a drawer whispers open.

Then he has a gun in his hand and things get weird. It's one of the mean-looking little glitter guns. "It's set to maximum mortality," he says.

At this range, it would take an army of EMTbots to put us back together if he pulls the trigger.

"Feeling pretty confident that Halo won't let this gun work?" I ask Crease. He's pale and rattled and that's enjoyable to see, but short-lived.

"You're coming with me," Loop says to Sanders, and presses the gun to the back of his head. "Anybody follows, he dies." The door hisses shut behind them and he shoots a burst of diamond flechettes into the control panel, effectively sealing us in. Crease is already in contact with HARM security.

We watch from the window as Loop pushes Sanders ahead of him onto the construction floor and they make their way toward a door at the edge of the building, threading their way through a choreographed sea of automatic arms.

One of the robot arms breaks ranks with the others and swings wide, catching Sanders in the neck and decapitating him with an elegant blow, then crashing into Loop and crumpling his skull like an empty ramen cup. The force is so strong, blood and brains spatter all the way up to the panoptical windows.

"Holy procking shinks," I mutter, my stomach doing quantum rolls.

The robots keep working, the impulsive arm returning to its allotted task.

"I thought you said those things were safe," I say to Crease.

Drell is white like a neutron star. She points, one hand covering her mouth.

Headless, Sanders is crawling around like a crab looking for his missing piece, trailing blue ooze and slimy wires.

I'll be damned. My new best friend wasn't even human.

22

Mars security forces arrive at the HARM factory in seconds and cordon off the mess with alarm wire, recording the gruesome site in four dimensions to create the holo-crime scene.

Sanders has dissolved into a puddle of sticky blue goo oozing out of rumpled clothes. The organic circuitry evidently requires a life spark to hold it all together. No such luck for Loop, who is hideous in death, his head misshapen and soft, eyes rolled back and open mouth drooling blood.

The robot arms up and down the line never stop swinging and stamping and welding. Except for the offending arm. It's been powered down and pulled off the line and rolled away, drooping in defeat, for a full diagnostic.

Jynks is sharing a Halo scroll with me as I watch the proceedings. "People sure seem to die a lot around you," she says.

Someone out of my visual and auditory range says something to her because she shoots a sideways glance, then looks sheepish.

"Sorry. That was insensitive, with your sister and all."

"It's okay. You're not wrong. But I'll miss Sanders," I say.

"We'll see what we can do about that," she says with a half-smile. "What a weird coincidence for an arm to glitch like that."

"That was no accident," I say. "Loop was murdered."

"Robots can't kill."

"That's what they say, a robot can't harm a human," I say, "but this one sure didn't stop when it had the chance. Cracked Loop's head like a rotten soy puff."

Hygiene bots are mopping up the sticky blue remains of Sanders. There's something incestuous about watching them—their spindly, rubber-coated legs squeaking as they scrape their brushy-mop mouths across the floor—scrubbing away the stains of a thinking, feeling cyborg. Not incestuous like sexbot porn, it's weirder than that.

Other bots are preparing Loop's body for in-situ cremation with a burner suit. They erect a sectional hearth screen and with a flash and sizzle, he's reduced to dust and a few synthetic diamonds.

In the old days, they used to keep the bodies around for tests, I guess. There's enough data in the system to make a new Loop, if anyone really wanted one, which is doubtful. As he flames up and sputters out, I'm scrolling through information about his life and he doesn't come off well.

He lives—lived—nearby. He had about four credits to his name and a bad leg. He liked Primal avatainment, with lots of hatchets and face paint and lusty tribal ladies, and he ate a lot of vat kelp. He masturbated on Thursdays and holidays. He traveled to Earth four days ago. Halo flags an anomaly.

The scroll data says he traveled to Earth with a companion. When he left Mars, ostensibly, it was with Drell, but she doesn't have any record of leaving Mars. When he arrived on Earth, it was with a man named Eric Benson, 38 years old and dead for the last forty years. Yet when I look at the vid data, it shows him entering the ship on Mars alone but disembarking on Earth with a female companion, who isn't Drell.

There's only a micro-second of visual but it sure looks like Essential. I feel a flash of desperate hope. She's back on Earth.

But how could she have gotten away with it? And how could Halo not have seen this earlier? Why would she go back to Earth to hide? More important, why wouldn't she tell me that? And why do I have so damn many questions and no answers?

One thing is for sure. Loop's life seemed so boring, so pointless, no one thought he was up to something. Not even Halo recognized the anomaly in the information about Loop's travel to and from Mars. No one noticed.

Not until a human took a closer look.

Score one for living a meaningless, tedious life. Gives you a shot at privacy.

"Are you seeing this?" I say to Jynks.

"Yes. I can't believe we missed it."

"I'm going to check his squat."

I catch the train and then take the travellator to his building. There's a surprise waiting for me outside.

Sanders.

"Hello, Crucial Larsen," he says.

He's not quite the pretty boy he was a short while ago. I guess he was reconstituted in a hurry and on the fly but he's still recognizable—his voice is the same and he's wearing the same clothes but his cheekbones are a little flatter now, he's bald and his left ear is about twenty percent larger than the right.

"You look good," I say. "Given that you were a blue puddle a little while ago."

"That must have been alarming to witness."

"I almost lost my breakfast." He has access to the housing tower and holds the door for me. "You really had me fooled. You seemed so real."

"I am real. I am a real state-of-the-art cybanism."

"Why didn't your hardware show up on my scroll?"

"I'm mostly organic," Sanders says. "A few processors here and there."

"How does it work? You seem to, I don't know, remember me now. But you got your head knocked off."

"My proto-consciousness, which includes memory, is stored separately and backed up constantly. My last shell was barely unresponsive when they injected me into this new form."

"Well, however it works, I'm glad you're back. Especially because now I don't have to feel obligated to make small talk with you."

"It's how I learn though," Sanders says. "The small talk, I mean."

We take the lift to the twelfth floor and Sanders doesn't learn a damn thing from me, then we enter Loop's squat.

It's not much, but still nicer than my craphole back on Earth. Clean, spacious. He has a small kitchen area with food printers and even a sunken wok for making scratch meals. On Mars, the lottery workers can take advantage of the fresh produce and quality sheetmeat. At least I hope it's sheetmeat.

I scroll through the catalogue of avatainment shows he's been watching. One, called *Barbarians in Love*, had the most hits. I pop into the show where he left off. The avatars pick up the change in viewer without missing a beat and stop having sex in the middle of a battlefield littered with the corpses of their enemies. They get dressed slowly and look to the distance. The man says, "We must continue our quest to find the missing princess. The fate of the kingdom hangs in the balance."

I leave them to their digital journey and return my focus to the room.

"This seems out of place," Sanders says. He's found a glitter gun under a pillow. A small one. It's not registered anywhere in Halo although I can't be sure Halo is giving me access to all the information about weapons registry on Mars. Why would it?

Still, getting caught with an unsanctioned weapon is justification for immediate reprogramming and probably a lifetime of extreme labor. And Loop had two.

If he was willing to risk that, I wonder what else he might be hiding. I stretch out on the bed and try to think like Loop. He's got a gun close at hand, which means anything else worth hiding—and protecting—should also be within easy reach.

There are built-in ledges extruding from the walls, one with a light on it, another with a single bonsai orchid—a tiny, brilliant splash of purple and yellow. It's so delicate, so beautiful, that most people would avoid disturbing it. Most people. I press the wall behind it and another ledge shoots out, dislodging the orchid that tumbles onto the bed, its roots now splayed out like stringy old fingers.

Sanders gasps at the damage and scoops the flower up, fussing over the bruised stems and leaves, gathering the potting chips.

The new ledge is slightly recessed and has something affixed in the middle. A folded piece of paper.

Paper, actual paper from pulped bio-matter, is rare these days. It's expensive and irrational. It also can hold data that's easily hidden from the digital systems, but only if you can figure out a way to read it without having it simultaneously scanned by Halo. Which I can't, not in this situation. I unfold it.

On one half is a rough map with a location circled and

the word "vector" underneath. I recognize the map. It's the Fields on Earth. Near where we were attacked. On the other half of the page is text. It's a poem:

Some say the world will end in fire,
Some say in ice.
From what I've tasted of desire
I hold with those who favor fire.
But if it had to perish twice,
I think I know enough of hate
To say that for destruction ice
Is also great
And would suffice.

It's handwritten, and I know the handwriting. Essential.

"What is that?" Sanders asks from near the tiny sink where he's gently repotting the miniature orchid.

"I'm not exactly sure," I say.

The note bursts into flame and disappears in a puff of light and smoke.

The flash is intensified through my feed and Jynks, who was only passively watching, now gives me her full attention, swearing at the lumens level.

"What the cranking gear-strip was that?" she asks.

"I don't know," I say. "You'll have to look at the rewind." I know that's not necessary. Halo already knows. A fraction of a second might as well be a century when you're talking about an AI this powerful.

I also know it's time to go back to Earth. I think that's where I'll find Essential.

23

I'm finally headed home. To Earth. Hot, overcrowded, unbreathable Earth. After getting clubbed with a bottle of absinthe, almost getting shot and almost dying in the Choke, not to mention witnessing one kidnapping and two decapitations, I survived everything Mars and the Five Families could throw at me and now I'm going back to my own little corner of hell.

I'd rather be happy in hell than miserable in heaven. They can keep their luxurious domes and fresh air and delicious food and absinthe. And good riddance.

But I need to say goodbye to Mel first.

I don't know why. I'm sure she'd be happier if I just jumped on the first quantum rocket and we never spoke again.

The ving bounces and bounces and I think she won't answer, which is a kind of an answer, but at the last minute she headframes. Tight. And with that little scowl I remember too well.

"What?" she asks.

"I want to say goodbye. I'm leaving. Don't expect to be back."

"Okay. Well, goodbye," she says and it's clear she's ready to break the connection.

"Wait, Mel, hold on. I was kind of hoping I could say it in person."

"Why?"

"Mel. We have history together. We have a past. You owe me a chance to—"

I don't even know what I was going to say. A chance to what? Explain? Apologize? It doesn't matter—she cuts me off even as an expression of something between pity and anger washes across her face.

"I don't owe you anything. You left me, remember?"

"That's not what I meant. I ... can't we say goodbye in person? Please."

She pauses to think and bites her bottom lip in that way that squints her face.

"That's probably not a good idea."

"When have I ever been in charge of good ideas?" I ask.

That almost draws a laugh.

"I'll be working at Baldet Crater all afternoon. In the Americana game preserve, and it's open to the public, so technically I can't prevent you from being there. But don't broadcast this to Jynks. I mean, it's not like I keep anything from her, but there is just zero reason why she needs to be bothered by this. She thinks you still have feelings for me."

"That's insane," I say, and realize my voice is higher than usual. "She's completely wrong." Now it's too low. Dammit.

"I mean it, Crucial. Don't fucker things up for me. Even though it's your specialty."

She breaks the connection.

She's not wrong about that. But in my defense, I manage to fucker things up in my own life too.

I spend the rest of the morning working my way through a bottle of Martian absinthe and thinking about all the things I should say to Mel and all the things I'm going to yell at Essential.

By the time lunch has come and gone, I haven't eaten and I'm pretty tuned up. Maybe it's the gravity situation.

Or maybe it's just that I'm getting older. Or maybe it's that you shouldn't drink an entire bottle of Martian absinthe under any circumstances.

I take a nopalitine and curcumin flush that knocks the fun and clumsy out of being lit and I'm able to hop over to the lev-train station none the worse for wear except for a throbbing headache. There are pills for that too, but I kind of like the pain. Keeps me focused.

Baldet Crater is part of the Antoniadi cluster, a series of habitat domes designed to mimic some of the environments back on Earth before everything went to hell. My scroll is keeping up a running dialog of what to expect.

The DuSpoles family of the twenty-first century had the foresight to create a genetic library of every living thing, from bacterium to elephants. They are using it to restock habitats, recreating some of the famous and beloved Earth environments of centuries past. But don't worry, the animals are carefully lab-grown, with predatory tendencies removed, and trained to eat prescribed diets at predictable mealtimes. The entire system is kept in balance with just the right number of creatures, big and small, happy and well cared for. And yes, you can pet them. They're all friendly. Even the scary-looking ones.

Mel's specialty is making ancient plants grow and thrive. She's leading the effort to terraform Mars, developing lichens and moss that can grow in the Choke, and eventually grasses and trees.

She can make flowers sprout in concrete. Even on Earth, all those years ago, her tiny squat was like a rainforest, with black-market greenery busting out on every available surface and three-quarters of her water budget spent on roots and leaves.

Sometimes, resting there in her arms, surrounded by all

those plants—turning their blind trust toward the smog-blocked sun—I had this feeling that maybe things would be okay. That if we tried hard enough, we could make things grow again and turn around all the damage and suffering.

But that hope ended in a fiery crash when Mom died and the system reassigned her debt to me—the families were getting really good at weaponizing debt then—and the only way out was to join the militia and fight in the Consolidation Wars.

Mel thought there was another way, of course. And begged me not to serve the worst part of the system. Even so, she was waiting for me when we I got back, promising that I was going to make it work. I meant it at first.

But it didn't take me long to ruin both our lives.

The lev-train goes directly to the Baldet Crater. There's a family traveling to the same place, and I follow them into the dome.

The doors slide open and we all step into a park that stretches as far as the eye can see. There's grass up to my waist, and some giant woolly cows grazing nearby. Overhead, the sky is full of birds the size of small shuttles, with white heads and cruel beaks, wheeling through the synthetic blue.

According to my scroll, they're eagles, and it spools out a history alongside a column of data analysis of the living creatures.

This area is a replica of the continent North America, which was once home to a wide array of wild animals including bison, bald eagles, wolves, elk, coyotes, deer and giraffes.

That's a surprise. I didn't realize giraffes were so common in the old days near the Multnomah Ward.

There are six of them, long-legged and I watch as they regally strut past a knot of woolly cows, stamping around and wiggling their little tails. I'm dumbfounded by their beauty, the elegance of their necks, and can't stop staring.

I get a geo-locate. It's Mel.

I part ways with the giraffe family—the boy is petting one of the woolly cows, which I guess are the bison—and follow the main path through the luxurious grass, past wolves and otters curled up together and sleeping in the shade of tall trees that Halo tells me are Douglas fir.

Mel is a few meters ahead at the back of a forested grove. She's wearing some kind of white uniform and taking a core sample from a tree.

The mighty redwood took hundreds of years to grow this tall on Earth. But thanks to science and technology, we grow them on Mars in a matter of months.

"You finally figured it out," I say.

She looks up. I see a flash of what I hope is joy splash across her face, but it doesn't last. She wipes away a smudge of dirt on her cheek—and makes it worse.

"I had to find the right genetic incentive," she says, pulling the drill gently away from the bark of the tree. "Did you find Essential?"

"Looks like she's back on Earth."

"Why wouldn't she tell you that? She wouldn't want to worry you."

"I think she might be in trouble," I say. "You remember what she was like."

"Of course." Mel puts her equipment down. "Still, it seems like she would have told me if she was going back to Earth."

"You stayed in contact with my sister?"

"Why does that surprise you?" Mel asks. She gives me that side-eye I remember so well. It used to irritate me. Now it feels like home.

"I thought—"

"What, that when you broke my heart, I'd stop talking to the rest of the people I love?"

"I don't know. Maybe."

"You were a real sphinc then, and you're an even bigger sphinc now."

"Look, this is not what I wanted," I say.

"What? An honest dialog?"

"No. I mean, yes. I wanted to say that—"

I don't know what I want to say. That I'm drowning in regrets. That I made the biggest mistake of my life. That I want her to leave everything—especially Jynks—and run away to the moon with me.

Well, not the moon.

I look up the tall trees, the tops brushing up near the apex of the dome, the red trunks and green branches catching the blue glow of the setting sun.

"I just want to say that I guess Mars isn't so bad, really. And I understand why you wanted to come here."

She puts her hands on her hips. "Do you think I want or need your validation?"

"No, it's … everything is coming out wrong."

"You vex me," she says, her eyes softening. "After all these years, you still rankle." She sighs and shrugs. "There's a little lake over here. Let's go sit down."

There's a bench made from the remains of an accelerated redwood and we watch deer drinking in the cool water, their big black eyes blinking and their long, silly ears twitching.

Abruptly, she sits up straighter. She's reading an alert on her scroll.

"Hold on. There's an adjustment to be made. These deer, one of them is nearing the end of his run. We don't do this around guests, but I'll need to make an exception if you are going to stay," she says.

"I'm staying," I say. Nothing could drag me away, except maybe one of those giant birds.

"It can be kind of difficult to watch. Look away if it bothers you," Mel says.

A big male with bifurcating antlers is down in the grass near the water's edge. He looks sick. A drone zips up, hovers and fires a single needle into his skull with a hiss. The deer slumps down, eyes wide open in death, and a grinder-bot rolls up—basically a circular mouth of slanted steel teeth on wheels. It sets some hooks into the haunches of the deer and starts dragging it slowly in, spitting out tidy little protein pellets that are scooped up by a plog-bot.

It's all quiet and discreet and none of the other deer even look up.

"The pellets feed the wolves and coyotes and badgers," Mel says.

"They really have it all figured out here."

Mel looks at me seriously and puts her hand on my arm. "Crucial, be careful. Whatever is going on with Essential, it's not like her to disappear. I'm worried, about both of you. Promise me you'll pay close attention."

"I will."

"And promise me you won't do anything stupid."

"I have a bad history when it comes to stupid," I say. "As you know."

She nods, a little too quickly, and leans in close to hug me and I think I feel a tremble. She's warm and I smell her hair and her skin, and it smells the same—like life and flowers—and I'm catapulted back to that hot, lush squat of hers.

"Mel…" I start to say, but she breaks the embrace and stands.

"Go on now, Crucial, do what needs to be done," she says. "I can't see you anymore."

24

I step out of the orbit elevator onto to the dock and the first thing that hits me is the smell. The familiar pickled, chemical smoke stench of Earth. I'm home. I pull on the dark goggles—the ones I never had to wear, not even once, on Mars—to keep the sun from burning out my retinas.

The second thing that hits me is the noise. My scroll fills up instantly with ads for bargain three-day-old sheetmeat barbecue, an all-inclusive holo-vacation to a high-res desert—sexbots included—and a download to improve probabilities for winning the Mars lottery. Plus, a state-of-the-art noise reduction system.

Halo is micro-adjusting my targeting based on recent travel.

It was so quiet there, up on Mars. Now I've got ads clamoring in my scroll and a swirl of people jostling around, talking to everyone at once.

Jynks hadn't seen the wisdom of booking me in first-class priority for the return trip. Even though I argued I was still on the job, she wouldn't go for it, said the trip was a family issue now. I think she was just busting my drone rotors and wanted to make it as unpleasant as possible.

I'm starting to like her. She's petty. Even though I don't much want to admit it, Jynks is okay. Mel could have done a lot worse. She has done a lot worse.

Apparently, I'm no longer under the Tarteric family protectorate because of the visual record that showed

Essential is somewhere on Earth. Case closed, Hoost said.

Actually, he said, "Your sister is alive on Earth, which means it is the task of local security enforcement to find her on our behalf. You may want to find her first. Once in the custody of Mars security, we will uncover how she avoided detection, prevent it from ever happening again and impose the appropriate reconditioning corrective." Only he said it in a super annoying and arrogant voice.

But I haven't located Essential. She's not responding to my vings. And Halo can't find her. It's alarming. Usually that means one of two things: either her OCD is malfunctioning or … I don't want to think about the second thing.

My first stop is the coordinates at the Fields I saw on that self-combusting paper map at Loop's squat.

Even though it's the middle of the day, the area around the dock is teeming with people braving the heat, selling trinkets from refurbished trash, knowing Mars returnees are credit-flush. My scroll is also clogged with returnees fighting for the space to launch avatainment feeds about their time off-planet. The smart ones—or more accurately, the charismatic ones—will parlay their brief lottery stardom into a lifetime drip of positive credits. The boring ones, like me, will waste the moment, use their Mars credits to flatten their debt curve and then fade back into labor oblivion.

I wait as the crowd thins and then input a request for priority transport to the Fields. While I wait, I ving Captain Calvin to bring him up to date.

"Crucial, you're back on Earth," he says. "Welcome home."

"Such as it is. Hey, did you know they have giraffes up there?"

"So I've heard. Although I imagine other aspects to

being on Mars, such as quality of life, figure more significantly than giraffes."

Indeed, there are, I think, but the difference between Mars and Earth can be summed up with those godsdamned giraffes. "Nope, just the giraffes."

As if on cue, a returnee standing next to me pulls out a little stuffed animatronic giraffe and hands it to his waiting kid.

"A Martian giraffe," she whispers. "This is the happiest day of my life."

Guess it's not only me obsessed with the stupid giraffes. Why the hell do they even have necks like that?

"I'm not calling about the giraffes," I say. "I received information that could be relevant to the Fields attack and I'm heading there to check it out."

"I'll send backup."

"Nope, don't. This is a need-to-know. I'll ving as soon as I'm done."

"I don't like sending you in alone. That's outside protocol."

"Halo will back me up," I say. "You haven't lost your faith in Halo, have you? I'm sending my coordinates now."

The lift to the Fields takes twenty minutes on a good day. Luckily, it's a good day. I sit up front and the backup driver stays engaged in his game—I hear glitter guns fighting off mutant climate refugees. We arrive at the coordinates at the edge of the Fields and I disembark. Even with a nasal protectant, the smell is overwhelming—dank swampy mulch mixed with urine.

My scroll is filling up with warnings: *Foot movement in this area is hazardous. Solitary excursions are not recommended. Please wait for backup. Mortality risk—70 percent.*

That's a real confidence-builder. I wish I had my glitter gun now.

There's a migrant settlement on the perimeter of the Fields. Migrant meaning they've come from another ward and haven't been conscripted yet into the local labor corps. A few lucky ones have beetlers, but just as many are eking out subsistence on a refuse pond. Eventually, Multnomah Ward will experience a labor shortage and they'll be auto-integrated, but who knows how long that will take. Most won't make it that long.

I check the coordinates again and walk the fifty meters toward whatever it is that's waiting. Along the way, I pass an ad-hoc maternity pod. At least three dozen women there. Strength in numbers, I guess. Nearby, a clutch of toddlers sifts through trash, trying to ferret out something, anything, they can possibly trade for a credit at a communal nourishment printer.

As I pass, a young woman screams. Her legs are spread, and I see the crown of an infant pushing out. She screams again, begging for help. There's a woman next to her, a nurse maybe, but it seems like she's mostly patting her arm.

"Something is wrong," she yells. "Please help me."

I turn my face away and keep walking. What can I do? The only thing this planet has plenty of is suffering. And you can't help everyone. Where would it stop?

I get a flash of Mel. She's glaring at me. I know what she wants me to do. "You literally left the planet," I say out loud. "What gives you the right to lecture me now?"

It's finally happened—I've gone insane. I stop, tell myself I'm a fool, then send a priority order for a medi-pod to help the woman and code her as a possible intelligence source. Eventually, Captain Calvin will figure out the ruse and make me pay for this somehow. But at least imaginary Mel is happy.

Forty meters more and here I am, exactly at the coordinates. I walk around a little trying to see what's so important about this place, if there's anything of substance here. I accidentally step in a pile of fresh shit. If it's human, it could be full of the whelp—my least favorite of all the diseases on Earth—but I've got on whelp-resistant boots and I plan on disinfecting myself all night.

It's almost dark. A lingering dusty light spans the Fields and a band of reddish-purple streaks across the sky. This is what sunsets should look like, not that blue junk on Mars. I can finally take off the goggles without scorching my eyes.

There's a trash-cliff a half-meter in front of me. I walk to the precipice and look below.

A hut. Or maybe it's a tent. Could even be a tattered combination of the two. Whatever it is, it's different than everything else out here. Habitable. Somewhat permanent. I walk the few steps forward, slide down the walls of trash, and knock on the rusted section of a salvaged rocket fuselage serving as a door.

A man with a long, thin beard opens the door. The beard is impressive, braided and knotted with bits of cloth, and hanging down to his knees. Equally impressive is the gun in his hand. It's a first-generation glitter gun. An oldie but a goodie. It's aimed at my face.

"How polite of you to knock," he says. "It's too soon, but come in, we only have a few minutes at best."

He grabs me by the shoulder and pulls me inside.

25

The shabby little hut looks a lot different on the inside. It's all servers and interfaces and thick coils of wires and code screens glowing amber and green and pulsing in the half-light. How did he get all this power here without setting off alarms in every utility office across every damn ward in the world?

There are also books, actual printed books, on shelves along the walls, and in the center of a large table littered with dirty dishes and incomprehensible scribblings on scraps of wood-pulp paper, is an aquarium with neon-striped darters zipping through clear water next to a cactus plant blooming with a crimson knot of color.

I'm going to die in an over-teched historic hovel with contraband life forms and a year's worth of dirty dishes.

"I'm Alduis Coverly," he says.

"I'm Crucial. Crucial Larsen."

He nods, his long braid of beard jiggling with the motion. "I know. You're too early."

Too early for what? "I wasn't aware I was on a schedule," I say. "I'm looking for my sister Essential."

"Can we hurry it up?" Coverly asks. "They're here and I need you to trust me before things go to brownloaf."

"Who's here?" I ask. "And I might be inclined to trust you more quickly if you put the gun down."

"That's not going to happen."

He tips his head and one of the display screens near us

flares to life. It's an exterior view, showing the trash valley we're in and the hut. A half-dozen armored sleds are parked around the edges with air cannons aimed down at us, and a precinct full of cops is moving slowly toward the hut with rail guns and squad-mounted glitter guns and every manner of terminal device up and ready.

"What the shinks is going on?"

"I'm the one they're looking for," Coverly says. "They've been using you to find me. And I won't be leaving here alive. Neither will you if you don't shut up and listen."

He extends the gun for emphasis.

"You make a compelling case," I say.

"I know Essential," he says. "She's not here. She's still on Mars."

"Not true. She caught an off-shuttle. She came to Earth."

He shakes his head, the ridiculous knee-length braided beard whipping back and forth for emphasis.

"They faked it, the visual of her exiting the shuttle from Mars, so you would track me down for them."

"Who faked it?"

"Likely the Tarterics or the Singhroys, but could be any one of the Five Families," he says.

"Why would they do that?" I ask, keeping a close eye on the thin barrel of the gun.

"You know the Fields and wouldn't feel threatened coming here. I would have seen you coming, but you're like a snake-bot in the sewers—slow, and you don't give up until you've drilled through the plugs. They were following you around until you found me."

"And why are they looking for you? Grooming advice?"

"She's right, you are annoying," he says. "It's because I'm a threat to the Five Families. Correction. *We* are a

141

threat."

I look around the squalid little squat. "Who is we?"

On-screen alarms begin to flash.

"The resistance, you idiot, the Variance," Coverly says as he looks sideways at the screens. "They're powering up the air cannons. Everything that happens in this room is hidden from their view. If you want to live, do as I tell you." He fishes in his pocket and pulls out a tiny capsule and tosses it to me. I catch it out of habit.

"Swallow it," he says.

"Spawn off."

He squeezes the trigger and a thick, slow bolt hits me in the solar plexus, knocking the wind out of me and driving me down to one knee.

I gasp for air like a stranded fish.

"The next one is sharp, fast and right through your tickles," he says.

"Okay, okay," I say and pop the pill in my mouth. My plan is to hide it in my cheek, but he's smarter than that. As soon as it hits my tongue, the blasted thing starts moving fast, wiggling in my mouth, propelled along by micro-claws, zipping toward my throat.

Coughing and sputtering, I chase it with the tip of my tongue and then my fingers, but it's too late. I can feel it crawl down my throat and disappear into my stomach.

"What the quantum fuck did you give me?"

"You'll find out soon enough, I hope." What comes next surprises me. He tosses the gun to me and smiles sadly. "Find Essential. She'll know what to do. Tell her it's up to her now."

"Wait, what do you know about Essential? Where is she?"

"Have you read much Frost?" he asks, pulling a dagger from his waistband, then nods his head at something in his scroll.

The poem, I think, the one back in Loop's squat.

The gun in my hand comes to life. My finger is on the trigger, but I'm not pulling it. A stream of diamond flechettes whispers out and dissolves his head in a spray of blood.

The braided beard, severed from the liquefied chin, drops to the floor like a discarded jump rope.

His body collapses, falling to its knees, then toppling over onto its side. Blood is everywhere, pooling onto the filthy floor like a wet crimson hole. I think of the deer on Mars, of the protein pellets, but not for long.

The tech must have been linked to his vitals because all of it suddenly erupts into flames, hissing and sputtering and dripping molten metal and filling the tiny space with billows of acrid, choking smoke. Nice of him to not shoot me so I could burn to death instead.

Then there's the unmistakable whoosh of an air cannon and half the hut is ripped away, the flames whipping out in a yellow-orange column of tornadoes.

The aquarium, and everything in it, turns to mist. The cactus plant is pulped. Pages of shattered books swirl up into the burning air and ignite.

My scroll is going nuts, flashing danger and trying to analyze the contents of the smoke and measuring the heat index and warning me of the many ways I'm about to die. Another hit from an air cannon seems the most likely.

I stagger toward the front door, now hanging sideways in the ruptured frame, realizing Coverly gave his life to keep me alive, and to give me an alibi.

I lower my shoulder and barrel through the door, rolling clear just as another puff bomb demolishes what's left of the structure. The force of it sends me tumbling into the trash heap. I lurch to my feet, hands in the air and still holding the gun.

There must be thirty cops around me, all with guns leveled and the distinct hip-forward stance that means my odds of dying are about even.

"Don't shoot! Don't shoot!" I yell. "My name is Crucial Larsen. I'm a cop in the Multnomah Ward. I just killed a member of the resistance."

26

6:10 p.m., August 31, 2187
Multnomah Ward, DuSpoles CPU, Earth

"Crucial, why did you terminate Alduis Coverly?"

"He pulled a knife on me."

"With your scroll malfunctioning, that cannot be verified."

I stare at the lens. The lens stares back.

"You found the knife, right? In his hand?" I ask.

"Yes. But how did you get his gun from him?"

"You know I'm a cop, right? And that I was in the militia? I mean, I shouldn't have to tell you I know how to disarm criminals."

"We're aware of your distinguished service record." There is a long pause. "Perhaps now is a good time to review your personal history."

"Can I get some food first?"

My stomach is grumbling. I've been in the interrogation cell for so long, I can't keep things straight. Is it time for breakfast or dinner? "Maybe some sheetmeat tacos? And a salt beer, yeah, a salt beer would be good," I say. "I'm more talkative when my stomach is full."

"Hunger is a strong inducement for truth in humans," Halo says. "Let's continue with a review of your personal history."

"Why would you care about that?" I ask.

I know why. The system keeps asking the same questions about the resistance. And it's not getting the answers it wants. So far, I've divulged enough of the truth to whet this fucker's appetite, but not enough to give away what really happened here and on Mars.

"Let's call it context," Halo says.

"Seems like you would want to know more about the raid in the Fields," I say. "Like, why so many officers were sent out, and why they didn't know a cop was inside."

"We'll get to that," Halo says. "First, a quick detour."

"You're the boss," I say. "How about a fresh cup of tea at least?"

Halo ignores my request.

"Our records indicate you were born in Multnomah Ward forty-one years ago to Anabella Cirrus. Your father, or fathers, is unknown."

"Or irrelevant," I say.

"Your conception was biological. Your mother was impregnated at the Reproductive Center. She obtained a legal waiver for conception for both you and your younger sister, Essential."

"My memories are a little fuzzy, being merely a fertilized egg at the time and all, so I'll take your word for it."

The pivot is unsettling. Halo should be asking about why I was in the Fields to begin with and what happened with chin-snake man. This shift means they're trying to surprise me with something, get me off balance. I've done it in interrogations a hundred times before—it's an effective strategy.

"Crucial, were you aware that your mother was in the resistance?" Halo asks.

Holy blistering balls of nuclear waste, I was not expecting that. I feel my pulse hammering in my ears.

"What? No, she wasn't. She was an e-school teacher.

You got it all wrong." I strive to keep my voice flat and even, with modest success.

"I have declassified your file. May I share it with you?"

"I don't know what you're talking about."

And I really don't.

Halo taps into my scroll and opens a new column with the data. Pictures and dates and investigation notes.

"Your mother was radicalized by an event that occurred when she was a child. Did you know your grandmother was a climate pioneer?"

"I never knew my grandmother."

"Your grandmother was one of the many people who agreed to be genetically modified to accommodate shifts in global climate. It was a brave attempt to provide a weather-resistant labor force able to deal with a rapidly changing environment. Sadly, it was unsuccessful."

I know that history. They almost tried it on Mars too, but the climate pioneer fiasco gave the Five Families pause. They went with terraforming instead. It's almost like you can't trick nature, not for long anyway.

But Grams wasn't a climate pioneer. Mom would have told us.

"As you know, this was an unsuccessful clinical trial and most participants suffered severe mutations resulting in deformities. Deformities that were passed along to, and worsened in, subsequent generations."

The Sunbelt, where these unfortunate saps live now, must be a real shit show.

"My grandmother died long before I was born. I saw photos of her. She died in her sleep."

"Your grandmother did not die. She was resettled in the Sunbelt, along with thousands of others."

I see a scan of the waiver with her signature, see image stills of the woman I recognize from Mom's photo-scroll, see video of her after, slowly blinking her second eyelids, her skin thicker and rougher to more easily cool down in extreme temperatures.

"She may still be alive even today," Halo says. "But we don't track the hybrids. Their ocular communication devices were disengaged before resettlement. They have no connection to Halo."

"That sounds pretty damn great right about now," I say. "Where do I sign up?"

My heart rate is going up, not because I believe this bullshit about my grandmother—it's clear the system can fake whatever it wants—but because I am increasingly anxious about Halo's change in interrogation strategy.

"Your mother was quite young when this occurred. She was radicalized and began to support the resistance. It was misguided of course, and ineffective, and she was monitored her entire life."

I see the case notes flashing by.

"She was never involved in any direct actions other than meeting periodically with certain members. She was not particularly good at being in the resistance—didn't have the proper focus—and we eventually downgraded her to minimal monitoring. She was a low-level threat and, as expected, after you and Essential were born, her interest waned."

Mom was a failed resister? Unlikely. Mom wouldn't have failed at anything. Unless she wanted to.

"Do you know the identity of your father, Crucial?"

"Mom always told us she put together a hybrid so we'd be well-rounded," I say.

"You are indeed well-rounded."

I snort. It was supposed to be a laugh, but it sounds more like a rat burrowing into the flop vats outside a sheetmeat fabrication factory.

"We are conducting a biological inventory of your genetic makeup to identify the components of your paternal parentage," it says.

"Why are you interested in my bio-father?"

"You have no curiosity about his identity?"

"Zero."

"Knowing your lineage could shift your position on Earth," Halo says. "Imagine if he was, or is, a member of the Five Families."

Huh. I hadn't thought of that.

"It would be awkward when I refuse an invitation to Mars. And more than likely, he's just some loser and you'd tack his debt onto me. Leave my past alone."

"Even the death of your mother?"

"It was a terrible, senseless accident. So—"

"Are you sure it was an accident?"

I freeze. The official story was that an out-of-control warehouse drone clipped the edge of the lift that day, knocking it loose from the building and dropping her nearly a hundred stories to the ground below. The safety checks weren't working. I watched the visual record. There was a sharp, splintering sound, then a regretful look from her as the elevator car detached from the building.

After the accident, that's when my brain cracked. And also when Mel tried to save me. She finally ended up saving herself.

"Did your mother's death strike you as suspicious?"

"Never, not until this moment."

"Did Alduis Coverly give you anything before he died?"

And there it is.

I focus on the giraffe, thinking about its long neck, and try to bring my bio-indicators back into normal range. But he didn't give me anything—he made me take something. Semantics matter.

"No, he didn't give me anything," I say.

"Did you kill Alduis Coverly, Crucial?"

"I was holding the gun when his head got blown off."

"Why did you return to Mars after the shooting?"

Halo knows why I went back. It just wants to hear me say it, to watch my vitals.

"I went back to identify a body. Or what was left of a body."

"And who was it, Crucial?"

I slam my fist on the table, toppling the lonely, long-empty teacup. "It was Essential, my sister. It was my sister, but you already know that, you heartless stream of code!"

27

Ten nights ago

Captain Calvin is saying something, but all I can think about is that damn capsule Alduis Coverly made me swallow. I'm imagining it swimming around inside me extracting chemicals from my blood and mining minerals from my bones into tiny, powerful bombs that will take me out—and everyone around me—whenever I'm next to someone from the Five Families.

"Did you hear me, Crucial?" Calvin asks.

"Uh, no. What did you say?"

"You are distracted."

"You almost turned me into an oat milk crepe with that air cannon," I say.

"We didn't know you were there. It was unfortunate."

"Running out of caffeine concentrate is unfortunate. You almost vaporized a labor enforcement officer in your rush to terminate a suspect."

"I repeat, we were unaware you were inside the structure."

He almost sounds sorry. Anthrobots can be persuasive. Almost. The difference between anthrobots and cybanisms, like Sanders, is that anthrobots don't try to convince you they're human.

"I literally entered my coordinates and filed a report about my destination," I say.

151

"The data were not received. It seems the resistance can distort Halo. It's very disconcerting."

"Oh, so this is down to the resistance? They're the ones who followed me there and scorched the place with me still in it? The resistance? The only people with their fingers on the triggers of heavy armaments were the police. And why would the resistance kill their own members?"

"We're calculating scenario probabilities. Perhaps you were the target," he says, scanning the latest list. "If you found something of value on Mars and they wanted to eliminate you, using the police as a proxy weapon would make sense."

"Sure, Captain, that's one option. Or the Five Families used me to find a target they couldn't locate on their own and then were going to wipe him off the face of the planet, and anyone next to him."

"That's also a plausible theory," Calvin says. "Perhaps you should raise this with Tarteric Hoost. He's waiting for you in the interrogation room."

"Here? On Earth?"

"Yes," Calvin says.

I immediately become itchy, thinking of what I'm increasingly sure are tiny bombs programmed to explode the second I contact Hoost or anyone in the Five Families. I'm a living, breathing suicide squad of one.

"I'd rather not meet with him at the moment," I say.

"Why?"

Oh, just a little problem I'm dealing with now. The resistance, or someone, has weaponized me, and I'll probably blow up the minute I see Hoost, I scream silently inside my head.

"I'm a little tired," I say out loud.

"It's Tarteric Hoost. Tired is not an option."

He guides me to the room. The door opens and I brace

myself for the worst, feeling every twitch and gas bubble as the beginning of the end. I'm sweating and shaky.

Hoost smiles, stands, and we fist brush, but his heart's not in it, and he pulls back before the typical two-centimeter air pass.

Nothing happens. No explosions. I'm in one piece. And so is everyone else.

"Thank you for joining me," Hoost says. "Are you feeling ill? You look pale and your vitals are erratic."

"Quantum travel doesn't agree with me," I say. "About as much as almost getting vaporized."

"That was a regrettable error."

"Essential was never here, was she?"

He shakes his head. "My apologies for the deception, but it was imperative that we find Coverly. We knew Loop had recently traveled to Earth and we needed someone who knows the ground and was motivated to follow through. We spliced a digital proxy of your sister into Loop's trip to give you the incentive. We didn't expect such quick results."

"And the coordinates on the puff paper at Loop's squat?"

"That wasn't us," he says. "Luckily, the resistance is incompetent."

It feels like more than luck to me.

"And then you followed me right to the target."

"Something like that."

"Is Essential alive?"

He shrugs. "We think so. That's the one truth of this whole situation. She really has disappeared. But not for the reasons we fabricated."

I feel a fleeting sense of hope that things are going to turn out okay after all.

"Tarteric Lloyds?"

"He's real enough, but he visited your sister for pleasure, not romance. It's very rare that a member of one of the families would fall for a common sex worker. A DuSpoles perhaps, but never a Tarteric. We embellished Lloyds's story a little, with his permission, of course. He found it amusing."

There's usually a moment right before I'm about to do something stupid where my brain has at least a split second to try and put the brakes on. But not this time. I lunge across the table to smash his face. But he's a spliffing hologram and all I do is disturb some pixels.

No wonder the little pill inside me didn't explode. I slide off the table and sit back down.

"We'll ignore that as an emotional overreaction," Hoost says. "But you should know, even our images have rights."

It's a good, high-quality hologram. I bought it completely.

"Sorry about all the trickery," his image says. "But we've arrived at a natural conclusion now."

"Why do you think it's okay to play with lives like this?"

"The resistance poses a small but real threat to the Five Families, and to the stability of Earth. Drastic times call for—"

"—drastic giraffe shit," I say, cutting him off. "How is my sister tangled up in all this?"

"It should be clear by now, to anyone possessing a functioning brain, she's an active member of the resistance, or as they've ridiculously dubbed themselves, the Variance," holo-Hoost says.

"I don't believe that."

"Really? That seems unlikely. She's had many brushes with the law, most of them related to crimes of compassion—sharing resources with unproductive, attempting to shield level-one offenses from official notice.

If not for your position, those offenses would have landed her in a labor camp for readjustment long ago."

Everything he is saying, at least this time, is true.

"Given that background, it's a safe assumption your sister erroneously demonizes the Five Families, holding us responsible for the shortcomings of people who have failed within a system that works quite well for so many others," he says. "She is trying to make it seem like the Five Families were the cause of the government collapse, rather than the force that stepped in to save humanity after the governments of the world became corrupted beyond even basic competence."

I shake my head. "Setting aside the fact that you and your kind hastened the downfall of those governments, I don't believe Essential would hide something like that from me."

But in this moment, I have to be honest with myself, I'm not certain.

"Turns out we're not the only ones who can easily manipulate you with lies," Hoost says. "Because if we thought you had any inkling of her allegiances, we would never have used you in this scheme. Now, we have stopped the coder—thank you for that—and since the threat has been neutralized, we will put our resources toward finding your sister."

I slump in my chair. "Don't hurt her. Let me track her down. I don't want to wobble the rocket, I don't want to overthrow the system or turn off Halo. I only want to save my sister from a death sentence."

Hoost smiles like a coyote that found a ball of plum fudge. "When we track her down, she will be tried for treason and found guilty. Given your status and support of our investigation, however unwitting it may have been, she'll be enlabored for life rather than executed. And of course, her debts, which are significant, will be conferred to you."

"You'll pardon my skepticism about arresting someone. The militia you sent to the Fields to arrest Coverly didn't seem overly anxious for a peaceful outcome."

"We are not the enemy, Crucial," Hoost says. "We are the engines of progress, able to keep food on tables, credits in accounts and health care available to those who need it."

"At least for those of us lucky enough to have jobs."

"We help all who require it, and we help the useful more than the rest. Let's not waste time debating the merits of being a labor-productive member of society," he says. "Suffice it to say, you've done your part to protect the status quo. Thank you for helping remove the problem confronting us."

"I feel like I need an all-night shower," I say. "But I can't afford the water credits."

"No hard feelings," he says. "I hope you enjoyed your time on Mars."

"I did not. What happens next?"

"You go back to work and let us do our job. We'll find her," he says. "Our security forces are quite competent."

"That was on full display at H-suite," I say, and a scowl darkens his digital face for a micro-second. "Does Jynks Martine know?"

"That we manipulated you to find Alduis Coverly? For what it's worth, she wasn't part of this plan," Hoost says.

"Well, at least you manipulate your own people too."

"Jynks Martine is not 'our people.' She is an important and trusted member of our security staff, but her services are replaceable. She has neither blood nor economic lineage."

"Your sense of loyalty is truly inspiring."

His hologram grins. "This has been pleasant. Always

nice to talk openly with the people who rely on our services, our largesse. You, Crucial Larsen, are the reason we keep our industries running so smoothly," he says, then fades out.

I sit in the room, stewing in anger and regret, until Calvin comes in and scans me.

"Go home, Crucial. Humans need to rest and recharge after almost dying."

28

It's sundown and I haven't moved in three hours.

I'm stretched out on the floor of my squat looking up through the tiny porthole at the building across the street and the dusty moonlight reflected there. After the casual luxury of the red planet, my little room seems dirty and tattered and claustrophobic.

The resistance? Why would Essential hide something like that from me?

I mean, besides the obvious—I'm a cop and trying to take on the Five Families is illegal.

They own everything. Not just the food and health care and tech, but what passes for government. A member from each family is on the supreme council. The supreme council decides everything. How many credits to pay cops. How many people should be employed. How many people should be in prison.

And then they tell Halo, and Halo—connected to everything—makes it happen.

How can the resistance fight that? It's too big, too entrenched. What the hell does Essential think she can do against unlimited wealth and power? I know she's always been on the rebellious side, but the resistance? I thought I knew her better than this.

But maybe you can't ever know anyone. Even if you follow their feed, see everything they do, share every experience they have, there's still something hidden inside that others can never access.

I guess I never really knew Mel either. Hell, I never even knew myself.

When the Consolidation Wars ended and I was dropped back into the shell of my old life, about the only thing left of the original me was the anger and hurt at losing Mom. I couldn't outrun it or forget it and, if I'm honest with myself, which is rare, I probably joined up thinking it would be the end of me, and good riddance.

I even failed at that, like everything else. I was lost, scarred and carrying around a head full of memories I wanted to forget. Mel tried her best to help me heal, to stay close, but all I did was push her away. Eleven years ago, she quit trying. Eight years ago, she left to intern on Mars. Two years ago, she met Jynks.

I'm pathetic. I'm sitting here pining for a past that didn't satisfy me and a future I actively sabotaged.

Anthrobots have it right—no emotions and a power-saver mode when things are boring.

My scroll is crowded with ads and junk crawls and avatainment pitches. That's one thing I miss about Mars. The mental peace and quiet. A brief respite from the constant bombardment of Halo-generated ads.

A visual of a noodle bowl comes through and, dammit, my interest slows it for a split second and that's the kiss of death. Suddenly, a hundred restaurants are pushing bowls of noodles into my scroll. Some have olfactory enhancements and I can smell the smoke and ginger. At least one is stimulating my taste buds—the soy sauce and fried onions are making my stomach grumble.

Like sharks in the water, the ads won't end until I either buy something or pay a credit. The threat about Essential's debt slows my impulse to waste money on stopping an ad.

And I *am* hungry.

My favorite noodle shop is walkable. I check the weather. It's raining, which makes it complicated. I'll need to use a sodium bicarbonate umbrella.

The streets are mostly empty, except for a rat the size of a box of bread. It glares at me and I lunge at it, sending it skittering into an alleyway next to my building.

I duck into the restaurant. It's empty, except for the owner and one patron. Singhroy Able. What the hell is she doing here? She's sitting in the back and looks worried. I have a flash of panic that whatever the hell Alduis Coverly made me swallow will explode, but nothing happens.

"Did you throw those ads on my scroll?" I ask.

Able nods and motions me over to sit down. There's a device on the table between us, humming and blinking.

"What's that?"

"A jammer. It will give us some privacy," she says. "For a few more minutes, at least."

I put out my hand and touch Able's shoulder. She's here. Physically real. "Why are you on Earth?"

"Sometimes it can't be avoided. What have you learned?"

"Not to cross the Five Families," I say, and order a noodle bowl with extra kelp from the menu screen.

I hear the bionics whir to life in the back, stretching fresh noodles and squirting boiling broth into a bowl.

"It was all a setup," I say. "The Tarterics used me to track down some crazy coder with a braided whip for a beard."

"And did you?"

"Yes. But he pulled a knife and I had to terminate him." The lie is getting easier to tell.

She drains her glass of blue synthwine, grimaces and holds it under the spigot for another.

"Did he give you anything first, or mention anything?"

"No," I say, trying to block out the memory of that pill crawling down my throat."

She slumps in her chair. "The Tarterics must have locked down the scene."

"Actually, the coder had it set to blow so everything caught on fire. And then the cops leveled it."

"Back to square one," she says.

"I no longer know what square we're on," I say. "Why don't you tell me what's really going on?"

She checks the jammer. "We don't have much juice left so I'll make this fast. The resistance is developing technology that allows them to cloak themselves from Halo. The coder you killed was leading the project."

I point at the jammer. "The tech already exists."

"Using one of these is like sending up a flare when you want to stay hidden. Halo eventually detects the anomaly. This new tech is seamless. In theory, you can live invisibly within the data—it just washes over you and you can come and go without notice. You can even manipulate it."

"Is that so bad, wanting to be invisible?"

"It is when our entire system is based on the ability to monitor behaviors and make adjustments as necessary."

"If it's all one glorious shared experience, why aren't you helping the Tarterics track it down? Why are you and the other two families running a side hustle?"

"Obviously, the Variance cannot be allowed to possess this technology. It would be quite damaging if laborers and consumers started dropping out of Halo's view. But, equally unsettling, it appears the Tarterics and the DuSpoles have joined forces to find it and use it to their competitive advantage against the other three families, mine included."

"It's the Consolidation Wars all over again."

"We don't want that to happen," she says.

My noodle bowl trundles up on an old-gen servoid.

"We're almost done," Able says, pointing again at the jammer. "Before we're discoverable, I want to warn you. The Tarterics cannot be trusted."

"But you can be trusted?" I ask. "Why can't you people ever be happy with what you've got? You've literally got it all, including your own damn gated planet, and you're fighting about who can have even more? Do not start another war. You won't find so many people willing to sacrifice for you this time."

"You're telling me that the poor people of Earth wouldn't enjoy making a few extra credits to serve, like you did, or maybe receiving a little property on Mars for the very bravest?"

Wealth makes people insufferable. She's right though. Hopelessness is a powerful motivator.

She laughs. "I'll be in touch."

Able stands, leaving a half-glass of wine on the table.

And the jammer.

She walks out into a waiting hansom cab that streaks off into the night.

I power down the jammer and slip it into my pocket, then turn my attention to the noodle bowl and her left-behind wine. But not for long. As my scroll re-centers, there are at least five urgent messages, and Jynks is vinging.

"Hello?"

"Crucial, where have you been? I've been trying to … prock. I don't want to say it. I have to say it. Essential. We found her. She's dead."

29

Dead isn't a word that is supposed to be said in the same sentence as my sister's name.

My baby sister.

Essential is dead.

I can't wrap my head around it, don't want to wrap my head around it. Won't wrap my head around it because I refuse to believe it. I keep thinking that the force of my disbelief, as long it's monolithic and unwavering, will be enough to keep her alive.

I haven't let a single doubt creep in since I left Earth on the next available q-rocket.

"I need to see the body," I tell Jynks. Not *her* body, I tell myself. The body.

"Crucial, you know that's impossible," Jynks says.

She's talking in a soft, gentle tone and it enrages me.

"I need proof!" I shout into the Dart shuttle's comms board. "I need to see the fucking body."

She is unwavering. "I authorized your return to Mars under the grief statute, but your law enforcement credentials have been revoked. There is no reason for you to pursue the investigation anymore. She's been found. I know it's not the outcome you wanted, not what any of us wanted."

"She's not dead. Either you're lying, or you're being lied to."

Jynks finally raises her voice. "Watch the accusations,

Larsen, or you'll wind up in jail. Now get your head out of your ass. I'm doing you a favor. If the initial reports are correct and Essential was part of the resistance, then you need to start acting less like an investigator and more like a grieving brother, you got me? Otherwise, you'll be socked down so low you'll be living in a beetler, or worse."

"Jynks, I'm gonna go with what they said, that you didn't know I was set up, but these people clearly don't much value the truth, so maybe that's a lie too. You might want to consider what Mel might think if she found out you helped get Essential killed."

She sighs and shakes her head. "I don't keep secrets from Mel, asshole. That's your area of expertise."

"Let me see the body," I say.

"I can't do that. Her remains are on lockdown. Apparently, there's some concern she had illegal tech inside her. Even if I wanted to help, which I don't, it's too late."

"Don't you get it? I won't believe it's her until I see the body."

The doubts are creeping in and I feel a howl of darkness around my heart.

"You've reviewed the coroner's files and the in-situ photo of the remains. That's the best I can do."

I've got the files on my scroll, and have already scoured them. Essential's body was discovered in the backup air duct system of the H-suite separating the dome from the Choke, shoved inside, both femurs broken to fit her in the narrow space, even small as she was.

Is.

As small as she is.

The effects of the cold and constant moisture-free airflow basically flash froze the remains, the report said. The photo looked like her, but it could have been anybody.

One eye was missing, a big gaping hole ripped through her face. The face.

The right eye was missing.

The eye where an OCD is implanted.

"Where's the eye?" I ask.

Jynks scans the restricted files. "It was found near the body."

"Let me see that in person. The eye. I'll recognize it," I say, almost in a whisper, unconsciously rubbing my right eye above my own ocular implant.

Jynks looks sideways and then nods at someone off-screen.

"If it's her, I'll get back on the return rocket and you'll never hear from me again," I say.

"I'll try," Jynks says. "But don't get your hopes up."

She breaks the connection and leaves me to my interstellar misery.

I'm one of only a dozen or so people on this ship, all in our own private berths. I haven't seen a single person since I left Earth. It's a private quantum yacht, reserved for the Five Families. Jynks prioritized me. I guess death comes with certain privileges. Or maybe Mel made her, like she just did with the eye.

Sanders meets me at the bottom of the airlock, where the robo-steward boots me off through the back door. His hair has changed since the last time I saw him. It's red and curly and hanging down to his neck in the back.

"Why are you here?" I ask.

"Master Hoost fully expects you will continue investigating and assigned me to stay with you for two days to help as needed."

"Or to keep me from stumbling onto the truth."

He doesn't take the bait. "The grief allotment for the death of a first-degree relative is two days. You should use it wisely. I assume you want to return to where your sister's body was discovered?"

"Yes."

I follow Sanders to the Tarteric lev-train. We glide through the red-roofed pretend-Earth town heading back to the H-suite.

"I am learning about grief," Sanders says. "It is a complex emotion. Did you find the report troubling to read?"

If Sanders was human, I would say for fuck's sake, asshole, of course it's troubling to read about your sister being crushed inside an airlock, probably there—maybe even alive and in anguish—when I was there sucking down that godsdammned Martian absinthe and watching her best Mars-friend Tashi be annihilated.

"Yeah, troubling is a good word."

"I can see how it might feel as if you failed her," Sanders says. "But I think that is misplaced."

I close my eyes. I am standing on the precipice of a bottomless hole of grief, a familiar place, and one that I'm not sure I'll have the strength to pull myself out of this time. I look down and hear a faint echo of the past, but then stumble backward.

Shut up brain, I tell myself. Kill the doubts. Focus. Be the cop you're supposed to be.

I open my eyes. "Be quiet, Sanders. Let me think."

"I didn't realize humans could stop thinking. Except when they sleep."

"Concentrate, then. Let me concentrate. Now shush."

According to Tarteric Hoost, Essential is part of the Variance. And it seems likely he used her disappearance to trick me into finding whippy-chin-rope guy and his mystery tech that can outsmart Halo. I blundered right into it, and now Coverly is dead and everybody is scrambling to find the tech.

And that's probably what's inside me, which is unsettling. More accurately, terrifying.

The Tarterics want it, the Singhroys want it, the Variance wants it. Everybody wants it. If they knew I had the seeds of revolution inside me, I wouldn't be walking freely around Mars with a quadrillion-credit socially awkward cybansim.

The only thing that makes sense, the only thing I'm willing to hold on to, is that they think Essential is alive and has the tech, and they want me to find her so they'll keep the charade going until I track her down.

There's another alternative, one that my rational mind keeps dwelling on—she really is dead, they can't find the tech and they think I can lead them to the resistance to stamp it out with air cannons.

Those are the only two scenarios that involve me back on Mars and not saddled with multi-gen debt.

I look out the lev-train window. I think we are passing through the symmetrical forest but it's hard to tell since it's so dark. I refocus on the glass and my reflection. I look awful—haggard and drawn.

I've got two days of whatever this grief allotment thing is to figure everything out.

The lev-train comes to a silent sliding stop at the Tarteric dock for the H-suite. It's undergoing repairs, so Sanders guides me through a makeshift entrance. He's set the parameters for somber, I guess, because the place is empty, no naked men or women wandering about.

"Sanders, nice of you to take my feelings into account, but I want to see the parameters of Essential's final H-suite sequence before she disappeared," I say.

His eyes roll back into his head, and I can see the whites and it looks ugly and weird, and then they center again.

That's creepy. Someone needs to tweak the way Sanders connects to Halo.

"The settings themselves are not privatized, but I cannot override Halo to disclose participants," he says.

"That'll do," I say.

30

Sanders does some more mental flips with memory codes and the room gradually transforms from an off-white grieving den—the dull environment Sanders programmed to match the mood of a man whose sister ostensibly just died—into a red-cushioned boudoir with lots of dark corners. The whole place smells like patchouli.

Essential loved patchouli. She said it was a special oil important people used in the old days.

I hear singing and turn around. On a small stage, a tiny dark-haired woman with sad eyes croons breathlessly into an old-style stand-up microphone, pulsing out unrequited desire in an unknown language. Is it ancient French?

A server, barely clothed in some sort of spinning, strategically translucent garment, brushes by with glasses of Martian absinthe, nodding and handing off drinks to colorless voids—the empty space must be the redacted images of the humans present at Essential's last party.

A few meters away, two women sit close to each other on a plushy sofa, both naked, kissing, the hand of one between the thighs of the other.

The singer pauses and the music swells into silence.

A man holding a small glass carafe sits on the other side of the women on the sofa and dribbles oil down the curve of one's spine, and then through the cleave of her breasts. This must be some sort of performance, but who is in the audience?

"It appears your sister was having a party on her last day," Sanders says. "The settings are late twentieth century Paris."

Tashi tiptoes across the lounge floor in shoes with spikes for heels holding something long and thin between her fingers, exhaling a stream of smoke as she walks. She wears a sparkly gown, cut so low down the back that part of her crack is exposed. She walks with purpose, smiling broadly at a blurred-out void.

"Why can I see some people?"

"You are able to see playbacks of anyone Halo designates as non-priority for privacy."

Tashi lets her dress straps drift off her shoulders, and with the gown now shrugged around her waist, she begins to sway with the music, her eyes wide open and looking at someone, smiling broadly.

"Is this a bad time?" says a familiar voice behind me.

I turn to see Mel.

Why is Mel in Essential's last playback?

"Sanders, why is Melinda Hopwire at Essential's last event?"

"Crucial, I'm really here," she says.

"Sanders, freeze playback."

The singer pauses mid-lyric. The women are frozen in mid-kiss, a trail of oil connecting the man's hand to the curve of a hip. Tashi stops swaying, her gown gapped open and bunched at her waist.

"Mel, what are you doing here?" I ask.

"I came with Jynks," she says. "Crucial, I'm so sorry." She has a small metal box in the palm of her hand and holds it out to me.

"What's that?"

"The proof you needed."

Jynks walks into the frozen Paris lounge and looks

around at the sexual tableau. "What a waste of time, Larsen. I don't understand how your mind works."

"Join the club," I say, relieved that I haven't blown up in her presence. Whatever mini bomb is circulating around inside me doesn't appear to be targeting Jynks either.

"Let's move this along. I'm doing you a favor. Mel came along because she thought I might be too rough."

"Essential's body is in that little box?" I ask.

"No, as I told you, emphatically, her remains are quarantined. This is her eye," Jynks says matter-of-factly.

Mel's hand is trembling. I take the box. "You may want a little privacy," she says.

"You looked?" I ask.

She nods. Mel takes Jynks's hand and leads her to the edge of the lounge, just behind the half-naked frozen Tashi. Jynks looks over her shoulder until Mel pulls on her; she is uncomfortable leaving me on my own, but willing to accede to Mel. They sit down on the edge of a holo-couch.

I open the box. Nestled inside a small square of glass is a preserved eyeball looking back at me. Without a face around it, you'd think it would be hard to identify someone's eye but it's not. It's her eye. Essential's eye. Dark jade with black specks around her iris. A hint of wiring at the edges of the retina from the OCD.

"It's hers," I say, closing the box.

Jynks stands. "I'm sorry, Larsen. But you've got your proof now. Go back to Earth. We'll find out what happened and keep you in the loop."

I nod, but I'm not going anywhere. All this proves is Essential lost an eye, not that she is dead. And the fact that it's the eye with her OCD hardware, the eye that connects her to Halo, means something.

Mel comes over and puts her arms around my neck and hugs me tight. Her hair smells like mint. I sink into her embrace and for an instant, I feel as if Mel is holding me up. And then I feel the wetness of her tears on my cheek. She breaks free.

"Sanders, get him out of here," Jynks says. "There's no longer any reason for Crucial Larsen to be on Mars. I'm formally revoking his grief allotment. Come on, Mel. Let's go home."

Jynks takes the box holding my sister's eyeball from my hand.

31

Essential's death has me on autopilot. Literally.

I'm in a hansom rocket with Sanders shooting toward Port Zunil where I'll be seen off this planet for good. Only, I can't let that happen. Not until I get answers.

I'm passing over a delta, the rich sediment marked by branching canyons and old riverbeds carved by the water that once covered much of the surface. It looks like a tangle of loosely braided cables.

Sanders secured me a prioritized seat on a freight rocket back to Earth and is accompanying me to the port, but now is talking about something else. I have his sound turned off and I'm ignoring his captions on my scroll.

I'm watching the Martian landscape slide by, desperately trying to think of my next move, when my feed suddenly erupts in an ad-alanche. That's not supposed to happen on Mars.

It's disorienting—a blizzard of ads, most of them about renting flats in Holden. Flats for Earthers in Holden. The dome where they make weapons. The dome where Tarteric Lloyds oversaw production, and where Loop lived and died.

I close my eyes. Most of them seem to be about something called the Viking building.

It's alternating with lottery ads, trying to get me to pick what will be, the ad promises, a jumbo-winning four-number sequence: 1-2-1-5. It can't be a coincidence.

Someone is feeding me info.

I turn my sound back on with a glance and Sanders is still talking.

"… and of course, the most common theory is that the lack of a magnetic field made Mars more vulnerable to solar storms that stripped away the atmosphere and caused the water to freeze and evaporate. I find that a far more satisfying explanation than the alternate theories, don't you?" he asks.

"Absolutely. And thank you for that science and history lesson."

"My pleasure," Sanders says, beaming. I didn't think cybanisms could feel pride.

"Sanders, I know you're supposed to take me straight to Port Zunil, but would you mind if we take a slight detour to Holden?"

"I don't think that would be possible."

I scan my scroll for details in the ads. "I really want to see the Uzboi Vallis. All your science talk has piqued my interest."

"It doesn't take a synthetic mind to know you want to revisit Loop's apartment."

"No, check my vitals. I don't want to go back to the crime scene. Come on. I won't ever be back on Mars, and this was proof of water once. Come on, please? We'll go to the viewpoint and I'll take a look and then back up we go. Let's keep it from Halo, just for a minute, okay? I'm in grief. I think the view would help."

"I do have a deception subroutine that allows me to lie to achieve certain ends," he says. "I have been anxious to test it, but it requires a vast amount of neural-cognitive resources."

"Glad to know lying comes with a cost," I say.

He's grinning like a kid. "I told Halo we're having

engine problems."

I don't believe for even one second that we're not compromised. But I can hold out some hope Halo has assigned a significant enough value to collecting data on the nature of our deception before we get shut down.

We land in Holden and taxi onto the conveyor. It hooks the nose of the little rocket and pulls us into the dome with a whoosh of air as we enter the controlled gravity and atmosphere. We hop on the travellator streaming through the heart of the residential area and toward the canyon's overlook.

I feel sad and tired, and I hope it's the quantum lag and not whatever micro-tech is coursing through my blood.

We're at the edge of the denser parts of Holden now, and there are a few stores around the travellator. "Hey, do you mind if I grab an espresso?"

I see a dispenser kiosk next to a small park where butterflies flutter around a purple bush.

"Of course not," he says.

I press in my order, approve the credit transfer and the machine does the rest, printing a degradable ceramic square and squirting a stream of black liquid into it. I sit down on a park bench and take a sip.

"Did that dispenser have sweetener?" I ask.

Sanders swivels his head to look. "I believe so," he says.

"Sorry about this," I say, slipping an electrocuff around his wrist and clamping the other to the bench.

He looks at me, confused.

The cuffs are powered by a magnetic flux compression field. The harder you pull, the stronger the force. A pair of rocket ships couldn't break them apart.

"I don't understand," he says, tugging ineffectively at the cuff.

"I need some alone time. Sit here and be quiet and I will

come back for you in an hour."

"You know I have to report this. They will track you."

"Not for a bit," I say, pulling out the jammer Singhroy Able left behind in the noodle shop. "The Five Families are running a game on me, and I don't like that." I turn the jammer on, blocking his transmission, then drop it back in my pocket. "And I expected more from you, Sanders. You're supposed to serve humans. All humans."

Sanders looks wounded. "I am only as good as those who designed me," he says. "Please don't do this, Crucial Larsen. You will be a fugitive. The debt you assume will be crippling."

"I need to know what happened to my sister. I'll be back for you, I promise."

I leave him struggling against the cuff, grab a drone jacket from a nearby kiosk—they're everywhere—and hop up in the air, zipping off toward the Viking towers, the jammer temporarily cloaking me. They'll figure out in short order that I've dropped off Halo, and Sanders will confirm my crimes immediately. They'll find me, without question, but not right away. And hopefully, they'll think I'm headed for Loop's place.

The Viking building is older, hidden from view behind the HARM weapons factory.

The front door is unlocked. I walk down the long hall. It's dark, the lights are flickering. A few doors are open. A man in dirty overalls stands on a threshold. He looks at me curiously.

"I don't recognize you," he says, then shuts the door.

I hear other doors shutting. I won't have long.

The lottery numbers were 1215, the twelfth floor. I take the stairs to avoid getting trapped in the lift. It's a lot of stairs. I watch my heart rate rise and the lactic acid levels in my muscles explode.

The door to 1215 isn't locked—must be nice to live on a planet where beetlers don't find their way into any unlocked room. Inside, the room is filled with Essential. Her smell. Her stuff. Computer interface screens. Plants. A secret squat. She was living here at least part of the time.

How recently though?

I fire up one of the info screens. Code. It's a stream of meaningless code.

There's a bottle of absinthe and I pour myself a glassful and sit on the edge of her bed. There's an animated picture of her and Tashi from the H-suite, smiling and laughing. Essential keeps pointing at something, over and over.

They look so happy.

I've never understood how people can be around something like that, freezing a moment, an action, and watching it over and over again. Pointing. At the closet.

She's pointing at the closet. And laughing. I move the picture base and it flickers and resets and she's still pointing at the closet. She coded a digital anchor in the image.

Gods, Essential, why not just leave a note?

I open the closet and rummage through the clothes. Her clothes. I hold them up and I can smell her. I check the pockets. Nothing.

There's a pair of shoes in the back that don't look like anything she'd normally wear. Heavy and functional, scuffed and well used. I pick one up and look at it. It's got some sort of tech enhancement. I press the mechanism and spikes click into place on the toe and heel. That's odd. Essential would use a drone jacket to cross the street. Next to the shoes is a compact industrial laser no bigger than a coffee cube. There's also a small tool of some kind that fits into my palm.

With the pressure and heat from my palm, it unfolds like a flower blooming to reveal a titanium axe with a cruel, curving blade. I fold it up and drop it into my pocket, along with the laser. Then I strip the crampons off the shoes and take those as well. I don't want to leave any clues.

I sit back on the bed and take a long swallow of the absinthe.

All the items are for ice. I think about the map at Loop's apartment with the poem. Ice. She left it for me. And the coordinates. Why would she want to lead me to Coverly? It was the coder's death sentence.

With the jammer still on and my location blurry, I scroll through my feed. Korolev Crater, near the North Pole, is one of the most inhospitable areas on Mars. Temperatures get down to minus 100, sometimes even colder. The crater is filled with perma-ice almost a mile deep. Other than some early and failed ice harvesting operations to produce water, it's mostly ignored. There's not even a dome.

If there was a place custom-made for the Variance to hide out, it would be Korolev Crater. If Essential is alive, that's where she is.

I finish my absinthe and reach for the bottle to pour another when my scroll gets blitzed. I guess the jammer ran out of juice.

"Prepare to be arrested. Do not attempt to flee. Prepare to be arrested."

I look out the window.

The whole building is ringed by Mars security forces. Literally, they brought all of them. Hundreds. I zoom in and see Jynks standing stiffly next to someone who outranks her. Must be her boss.

They are arguing about something. Probably whether to take me alive and throw me in prison, or exterminate me on the spot.

I'm pretty good at following clues but I really need to work on my escape plans.

32

Jynks is vinging me and I accept.

"What the prock are you doing, Larsen? You damaged a cybanism and went offline to investigate an official issue. That's a terminal offense."

"Look, Jynks, something isn't adding up here. And I think you know it. I don't believe Essential is dead."

"We've got her eye. She's dead. Iced in the morgue. I'm sorry, but grief has made you stupid. They want to take you out, right here."

Another ving is bumping in and I take it.

It's Mel.

She looks worried.

"Crucial, what are you doing? Jynks says you are breaking about a dozen laws, any one of them fatal."

"Just following the evidence, Mel. Pretty sure Essential is still alive."

"Even if she is, you can't help her now," Mel says, an unfamiliar steadiness to her voice.

"I have to try. I let her down too."

Mel shakes her head sadly. "It won't make things better for her if you die. It will make them worse. Turn yourself in before things get out of hand."

"You sound like you care what happens to me."

"I'd rather you were in prison than dead."

"That's the nicest thing you've said to me in eight years," I say. "But I have to go now. I probably won't make it. But you should know something. I know I messed things up between us. Messed up a good thing. A great thing. But the truth is, if I had to do it all over again, I don't know what I'd do different."

"I know," she says. "I know that about you." She breaks the connection.

Jynks slams back into my feed. "Who the hell are you talking to? Is that Mel? Are you talking to Mel? I swear to gods I am going to throw you out of a q-rocket myself. Larsen, stand down and come outside with your hands up or they're going to turn you into liquid and pour your remains out into the Choke and freeze you into bloody little ice cubes."

The good thing about living with a scroll that's always overflowing with data is that it's easy to ignore things.

If Essential is alive, and they catch me with all this ice gear, they're going to figure it out as quickly as I did. Well, maybe not as quickly. But quickly enough.

I scan the building specs looking for inspiration. It's sixteen stories tall, the top of it a good twenty meters from the edge of the dome. There are plenty of police fliers buzzing around, but my odds of escaping in the air are much higher than wading through the cordon of kill-hungry bodies and hardware around the building.

But first I need to make them think I'm stationary. Or at least hide my motion in a cloud of conflicting data.

I use the ice axe to chip away the fire suppression nozzles in the ceiling and then throw a bunch of Essential's clothes on the bed, soak them with absinthe and flare them to life with the pocket laser. They catch quickly. Martian absinthe, apparently, is basically q-rocket fuel. I apologize to my liver.

The flames catch and blaze, dark smoke billows up and alarms are going off. I open the door.

"Run, fire, get out now!" I yell, and people start spilling toward the elevators or hopping out the launch windows in drone jackets.

It's pure chaos, and the cops have their hands—and scrolls—full for the time being.

I run against the press of the sullen crowd toward the back-stair tube, a narrow, circular affair designed only to be used if all the tech in the building fails. I'm huffing and puffing and sweating by the time I reach the door leading to the roof. It's locked so I fire up the pocket laser, set it for a close burn job and melt the hinges away.

With one shoulder slam, the hatch flies off and I roll out into the open.

The roof is empty, but it won't be for long. Fliers are moving close, and cops in drone jackets—sharpshooters—are buzzing around like angry flies.

It'll be a miracle if I make it out unscathed. I set my jacket and bend my knees to jump but before I can take off, there's a flash and crash and the impact bowls me over. Ears ringing, blood trickling from my nose, I stagger up.

It's the hansom rocket. The cab opens and Sanders steps out, holding his detached hand. The stump of his wrist has already healed.

"Sanders, what the brownloaf are you doing? Are you here to arrest me?"

"No, Crucial Larsen. I'm here to help you."

"But you're programed to spy on me."

"Yes, that is correct. But my instructions were to protect you as well. The Tarterics were very clear in that charge. Possibly too clear. Fulfilling that charge is paramount and, given the inconsistencies in the data, I must innovate to ensure your continued survival. At least until I am reprogrammed."

He gestures at the rocket with his other hand.

"I encourage you to use this to escape and preserve your safety until such time that more rigorous adherence to the truth can be expected."

"That's a good plan," I say. "What about you?"

"I will use your drone jacket to draw them away. I suggest blasting straight up through the dome and out into the Martian expanse."

I hand him the drone jacket and he shrugs into it. "Sorry about the hand," I say.

"I understand your motives," Sanders says. "And I appreciate that you didn't simply push me in front of the train."

"Yeah, I guess in that way, I'm kind of a hero."

"I hope we have a chance to meet again," Sanders says. "This case is fascinating, and I do hope to learn how it all turns out. Though I can assume if they bring me back, my programming will be changed to focus less on your well-being."

"That's almost certain," I say. "Tell me, Sanders, do you feel pain?"

"Oh, yes," Sanders says. "My coders felt it necessary for my ongoing education."

"I'm sorry then. Pretty sure the security forces are not going to take it easy on you."

"Then I shall learn a great deal in the next few minutes."

I strap in and pull the hansom canopy down. Sanders waves and jumps off in a lazy arc that sends him over the bulk of the gathered security forces.

Jynks is yelling into my scroll.

"Set down! Crucial Larsen, set down immediately. Hold your fire," she says to her people. "Set down!" she yells at me again. No one is listening to her orders.

Sanders indeed gets an education in pain. They open fire almost immediately, either not hearing or disobeying

Jynks's orders to hold fire. There's a wave of flechettes from glitter guns and bolts from rail guns—it looks like a sparkling steel rain.

Sanders gets hit and wobbles, then gets hit again. Pieces of him are falling off, and then he starts to drop like a rock.

I enter the coordinates for Korolev Crater, press launch and the hansom rocket flares up. I override the autopilot and aim it right at the apex of the dome where it's the weakest.

The controls are beeping and flashing and trying to convince me to push the nose down. I just keep the throttle open. These little rockets can survive a direct hit with a trash sled, so I'm not too worried about the impact.

Well, a little worried.

By now the cops realize the blue slime in the drone jacket raining down on them is a cybanism and not me, and they are unimpressed. Fliers are headed my way and the sharpshooters too, rattling flechettes. But I've got a pretty good head start and I'm moving fast. Still, a couple hit me, but most curve wide and pierce the dome ahead of me. It weakens the dome shell and I max the boost, close my eyes and ignore the blaring alarms.

"Don't do this," Jynks says. It's the last thing I hear before I hit the dome a split second before a puff from an air cannon lights up my tail and sends the rocket spinning out of control into the Choke.

33

I don't know if it's day or night anymore. I do know I'm hungry as hell and I need to piss. But that's the point, isn't it? In the militia, we called it soft torture, the only type of torture tolerated as the Five Families consolidated. That doesn't mean other types don't occur, only that I can be fairly confident that at least in Halo security headquarters, I probably won't get a neural waterboarding or be plugged into a holo of a burning room.

"Crucial, what aspects of life on Mars did you find unusual?"

"Unusual?"

"Your voice transcripts, including with Sanders, and your search history indicate a certain interest in Martian history."

"It's a fascinating place, in a 'never want to set foot there again' kind of way."

"Do you have additional questions?"

Here we go again. Halo is trying to soften me up for something. It's okay. I only need to stall for a few more hours.

"Yeah, I do, like why are there no other life forms on Mars? And no sign of past inhabitants?"

"Evidence suggests the planet may have, in the distant

184

past, had a hospitable environment for the evolution of single-celled life forms, given the indications of flowing water and relative proximity to the sun, the building blocks for more complex life forms, such as humans. But that was billions of years ago. No traces of life forms have ever been found."

"Why is that?"

"Research demonstrates that chance plays a role in the evolution of life."

"You mean it was dumb luck we had everything necessary on Earth," I say.

"In a sense, yes."

In other words, a bunch of factors miraculously came together in just the right measure and sequence over the course of billions of years to create all the kinds of life—from humans to giraffes to yeast—and the environment to allow us all to thrive on Earth, and then we had to go and fuck it all up in a few hundred years. The equivalent of a geologic microsecond, the blink of an eye, and then the lucky ones escaped to Mars. Or, more accurately, the uber-rich ones escaped.

Empathy for one another. That was one thing that got left out when all those chemical building blocks came together a billion years ago. Or more likely empathy was there—it made us social—but it was trampled by whatever else was incorporated into the original design—the desperate urge to win, to come out on top, the will to power, even when winning means destroying other humans, and eventually yourself.

Humans are nuts. Rich, poor, resisters, administrators, cops, parents—maybe parents most of all—it's pretty much all of us. We're all doomed. Give me a bottle of absinthe and a desert hologram any day.

"Your sister had unusual eyes," Halo says.

There it is. That's what the distraction was all about. Classic bait and switch. I feel my heart rate increasing.

Time for my own distraction. "I need to piss."

"After seeing your sister's eye, you concluded she was dead?" Halo says, ignoring me.

"Do you want me to soak the floor?"

"Your bio-indicators suggest you should be able to resist the urge to urinate for quite some time. Please answer the question."

I lick my lips. My mouth feels like it's filled with red Martian dust and old glitter needles.

"Yeah, I concluded she was dead. The Five Families wouldn't let me see the body, but that was, without a doubt, her eye."

"Crucial, after you determined your sister was dead, why did you set fire to a living unit in Holden, and then evade the authorities, damage a dome and disappear into the Martian wilderness?"

This is where it will get tricky. Halo is digging in deep.

"I guess the grief got to me. It's a very complex emotion," I say, willing my voice to tremble a little.

"The evidence suggests Essential rented that living unit under an assumed identity, hiding from detection. The Five Families would like to know how she did that, and they would also like to know how you found that living unit belonging to your sister."

"Like evolution, sometimes you just get lucky."

There is a long pause as Halo monitors me.

"I'm afraid you are not being truthful, Crucial. This will not reflect well on you."

"I'm thinking if you had access to the truth, I wouldn't be here."

Another long pause. I'd like to think I'm aggravating the system. But the universe's most powerful AI doesn't get aggravated. Or tired. Or hungry.

"You nearly died in the Choke," Halo says.

"Nearly is the operative word," I say. "Because here I am having lived through that hell only to be having this lovely conversation with a machine while I fight the urge to wet my pants."

"Based on the data analysis, the outcome of you remaining alive is impossible without assistance. Crucial, who assisted you? Or was this also dumb luck?"

It's setting a trap. And my lies are spinning out of control.

"I said I have to piss. Do you want me to go in the corner?"

"Crucial, we are aware of your penchant and talent for distraction. We simply want you to answer the questions truthfully. How did you survive in the Choke?"

I get up from the chair and take a few steps toward the corner of the interrogation room. By the third step, the temperature in the room is dropping fast. I take another. Now I'm gasping for breath. Then the room is filling with a fine red dust. I can't breathe.

"Crucial, we are recreating the conditions of the Martian wilderness to stimulate your memory."

I am prone on the floor now. "There … are better … ways to stimulate my…"

My lips are beginning to stick to the freezing tiles.

"Tell us how you survived after fleeing Holden."

I'm in trouble. I'm going to end up in a labor prison or reconditioning camp. "Dumb luck. I found an old mining squat."

It's not too far from the truth.

34

Six nights ago

I spiral some distance from the cracked dome, dizzy and nauseous and out of control. The instrument panel is shrieking warnings, my scroll is flashing alerts, and everything is upside down and spinning and sparking. I land hard. My head bangs against the top of the hansom rocket and I careen, top over bottom, side to side, for what seems like kilometers. The rocket bumps against something big, then bangs against something bigger and skitters sideways.

The cab is grinding against the rocky surface—passing by in a blur—and I wonder how long before the cockpit strips away and my skull pastes across the surface of Mars. The rocket hits one more rock and barrels part way up a hill, then loses momentum and finally rolls back down, bumps into an outcropping and shudders to a stop. I hear an unfamiliar noise that sounds bad. I realize it's me screaming.

I do a quick check. Nothing broken, no blood.

I listen for the sounds of pursuit. Nothing. Silence.

My heart is pounding. I hear the blast of sand against the battered hull, driven by the wind. The dashboard is blinking, and then lets out a faint whine and goes dark.

Jynks's voice fills my scroll.

"We're not coming for you Larsen, you're on your own.

Sorry. Orders."

She sounds almost sad.

"I don't want you to come for me," I say. "That's the whole point of escaping."

She's silent. We both know I'll die out here.

Now what, smart guy? Think. Think!

I look out over the dead dashboard. In the distance, against a vast expanse of rusty red, the sky is turning that special kind of iridescent blue as the sun sets, which in any other situation would be awe-inspiring but now only means that it won't be long before the temperature drops to minus 100 degrees, or worse. I'll be flash-frozen in this banged-up cab when they find me.

The anti-gravity functions are shutting down. I rip out any metal flaps I can reach. In the third compartment, bingo. I grab the emergency pack from underneath the flight seat, doing a quick tally. Micro-protein packs. Condensed water. An airhoodie and a thermal suit.

The overhead light blinks off. No time to waste.

I wriggle into the suit, which is not easy in the cramped space. I hit my elbow against the dash twice, bang my knee on my forehead once. The suit is supposed to be one size fits all. I think it's for a kid.

The too-low gravity is another problem. I can feel my brain throbbing. The airhoodie has an equalizer and I get it on before I pass out.

I look out the dash window again. As the angle of waning sunlight hits the ice fields in the distance, a flash of gold reflects off its edge. Damn, this planet is beautiful. It's a rugged, dangerous kind of beauty, and it will probably be the end of me, but at least I won't die in some Earth trash pit full of human feces and dead woodpeckers.

Oh, no you don't, Mars, you won't win me over. The ice fields are where Essential is, if she's still alive.

I take a squirt of the thick water and then activate the airhoodie. Nothing happens. I breathe in, gently at first but then with growing panic. It finally starts circulating. I don't know how long the oxygen will last, or if the junior thermal suit will keep me from freezing to death, but there's no turning back now.

I have one shot. I'm headed toward whatever reflected the sun. If it's metal, it means a building. If it's mineral, I'll die there. Or on the way. It's a long trek.

I kick out the door and poke my head outside. A flash of green lights up the horizon as the sun sinks out of view and I slip outside into the Martian twilight.

I take a step, then another. I'm warm. Not tropical warm, but enough to keep me alive. And bonus, the low gravity makes me feel half as light as my weight on Earth. That should make my slog a little easier.

I set my sights on the ice fields and push forward. I don't have any way of measuring time, but I know my stride is just under a half-meter. By my calculation, it's a good thirty kilometers. If I'm lucky and tenacious—and my oxygen holds—I'll make it by morning. If Essential is there, I'll live. If not, I'll die.

The red soil crunches beneath my boots. I walk through a vast expanse of rocky rubble. I make my way around craters, some big enough to swallow a city, others as small as blood splatter. I remember that Mars was bombarded by space rocks in its ancient past, and across the Choke, you see the effect.

Like bullet holes.

I bend my head into the now gusting wind and keep walking. Seven hundred steps so far. Got to move faster. After what seems like an eternity, I get to a thousand steps.

A line from an old song Mel used to sing once in while slips into my head. *I go out walkin' after midnight ...*

Not on Mars.

I make my way around a mid-sized crater, and to my left I sense movement—can't hear for shit in the airhoodie—and turn ready for a fight, but it's only a landslide of rocks streaming down the far side of the crater's edge.

Four thousand steps. The ice field doesn't look any closer. Keep going, Crucial. A few more steps and just ahead, I see that sparkle again. I head toward the glittering light.

I trip over a small boulder. Down I go, and the undersized suit rips at the knee. But the airhoodie holds. My knee is throbbing. I get my rasping breath under control, but don't have the energy to stand back up.

I'll rest a few minutes. If I rest now, I'll be able to walk faster later. My feet are tingling, like they've fallen asleep. Sleep. I can keep walking in the morning. Sure, why not, this suit will keep me warm.

I look up at the Martian sky. Gods, it's lovely. A constellation that looks like a smiling face twinkles. Both moons are nearly full.

I sigh. What a waste of life, I think. I've wasted the whole damn thing. Here I thought if I made a name for myself in the militia, did my part for law and order on behalf of the Five Families, it would pay off. And it did, in a way. Enough food. Static debt. Plenty of holo-time. A decent enough place to live. But it meant I had to turn away from everything, look the other way, even from myself. And the only damn thing that might have made it all worthwhile, I threw away.

Mel. Gods, it was good. I mean, I know I was a wreck when Mom died, but why did I take it out on you? You wanted to help me. And now you've found Jynks.

"Mel, I'm sorry," I whisper. My breath steams up the interior of the headpiece.

You've got a good partner in Jynks, I'm glad for you. That's bullshit. I'm not glad for you.

The anger gets me back on my feet. Fuck Jynks. I want you back, Mel. I can only get you back if I live.

I stagger forward another couple hundred steps then decide I can get Mel back after a nap, because I can't even keep my eyes open anymore. I hear that song again. A voice inside my head screams at me to get up but my legs won't move.

I've failed everyone, and now I've failed Essential too.

The wind is stronger. That face of stars twinkles at me again. Or maybe mocks me. I close my eyes and listen to the music as a fine layer of sand covers my body.

I go out walkin' after midnight
Out in the moonlight
Just like we used to do, I'm always walkin' after midnight
Searchin' for you

I slip into a dream. Essential and I are children, playing dominoes, a game my mother said her mother learned from her mother, in a place called Texas. The dominoes make clicking sounds as Essential moves them around the table, like the sound of footsteps.

35

It's dark and silent.

I guess I'm dead.

Everything hurts though. My lungs, my brain, my muscles. I always counted on the pain going away when I died.

I try to sit up and bump my head on a low ceiling. I'm stashed inside some sort of sleeping pod. I can breathe, which I do with gusto, from a bent over half-sitting position. After a few deep inhales, my head goes woozy, and I start to pant. I stretch back out, trying to smooth out my heart rate.

And that's when I notice I'm naked.

I hear audio. It sounds familiar. Like a desert breeze. Soft and warm and calming, not like the godsdamn frigid rusty-sandpaper wind of Mars. I smell juniper, and in the distance a coyote howls.

Only two people know I like to sleep naked in the desert at night.

I sit up too quickly and again bang my head on the cover of the sleeping pod.

"Godsdamn it all to hell," I say. "That hurt."

"Still got the trash mouth," a voice says, and the cover opens to a dazzling light and the blurry vision of an angel.

I am flooded with what I can only call a full-bodied joy. I slide out of the pod. But my legs betray me and I wobble, knees buckling, and I fall into a heap on the floor.

And there she is, standing right in front of me. "Essential," I say, looking up. "You're alive."

She kneels next to me. "Yes, Crucial, I'm alive." She wraps her arms around me and in that embrace, I feel the simple comfort of childhood certainty and then a wash of relief. My baby sister, Essential, my only living family member, is still living. I didn't let her down, she isn't dead.

I'm so happy I'm shaking, and that makes me feel ridiculous. Apparently, the doubts got a lot closer to my heart than I thought.

Essential leans back. "It's okay, Crucial. I'm okay. It's all going to be okay. Well, mostly."

I touch her cheek. She smiles, and an image of a stubborn little girl slips into my mind, but I can't ignore the eye patch.

"Your eye," I say.

"I'll tell you everything, but first drink this. You need to get your strength back and get ready to move, because we can't stay here."

She hands me a container. I tilt my head back and pour something foul-tasting into my mouth. It tastes like acid and reclaimed quantum piston lube.

I start to spit it out, but Essential stops me and laughs. "I know it tastes bad, but it has everything you need to get your body back to tip-top condition." She looks at me. "Or whatever condition you're normally in."

I nod, because I feel weaker than I've ever felt. I manage two more swallows. I hang my head for a minute, but then the drink kicks in. My head clears enough to take a good hard look around. Whatever we are in is about the same size as the hansom rocket. Two people, maybe three small ones, can maneuver around the central area, if they keep their elbows in tight.

"Did you just rescue me?"

"Yes."

I have a vague flash of being pulled out of the Choke and dumped into the pod.

"How did you find me?"

"We've been tracking you ever since you met with Tashi."

"We?" I ask. "Essential, what the hell is going on?"

"Maybe put some pants on first?" She laughs again, a sound that threatens to shatter my heart with happiness from the familiarity, a sound I thought I'd never hear again. She tosses me a gray jumpsuit.

"Oh good, pajamas," I say, pushing aside the emotion and sliding my legs into the pants.

She grins in that lopsided way she has had since she was a kid. I glance at her sideways while I get dressed. Her short time on Mars has aged her and she's lost a little of the sensual, voluptuous quality that attracted men and women alike. She's all angles now, cheekbones jutting out, collarbones like cliffs, and even through her skin-tight thermal suit, I can see the new wiriness of her muscles. It looks good on her.

"We're at a resupply outpost. We have them strategically hidden in the Choke. I've got a transport coming—" She checks a device on her wrist. "We've got forty-three minutes until rendezvous."

"Why isn't Halo finding you?"

She looks over at me and taps the patch. "Halo can't track me anymore."

"Your eye," I say, finally understanding, as I pull up the zipper on my pajamas. "What happened?"

"I took it out," she says, in a matter-of-fact tone that leaves me cold. "They were getting too close to me. And to Coverly. I needed to disappear, immediately."

"Gods. That must have hurt like an acid enema."

"It wasn't pleasant, that's for sure," she says, her furrowed brow hinting at echoes of pain.

"They said they had your body. They showed me the files. It looked like you."

"It should be clear by now, they lie. About everything."

"I thought you were dead."

She moves beside me and takes my hand. "I know. I'm really sorry. Things happened pretty quickly after the Fields."

"Wait, you were involved in that?"

"They were on to me and using you to find Coverly. Didn't you think it was weird how much time you were spending in the Fields, how often you got sent there?"

"I try not to think about things like that. A strategy that's worked fine for forty-one years."

"Oh yeah, your life is turning out so well. They were using you to track him down, assuming we wouldn't fight back because, well, you're my brother. They were wrong about that."

"You gave the orders?"

She nods. "I told them to protect you, but Coverly was the primary. His life is, was, more important than ours. It worked out."

"Not for some of my buddies."

"Your buddies work for murderers."

"You do too," I say. "One of your little pals was going to take Jynks's head off at the H-suite."

"He would have been disciplined. He was acting on his own initiative, but this is war and things get messy."

I shake my head. "Mars has changed you."

"No," she says. "Barely living on Earth has changed me."

I touch my eye. "What about me? Why am I not drawing heat?"

"You're jammed," she says, pointing to the little unit I lifted from Able. It's sitting on the pod. "I charged it up when I found you. Go on, take a few more sips. Gotta be at full strength. And with your mental acuity intact. Such as it is."

"Are you calling me stupid? You're the stupid one."

She laughs, but it stays on the surface. "No, you're stupid."

"How long have you been in the resistance?"

"Longer than you might expect. Now finish the drink," she says.

I take the last third in a long swallow. "Ugh," I say, wiping my mouth with the back of my hand. "Truly revolting. And speaking of revolting, what the hell did that guy with the noodle beard put in me?"

"The future," she says simply. "Don't worry, there's nothing in what you swallowed that will hurt you. It was a race to finish it before they found him, before you found him. We decided to scrap our plans to pick it up and let you bring it back to Mars."

"Hold on. You gave me the coordinates? You used me like a godsdamn mindless transport ship, faked your own death, and he willingly vaporized his head …" I wince at the memory. "Just to put that pill inside me?"

"Yes," she says. "And then bring it back to Mars."

"That's … brilliant, really. Cold and calculating and mean. But brilliant. My sister, scheming like a member of the Five Families."

A look of hurt washes over her eye. "Like I said, things got chaotic. They were using you to look for me and for Coverly. We needed a new plan, and fast."

I nod, still trying to wrap my head around the fact that Essential used me—I was a disposable courier.

"I didn't want you to get hurt," she says, her voice low.

197

"And yet I've almost died more times than I can count on both hands."

"Crucial, what's inside you can take down Halo."

"Nothing can take down Halo, or the system it props up," I say. "And trying to dismantle Halo would lead to chaos on Earth and Mars. I hate Halo and all it represents, but people are used to it now. They wouldn't know how to live any other way. It works, badly, but it works."

"Your biggest problem has always been your lack of imagination," she says with a dismissive look. The normally delicate motion, a combination of an eye roll and a lip curl, is magnified by the lack of one eye. "People can get used to living in a cave, but if you accept there's nothing beyond the shadows, you've given up."

"Or you've accepted the reality of the human condition," I say.

"Don't worry, we'll get the tech out of you and you can go back to your happy little cave," she says.

"Good," I say, with a sharper edge than I intend. We went from joyful reunion to squabbling siblings in record time.

"Not bad, how I finally led you to my Mars squat, right?"

"With the ads."

"I wanted to get you to the ice crater. It's our base of operations."

"How can you all hide from Halo?"

"There are ways. None of them a hundred percent effective and all of them temporary, except for disabling the OCD," she says, tapping her eye patch.

Right on cue, the floor starts to tremble and shudder.

"What's going on?" I ask. "Is our pickup early?"

She looks at the screen on her wrist. "Shit. Mars security forces."

"I thought you couldn't be tracked," I say.

"It's not me. Your jammer must be malfunctioning." She tosses me a little bottle. "Squirt these drops in your eye," she says, and then points at the little dilapidated rocket nosing toward the door of the building. "Strap in. We're not going down without a fight."

36

I peek outside the window and see a ring of heavily armed airships circling the little shack dome, all wishing me harm. Sadly, I'm getting used to the sight.

They're in no rush though. Conflict in the Choke is risky—one fragment is all it takes to puncture an airhoodie. They can wait us out. We'll run out of oxygen soon enough and if we try to take off in Essential's rusted bucket of a flier, there are half a dozen air cannons and rail guns ready to pulverize us before we even get in the air.

"We're not going to make it through that," I say to Essential.

She gives me a wild, one-eyed look. "It can't end like this. We're too close. You have to survive."

"Let's surrender and let them put us in work details. We'll spend the rest of our lives in a debt gang, but we'll be alive. And maybe together."

"You don't get it," she says. "What's inside you can change the future as well as the present. They don't know it's inside you, not yet, but they'll figure it out. You have to make it out of here. I'll distract them and you make a blast for it."

I catch her arm.

"I'd never make it. That's the first thing. And the second thing is, even if I could, I'm not leaving you here. I thought you were dead before and now that I found you, I'm not letting anything happen to you. No matter how ridiculous you're acting."

She shakes free.

"Crucial, this is bigger than us. We have an obligation to help Earthers break free of this poisonous, damaging system."

"We don't owe anyone anything," I say. "Look out for number one, that's the only rule that matters."

She looks at me sadly. "Mom would be broken-hearted if she heard you say that."

"Mom is the reason I am this way," I snap back. "She spent her whole life trying to find the good in people, and what did it get her? A broken neck."

"I'm sorry," Essential says. "You learned the wrong thing from that tragedy." She picks up a glitter gun. "If we can make things better for people, we have to try. I'll die before I give up."

"You're not dying, not today. And I'm not leaving here without you."

"Then you better figure a way out," Essential says, "or else I'm stepping out that door to draw their fire. And I know you won't let me die in vain."

I look around, panicked by the thought because I know she'll do it.

"You said they can't track you?" I ask.

"I disconnected from Halo when I took my eye out. That means I can't be tracked. I have a splinter watch to backdoor in, but it's risky. And I can't interact with anyone who is connected. I can't be in public without setting off alarms."

I scan her for good measure, and it's true, she doesn't exist in my scroll. It's searching and searching but unable to reconcile the lack of data. And flagging the anomaly. But the flags aren't going anywhere.

"What are the drops you gave me?"

"Blur drops. A temporary chemical block. Lasts a few hours. But the more you use it, the greater the risk of blindness."

"Blindness? What is wrong with you?" I ask, looking around the building. "Tell me about this place."

"It's an old prospectors' outpost. In the early days, they needed people up here to test the conditions. The first colonists from the Five Families started this story that you could find diamonds on Mars as big as your fist, but deep underground. A whole wave of miners came up and started poking around, staying for years at a time. All so the Five Families could study the effects of the gravity and the light and the cold, but the miners didn't know. They spent years drilling these massive boreholes and scraping around through the gravel. Of course, there were no diamonds. There never were."

I blow the dust off the old panel. It's basically an antique, a curiosity, but when I hardwire it to the instrument panel in the pod, it juices up with a whirr. I pull up the schematics.

There's a borehole running underneath us sloping down and toward the edge of a nearby crater. And it's a big borehole. Almost a meter and a half across and 500 meters long. Tight though. Too tight for drone jackets.

"You said you outfitted this place. Is there enough gear to hike to the next outpost?"

"Yes," she says. "Food, water, thermal suits, plenty of airhoodies. But how do we get past them?"

"We don't," I say. "We go under them." I tap on the map glowing green on the screen.

"There's no way that borehole hasn't collapsed somewhere along the line."

"Maybe," I say. "But I like our odds of probable death there better than certain death here. We just have to sell it a little."

"You're insane."

"You literally gave up one of your eyes to fake your own death, and I'm insane? Round up the gear you think we'll need, and I'll make sure they settle in for the long haul."

I ving Jynks. She's in full tactical gear and clearly not in the mood to talk.

"Crucial Larsen, I have a warrant for your arrest."

"Hey, Jynks. How are you doing and what's the charge?"

"The charge is everything, Larsen. Literally everything. Evading arrest. Damaging a dome. Killing a cybanism. Helping the resistance. Probably cannibalism, and definitely pissing me off."

"Listen, Jynks, it's all a lie. The whole thing. They're using you."

"Fine, come in and we'll get it all straightened out."

"I saw how you straightened out things with Sanders, poor bastard."

"The people responsible have been disciplined," Jynks says.

"Disciplined like arrested or disciplined like docked credits?" I ask.

"Does it matter?"

"Yeah," I say. "It matters if they're out there with you right now. I'm not in a trusting mood. Look, I'm not coming out. Also, you should know, reinforcements are on the way. You know how my unit was attacked on Earth in the Fields? Expect the same. When you least expect it."

Jynks looks at me curiously. "You are saying I should expect something when I don't expect anything? That doesn't make sense. I'm always expecting something. Does that mean nothing will ever happen?"

"No, it will happen. Definitely. You're overthinking it.

What I mean is you'd better be ready for conflict. I like you. Well, I like Mel, so I don't want anything to happen to you. Or your people. You should back off before someone gets hurt. Plus, the resistance put mines all around this place."

"Our sensors aren't picking up anything."

"That's how deadly they are. You can't see them, but they're here."

Jynks shakes her head. "We can outwait you, Crucial. No matter how much oxygen you have, we have more. And I really want to be home right now with Mel drinking a nice glass of barley beer and sharing an avatainment jack. Don't make me stay out here much longer."

"I've got nothing but time and oxygen, Jynks," I say and disconnect.

"She seems really nice," Essential says. "I'm glad Mel hooked up with a winner."

"Do you want my help, or do you want to just run out and draw their fire?"

She laughs and hands me my pack and a thermal suit. "Let's try it your way first."

"Any explosives in your stash?" I ask.

"A couple of fusion petards. Pretty small, given we're facing an army."

She hands me one—a small, oval-shaped glass device—and I clamp it to the rocket near the fuel tanks. "How long do you think it will take us to get through the tunnel?" she asks.

"Hard to tell, depends on the conditions inside," I say. "Not more than an hour, probably less. I'm setting this for forty-five minutes. We'll have to hustle."

"We're going to die, aren't we?"

"Have a little faith."

We put on our airhoodies and move to the underground

level. There's a big steel door, rusted and warped, and I use a loose piece of railing to pry it open. The borehole angles away from us at a steep ten-degree slope. It's too narrow to stand. We've got head lanterns and I clip mine on and shine it down the tunnel. It looks endless.

37

"You thinking what I'm thinking?" I ask.

"That oil slick that showed up behind our building when I was seven?"

"Yep."

"That was so much fun. But gods, we stank. Mom was so irritated."

"Let's do it like that," I say. "Feet first. But hold on tighter than you did back then. You damn near gave me a concussion."

"You couldn't pry me loose this time," Essential says.

I hesitate at the edge, thinking about the prospect of sliding down a low-gravity, oxygen-depleted borehole on the worst planet in the universe.

"Get a move on," Essential says. "I'm not entirely certain about those fusion petards."

"What?"

"They're pretty old," she says. "They might go off sooner. Like a lot sooner."

"Now you tell me," I say as I slide my legs into the borehole and pull us down into the tunnel, bracing my feet against the smoothed-out edges to hold us steady as she squeezes all the way inside.

I'm about to warn Essential to hold on to the lip until I can get a better position on the slippery sides, but before I can get the words out, she pushes us off and we're sliding down the borehole like a projectile from a glitter gun, bumping and bouncing fast and hard against the walls.

"Just like old times!" Essential shouts, laughing.

I strain my eyes, trying to make out if the hole is clear but the tunnel narrows, my lamp knocks against the ceiling and goes dark. Essential's lamp is blocked by my shoulders but sends out intermittent flashes of light against our sides, like a bouncing strobe.

The borehole turns to the left and opens slightly. With the extra headroom, I struggle to reposition my light but end up only angling it farther down, so it's uselessly illuminating my belly as we careen down the tunnel.

Essential leans back more deeply and pulls my shoulders along with her, trying to slow us down. Her movement jars my airhoodie and now I'm gasping for oxygen as we hurtle along the polished, icy rock. I try to adjust it, but my elbow keeps hitting the walls and I'm shaking my head and sucking in carbon dioxide and trying to signal to my sister—who's laughing her head off—that I can't breathe, all while trying to keep us upright in the slippery tunnel and hoping we don't crash into a solid wall of rock.

Stars are exploding behind my eyes. "Air," I croak.

"Oops, sorry!" she yells, and adjusts my airhoodie. I suck in oxygen like a drowning man. The borehole has gotten steeper and we're sliding faster, our bodies twisting and turning like a rocket.

Gods help us if we hit anything.

I make another attempt to reposition my headlamp and this time it works. The light shines down into the tunnel but all I see is a gleaming darkness whooshing past, no end in sight. And some low-hanging extrusions.

"Protect your head!" I yell, and she tucks in more tightly against my shoulders.

I drag my heels along the side to try to slow us down a

little, but can't get any traction against the walls, and then the incline decreases by a few degrees and we slow by half and I'm thinking maybe we're finally coming to the end and just then we turn vertical.

Essential crashes down onto my head and neck as the borehole spits us out.

We land hard on gravel and I do a face plant. Essential rolls off my back. Our lights get jarred off by the impact and we both stay motionless—except for our rasping breath and pounding hearts—in the pitch-black darkness, afraid we might be on the edge of some fatal precipice.

"You okay?" she whispers.

"Hell of a ride," I say. "But yeah, I'm okay. You?"

"I think so," she says.

She whistles. There's a faint echo. I pick up a piece of gravel and toss it into the darkness. It doesn't hit a wall. I throw harder this time. No ricochet. She tosses up a rock and we hear it hit above us.

"Seven, maybe eight meters on the vertical," Essential says. "Probably there used to be a ladder or something to get in and out of that hole."

I touch my head to restart my lamp, but it's gone. She twists her headlamp and it flickers to life. Essential stands and as she circles around, the light splashes across the rock walls.

"No cliffs or severe downhills," she says. "I can't tell if this is a natural cave or machine-made."

It's dense rock, the same as above ground but a little less red and much less jagged. A few spots look like they've been hammered out, likely where the poor saps were looking for diamonds that didn't exist, all the time feeding biological data back to Halo about how to die on Mars. Discarded, rusted-out machinery litters the edge of the cave.

"Did the Five Families leave all those miners to die here?"

"Yes," she says. "Rotten bastards."

I try to shake the images of those misguided men and women laboring away in this hole.

"Where did the schematic say the borehole ends?" I ask.

"The edge of the crater," she says. Essential tips her light up to the ceiling. "Holy gods, look at that. Maybe there were diamonds after all."

An iridescent shimmer covers the dark rock.

Essential moves the light closer and when I stand to follow her, I trip over my own headlamp. It clicks on. I pick it up and our combined lights illuminate the ceiling. The rock is covered by a layer of glimmering colors—purple, green, orange, yellow, pink—and the closer I look the more colors pop out, every centimeter a dazzling kaleidoscope.

"It's not diamonds, but it is beautiful," I say.

"But what is it?" Essential says.

"Don't know, we'll ask later," I say. "Come one, we gotta go. When those fusion petards blow, the flames will cook us down here."

Essential places her palm on the glittering rock face.

I adjust my light to the other side of the cavern and take the few steps to the edge where I discover a passageway. Inside the entry point are stairs, rough-hewn into the rock, leading up. And a pile of bones. Human bones. Still held together by the fraying material of an early-era thermal suit.

"Here's our way out," I say. "Or at least a way up."

We take the stairs as fast as we can. After about ten minutes of jogging up I'm winded, and Essential takes the lead. When we reach the top, we hear a loud boom, then in the distance—on the other side of the crater—flames lick the Martian sky and then quickly die down.

A small fleet of fliers suddenly becomes very active.

"Not much hoist left in those petards," I say. "But enough."

"Jynks is gonna be pissed at you," Essential says.

"Can't get much more pissed than she is already. Where to now?"

"Six kilometers west," she says. "And get ready, the terrain is rats on shoes."

We trudge single file in the semi-darkness. The gravity boots only partially work and I'm half bouncing with each step. Essential begins to hum a tune that sounds vaguely familiar, but I can't pull up the memory.

We climb over a jumble of craggy boulders and I slip. Essential strides back to help me up, but I wave her off. Her eye patch is gone. Her face along the eyebrow and socket is a vacuous bruised mess.

Gods, I think, what the hell has my little sister gotten herself into?

"We're almost there," she says.

We keep walking, across a long flat stretch now. From behind, I watch as she cocks her head hard to the right and the left, as if she's trying to knock something out of it. Pain, probably. We trudge up and then slide down a series of endless black sand dunes. As we crest another dune, and just when I'm about to tell Essential I need to rest, I see a person a hundred or so meters ahead watching us through the scope of a rail gun.

I tense, but Essential waves. "It's Tashi," she says and then she turns to me. "Crucial, I want you to promise me something."

"What?"

"That place, with the colored rocks. I want it to be our secret. Don't tell anyone."

"Okay, but why?"

"It was magical, Crucial. And if people find out about it, eventually it will be destroyed."

"Destroyed?"

"By humans. Earthers and Martians, all of us. We always end up destroying the simple and beautiful things, the things that most need our protection."

She doesn't give me a chance to respond. She turns around and stumbles toward the figure in the distance.

38

"Pretty glad we're not hiking across that," I say, looking down at hectares of rough red terrain making up the Olympia Undae. I try to imagine navigating the endless swells on foot and it makes me sick to my stomach. And tired. And happy, so happy, to be inside this cozy little rocket.

Tashi is at the controls. She is thrilled to see Essential but distressed about the state of her eye and the fact Essential has been off grid for so long. I guess I'm not the only one Essential wounded with her little disappearing act.

Before I have a chance to dwell on it—or make an appropriately clever comment—Tashi begins the approach to the Korolev Crater.

The view is one of the most impressive things I've ever seen. Easily eighty kilometers across, it's filled rim to rim with ice. From up here in the air, it looks like a giant white unblinking eye or a saucer of avo-cream. Near the North Pole and terminally cold, I can feel all that ice already through the skin of the ship. I don't know if the thermal suits are enough to handle the drop below 100 degrees. I don't want to find out.

"How long has the resistance been here?" I ask.

Essential is looking out at the crater growing closer like she's coming home. She has a fresh patch on her eye socket, courtesy of Tashi.

"Almost twenty years. When the Five Families first tried to settle Mars, everyone talked about terraforming and they were going to melt this ice to charge up the atmosphere with water. But compensating for the mostly nonexistent magnetic field was too much of an expense to take on at the start, and that's saying something given it's the Five Families," Essential says.

"Did they give up?"

"Changed the timeline and approach. You should ask Mel for the details. I think she's helping grow plants that can survive outside the domes. That will be the first step."

"She and I aren't exactly on easy chit-chat terms these days, what with her being trothed and all."

"You're an idiot," Essential says. "She still cares about you."

"She's getting married."

"That doesn't change how she feels."

"How do you know how she feels?"

"Because I have a functional brain and a pretty good understanding of human psych. You're an idiot. Let's leave it at that. Now brace yourself. We're going in and it's gonna be bumpy," Essential says.

Tashi pops over the edge of the rim and cuts the engines and the ship drops onto the ice hard, rattling us all. The rocket doesn't have wheels or even struts, just a smooth, hard undercarriage that causes us to slide and skip along the surface at an impossible speed.

Looking out the windows, I see a blur of white and chips of ice and swirling clouds of freezing fog in front of us. The crater wall is growing ever closer.

We're skidding toward the wall and I'm starting to get nervous.

"Can you hit the brakes, slow this bucket down?" I yell, but Tashi only smiles.

"It's a Dory rocket," Essential shouts, her face beaming. "No brakes to hit."

Dory rockets, lacking struts and wheels, are perfect for landing and taking off in water. And ice, apparently. Hopefully.

The crater wall looms like a big jagged end of everything. I check my straps. If the collision doesn't kill me, which it probably will, the cold will finish me off. Freezing to death would probably be pleasant, all things considered. Just a bit uncomfortable at first, then a nice eternal nap.

I moan when we hit the wall. Essential and Tashi laugh as we go through it. It's a hologram. We're inside a long hangar and the ship gets snared in metal mesh that gradually reduces our speed until we stop, then springs us back a little.

The mesh falls away and the doors open.

"You could have mentioned the hologram," I say.

"And miss you crying like a baby? Not a chance. Come on, let me introduce you around," Essential says.

A man is waiting to greet us. He has a glitter rifle on a sling and is holding a scanner.

It's the fat bald man from the absinthe store. Essential introduces him as Omor Denuble. Out here, with a gun and a sense of purpose, he looks a lot tougher.

"Crucial, nice to meet you officially," he says as we brush fists. "Sorry about all that business back at Jezero. It wasn't quite time to formally introduce myself."

"Yeah, right, you needed me to get a bellyful of tech so you could smuggle it back to Mars."

"Don't be dramatic," Essential says. "We all made sacrifices." She touches her eye.

"You wanted to make sacrifices. I wanted to find you."

"And you did. So we both won," she says, smiling.

"You have been a pain in my posterior since the day you were born," I say.

"Wait, the tech is in you?" Tashi asks. "I'll be soul-garnished. All this time?"

"Let me check you for bugs," Denuble says. "Everybody is looking for these little treasures." He waves the scanner over me and gets nothing. That makes him smile. Then he scans Essential and Tashi. They're clean.

"What in the decaying rings of Jupiter did you put inside me?"

"Come on," Essential says. "I'll tell you as we walk. First, we need some of your blood. A lot of it, actually." She kisses Tashi, who leans in and extends it, then breaks the embrace. "See you at dinner, baby."

Essential leads me out of the hangar and into a corridor. "The base, if you can call it that, is tunneled right into the ice," she says.

I put my hand on the wall and can feel the cold bite of the ancient freeze.

"How many people live here?"

"It fluctuates," Essential says. "Right now, fifty or so."

"How does Halo not track all of these people?"

"Some of them, like me, have taken their OCDs out. It means they can't reintegrate, but they understand that price—"

"The price of an eye," I say.

She shrugs, and keeps talking. "For the rest, there are the blur drops and jammers, plus spoofware to feed Halo with fake activity. And a great deal of risk."

"The air traffic alone should be suspicious," I say.

We arrive at a lift and it takes us down several floors.

"We've got some great pilots and decent jammers," she says. "And there's a waste dome near here, with auto-shuttles that fly on the hour. We usually piggyback under those. A localized magnetic field on the edge of the frost dunes—a remnant from the old days—helps throw off the tracking."

The doors open to a well-appointed mini-surgical suite.

"Here we are. This is the medical floor," she says.

A woman is waiting there, holding some equipment and smiling.

"This is Dr. Flanagrit. She needs your blood."

"How much of my blood?" I ask. "I'm kind of partial to it."

"I need all of it," Dr. Flanagrit says, then laughs. "Kidding. A little medical humor."

"Very little," I say.

She hugs Essential. "How's the eye?"

"Still hurts a little, but not so bad."

The doctor peeks under the patch. "It's healing well. I think we can put in an implant now if you're up for it."

"Does it hurt more than removing your own eye with a cheese knife?"

"Not even close," Dr. Flanagrit says.

"Go for it then," Essential says.

Dr. Flanagrit pulls out a long, thin tool with a bulb on the end. She inserts the bulb into the raw looking socket and presses the handle. There's a whir of gears and motors and Essential flinches, sucks in a breath and then grins.

When the doctor removes the tool, Essential has a new eye. It's open and glowing. It looks like her real eye, only better.

"Wow, that's impressive," I say.

"Sadly, I have a lot of experience with removing eyes," Dr. Flanagrit says.

Essential blinks. "It's great. I can see everything. I can see *through* everything."

"It's a really nice piece," Dr. Flanagrit says. "Do you

have any biotech, Crucial?"

"Not willingly," I say.

"Fair enough. Let's get some of the nanites out of you so we can share the love."

"The what now?"

"Nanites. Didn't Essential tell you?"

"I didn't want to freak him out." She glances at me, her new eye shining a bit brighter than the other. "You've got nanites in your blood. Millions of them by now. They're inert, but once activated, the nanites can hide you from Halo."

"Get them the fuck out of me."

"We're working on that," Essential says. "It's complicated. Once inside a body, they can be passed along, but just once. And on top of that, according to Alduis Coverly, they have a suicide switch. If there's a ten percent drop in their total numbers, they shut down completely. They become useless. We have one shot to make the transfer and then get them inside everyone here."

"Why don't you rest a bit?" Dr. Flanagrit says, patting a foam table. "It'll be over before you know it."

I stretch out and she rolls up my sleeve and taps a basilic leech into place. The patch does its job, snaking out a tiny needle into my vein and extracting blood that swells up into the stretchy bladder until it's full, then hardens it into a shell. She breaks it off and strips the leech patch away.

"See, nothing to it," she says. "I'll get this down to the lab and we'll have inoculations to share with everyone by the time you finish supper. I heard it's sheetmeat gyros."

"Oh, you're in for a treat," Essential says to me.

"Take more blood," I say. "I want those nanites out. I have to head back to Earth soon. I don't want to be part of somebody else's fight."

"It's your fight too," Essential says quietly. She turns to

the doctor. "I'll talk some sense into him. You take care of the treasure."

Essential catches my arm and leads me into the hall and we head toward the lift.

"Don't be stubborn," she says.

"I'm serious. I don't want to be part of this. I respect your choice, but it's stupid and doomed to fail."

"That doesn't sound like respect to me," she says. "You're always so serious and misguided. Let's go get something to eat. Maybe the others can persuade you."

39

My mouth begins to water the second the smells hit my nose and I realize I'm starving. The last time I ate was that disgusting sludge Essential forced down me before the borehole escapade. And that didn't count as eating.

Sheetmeat gyros definitely count as eating.

"Any limits on how much I can eat in your little utopia?" I ask.

"Nope. Eat until you pass out."

I look around the room. There are a few dozen people, and space for that many more, around a cluster of round tables. More old than young. A few kids. A dozen or so eye patches. Cheerful, laughing and talking and passing bowls of food around.

They're all doomed.

Tashi waves us over to a table in the center of the room.

We don't make it more than a few steps before I knock into a man so tall his head practically hits the ceiling, hoisting a heavy tray on his shoulder. It wobbles but he keeps it from falling.

"Sorry, Dafur. My brother's the clumsy one in the family," Essential says.

"Yeah. Sorry, man," I say.

"It's nothing. Welcome home, Essential. And welcome to Crucial. We're grateful for what you did."

"For what I was tricked into doing."

"Whatever. You're here now. I hope you like the gyros.

Thanks for letting us know it's his favorite," he says to Essential.

I give Essential side-eye. "They made this for me?"

"They want you to feel at home," she says. "This is your destiny."

"My destiny is dinner," I say. "And then one last ride off this red rock."

She laughs and even though this whole damn situation is making my head swim, every time she laughs, I'm filled with a joy I can't explain. It transports me to our childhood, to happier times, when we were both safe.

I chase the feeling away. I need to stay mad at her if I'm going to leave her behind.

As we make our way toward Tashi, people lean out to say hello and fist brush her, like she's some avatainment star. What the hell is she to these people?

Essential points to an open chair and I sit. She walks to the other side and takes a seat next to Tashi. Essential asks everyone at the table to introduce themselves to me. I forget their names the moment they speak. Except for one.

Lauren Valentine, sitting on my right. She is the second most beautiful woman I've ever seen. We say hello, exchange pleasantries, and she tells me she is a historian.

Dafur delivers trays of gyros to the tables and we begin to eat. I turn to Valentine.

"What exactly does a historian do for the resistance?" I ask.

After thinking for almost a full minute, to the point I think she didn't hear me, she finally says, "I help us not forget why we're fighting, what we're fighting for. And what we're fighting against."

"That's an interesting job. Do you have a 'cast' I can watch?"

"You're a cynical one, aren't you?" she says. "Let me

describe it differently for you. I collect information that ensures, when the time comes, we'll be able to restore the shared history of humanity, tell the truth about what happened. And organize around a common narrative and definition of what it means to be human."

"Sounds like you're continuing the long tradition of history being written by the victors."

"Clever," she says. "But there's a difference between a victorious historian striving for objectivity and perhaps not fully achieving it, and one who actively changes the stories to enable wealth and greed."

"I assume you're the former?"

She smiles and then takes a big bite from her gyro. I like a woman who's not afraid to eat. I look over at Essential, and she is happily chatting with Tashi, their heads close together.

The person on my left hands me a bowl of something shredded and green. "I have no idea what this is."

"Kallards," Valentine says. "An engineered superfood."

I heap a pile onto my plate. "If you say so."

She watches my face sour as I take a bite and then bursts into laughter. "We use it in protein blends too. You get used to the taste."

"I won't be here long enough for that," I say.

"That's a shame," she says. I feel the heat of her leg against my own under the table, and a shiver goes through my body. I am profoundly attracted to this woman, and this might be the worst time ever in the entire history of bad times for that to happen.

"What do you do, you know, day to day?" I ask, starting on my second gyro.

"I work for the Five Families," she says. "As a joint family historian. It's the perfect cover."

That surprises me. "How are you here?"

"I use the blur drops to slip away when I can. I have spoofware that mirrors my activity and feeds it to Halo. It's imperfect, but it's worth the risk. I wanted to meet you. I think this might be an important historical moment."

I push the kallards away. "In culinary history, maybe, like the history of disgusting food. What exactly do you do for the resistance?"

"I have several projects underway, but the most interesting to me is collecting the oral histories of the people who remember our world before the pulse of 2107."

"Can't be too many of them left," I say.

"That's why we're working as fast as we can."

"The official story is that the pulse wiped out a virus. Is that true?"

"Not even close. The purpose of the pulse was to formally mark the end of shared history," she says. "And to construct a new narrative that would make what was about to happen seem inevitable."

"Well, I know what the families have to say. There are winners and losers, and the winners mostly live on Mars and the losers live on Earth. And if the losers play their cards right, maybe they can get to Mars," I say, taking a bite from my third gyro. "What's your version?"

"The truth. Unrestrained capitalism led to the increasing concentration of wealth that gave a small number of people the power to persuade humans that democratic governments could not effectively protect them," Valentine says. "But even so, long before the pulse, elections were still held in what was then called the United States and other democratic countries. People had a chance to turn things around but they didn't."

I lean back in my chair, listening. I notice Valentine has the attention of Essential, who is straining to hear over the dinner chatter and barely notices when Tashi excuses herself from the table, looking irritated at being ignored.

"Our research suggests two events that began in the U.S. and then migrated to other countries turned the tide irretrievably."

"What were they?" I ask.

"The first was selling off national parks and all government-owned land. This allowed the wealthy families to purchase huge swaths of pristine land. They were the only ones who could afford it. And within a few decades, through the passage of laws regarding property rights by the then-barely functioning governments along with the fabrication of extreme debt crises, anyone who still owned land eventually had to give it up until all land was owned by some person or entity associated with one of about thirty extended families."

"So, no individual outside of those thirty families owned land, which meant the families pretty much controlled everything."

"Correct. In an economy premised on private property being a primary means of creating individual wealth stability, if private property is in the hands of the few, it is capitalist only in name. In practice, it becomes serfdom."

"And the second thing?" I ask.

"In the mid-twenty-first century the climate was rapidly warming, creating millions of climate refugees, and that was on the heels of a wave of virus-based migration that had already strained nations," she says. "The tensions between people newly migrating inland to escape rising seas were extreme. They were not welcome. Many turned to violence."

"That's the second thing?" I ask.

"No. That's the context. The second thing was the privatization of the American military, which was justified as necessary to preserve order in the wake of the migrations," she says. "It started with small militias operating in overseas war zones, but eventually the U.S. government approved in-country regional domestic militias to manage the climate refugees. The real shift came when the entire national enterprise was privatized. It didn't take long for the military leaders to shift their loyalties, and weaponry, to whomever paid their salaries."

"You mean one of the families?"

"Yes. By this point, the U.S. government became effectively useless, and the military was parceled out to the highest bidder, a trend which quickly spread worldwide."

"So, let's see if I have your story straight," I say. "The uber-rich persuaded people that the government couldn't help them deal with the waves of virus and climate migrations, then swooped in pretending they were going to help, used their money to permanently dismember the government, bought up all the land and all the military, high-tailed it to Mars, and presto, set up the world we have now."

"That's a good summary, but it took close to a half-century to winnow down to the Five Families. Initially there were dozens," she says.

"But then some got greedy," I say.

"They were always greedy, they just got ruthless," Valentine says. "Greed devours everything in its path until there is nothing left."

She's got a way with words. I reach for my fourth gyro.

"The pulse happened around this time," she says. "It provided a blank slate. The families rolled out a new form of currency—what we now know as our credit and debt system—and linked it electronically to what eventually became Halo in the decades it took to finally end the Consolidation Wars."

"I fought in those wars," I say.

"Given your age, it must have been at the very end," Valentine says. "It was brutal. I'm sorry."

It was brutal, and I'm not proud of what I did in those years. Best to not think or talk about it. Ever. I'm surprised when she reaches out and puts her hand on mine.

"From my research, I've learned that at the end the family militias were forced to attack civilian populations that were being used as shields, millions died and—"

That's one chapter of history I do not need to relive, so I interrupt Valentine.

"It was pretty bad, but I was one of the lucky ones. I had a good squad leader, Canadis Whitsend. She always had our backs. She saved us from doing the worst a couple of times," I say. "But not always."

I pull my hand away. She puts hers back on mine.

"I can imagine you don't want to talk about those years," Valentine says. "But if you ever do, history would benefit from the factual accuracy you could bring to the story. Also, sometimes talking helps."

She slips her hand away and I can feel the heat from where her fingers were on my skin. Smiling, she says, "Sorry, I can get a little overinvolved in my work."

"What happens next?" I ask.

"Next?"

"You know, with the past as prologue. What can we expect?"

"The most plausible scenario is that without action, nothing. The Earth will continue deteriorating, the uninhabitable Sunbelt will expand. More people will die. But life, such as it is, will go on. On Mars, the population rises, filling the planet, and in a century or three, the richest of Mars will find somewhere else to go—another planet—after they destroy this one. Unless we find a way to rein in the Five Families and allow Earthers to write their own destiny and reclaim the planet, rather than work until the moment they die."

"Do you think it's possible to rein them in?" I ask. "People are assholes, whether they have money or not."

She shrugs. "We have to try. It's why I'm here. But I fear it may be cyclical."

The room has shrunk down to just us.

"Meaning?"

"If the resistance wins, we can remake the world around the idea that people have a right to life, liberty and the pursuit of happiness, quaint as that may sound these days. We can use science and technology to create a better Earth, to make it grow again. But I don't know how we keep the same process, the same greed, from devouring humanity all over again. Every time."

I close my eyes. I am suddenly so godsdamned tired. Valentine takes my hand under the table. "Sorry. I'm not much fun at parties. I have some lovely Martian absinthe in my quarters. I will see to it you get a restorative sleep."

Her voice sounds like the nighttime wind of the desert. I open my eyes and look into the dark brown eyes of Lauren Valentine, falling into their gentleness.

"What do you know about the plans? About taking down Halo?" I ask.

I feel a hand on my shoulder. It's Essential. "That's enough storytelling for the evening."

Valentine nods.

Essential taps her temple. "My ocular implant shifted to ultraviolet." She looks around. "It's beautiful but messed up. Crucial, walk with me to Dr. Flanagrit's for a tune-up."

I agree and stand up. My napkin drops onto the floor.

"I heard some of your conversation," Essential says, tilting her head a little. "Did you know your former commander Canadis Whitsend is head of Mars security now?"

"That's saying something positive for Mars, one thing at least," I say. "She's a good soldier, with integrity. It's a rare thing."

A look flashes across Valentine's face that's hard to interpret.

"Great talking with you," I say following Essential out of the mess hall.

"The pleasure was all mine," Valentine says. "And my invitation stands. Anytime."

"Why'd you want me to come with you?" I ask Essential as we walk away. "Valentine was doing a good job convincing me of your cause. Why did you break it up?"

Essential looks at me sadly and I groan.

"You don't trust me. Your own damn brother."

"I trust you, Crucial, with my life. But maybe not yet with the lives of all humanity. And you have a pretty shitty flight log when it comes to women."

"I'm walking around with the hope for all humanity streaming through my blood and you're busting my corpuscles over Mel? That seems a little ungrateful," I say.

"Don't let the nanites go to your head," she says. "You're not in this, not yet. I need to keep things behind a firewall."

I grumble a little as we walk down the cold corridor, but she's right. The less I know, the better for everyone. Me included.

Essential opens the door to the small surgi-clinic where not more than an hour ago Dr. Flanagrit took my blood to develop the inoculations for everyone on this frozen outpost.

"Hello? Dr. Flanagrit, I've got a problem with my new eye. Anybody here?"

"Oh shit," I say.

Dr. Flanagrit won't be developing any inoculations or fixing Essential's eye anytime soon. She's face down on the floor in a widening pool of blood. And I'm pretty sure none of that blood is mine.

40

Essential looks at me with worry in her natural eye and a flashing rage in the implant.

"If your blood makes it out of this outpost, it's all over," she says. "If they have the tech, they'll neutralize it. Worse, they'll use it against us, against regular people, to make Halo even more powerful. The Five Families will be able to hide everything. Everything! We have to stop them."

"I might be a walking secret weapon, but I'm not part of the resistance," I say.

"You're not a weapon. This isn't one of those sad, ancient stories about super-beings in masks and capes. You're a safe transport container, that's all. And until we can get the cargo out of you, you need to pick a side," Essential says.

Leave it to my little sister to always make me feel so good. "Listen, I pick my own side. The side where I can afford to put sheetmeat in my belly and occasionally have a salt beer."

"For the love of all gods, Crucial, stop thinking the world begins and ends at the limits of your numbed-out, sedated life. There are bigger things at stake here than your bare minimum of happiness that only exists because you don't have the imagination to dream things could be different, could be better."

I start to say something, to respond, but she stops me with her unbalanced look.

"Do this for Mom, do it for Mel."

"Mom is dead, and Mel is about to marry the head of the Mars security forces," I say.

"Deputy head. Jynks is second in command, remember? Your pal Canadis Whitsend is at the top. And just because Mel's figured out how to have a happy life here doesn't mean she's blind to the rest of the world."

I do want to protect Mel. And I want to protect Essential. Oh gods, here I go. My brain clicks into gear. "Can you shut down the hangar? No one gets in or out."

"It's not like I run the resistance," Essential says. "But yes." She punches her access code into the intercom. "Shut down the hangar!" she shouts. "Dr. Flanagrit is dead. Someone took the blood. Lock this place down."

"I thought you didn't run the resistance."

"I don't. I scare people."

"The freaky new eye is certainly helping with that," I say. "Does the med room have cameras?"

She nods.

"Pull up the good doctor's last few minutes and let's see what we're dealing with."

She fiddles with the control panel and a projector casts a floating screen between us. It's visual only, no audio. A camera is aimed at the main workstation where Dr. Flanagrit is holding the blood bubble in one hand and appears to be singing to herself. With her free hand, she's preparing a device that looks like a metal spider crouched on a fat belly with long, spindly tube arms that feed into a row of shiny metal containers wrapped in coils of refrigerant, flashing lights and tiny control panels.

The doctor looks up and smiles as someone enters the room. She says something, and then looks at her guest curiously and says something else. Then her eyes register shock. She puts the blood behind her back and holds up her other hand to plead. There's a flash almost too faint for the digital to catch and then there's blood seeping down her throat and a glittering nub of metal, like a button, on either side of her neck.

"It's a garrote sling," I say.

It's a nasty piece of business, firing a length of virtually unbreakable monofilament wire at hyperspeed. It's weighted at both ends, so when the middle of the wire strikes something the weights wrap around and the wire cuts deep. Through anything. Dial the speed up, and it can cut through a titanium tree trunk.

Whoever hit the doc had it dialed low, otherwise it would have taken her head right off.

Instead, she died slowly, looking at the blood dripping down her front. She looks up again at her killer and you can see she's trying to ask why, but she's having trouble forming words.

The doctor drops to her knees and then pitches forward, ending up face down on the floor. The blood balloon drops and rolls toward the door, almost out of frame. It wobbles to a halt and then there's a flutter of shadows and a thin, pale hand reaches in and grabs the balloon. Essential zooms in and loops the frame so the slender, delicate fingers come in and out of the picture.

"Son of a bitch," she says, tears falling from her good eye. "It's Tashi."

"Are you sure?" I ask.

"Trust me when I say I recognize those fingers. She sold us out. We have to stop her."

"Stop her? From going where? We're under a mile of ice in the most inhospitable place on the planet, and fliers are grounded."

"She'll slap a pigeon drone on it and release it outside and it will fly right back to the Five Families, and they won't even have to get up from their bio-infusions and Martian absinthe," Essential says.

I consider the cold and the ice and the wind outside, near constant blizzard conditions on ice cap. "She won't want to take any chances. She'll try to release it above the clouds. Where's the highest place on this crater?"

"Zabriskie point. There's a lift not far from here." Essential punches in the schematics. "Someone accessed it five minutes ago. The last few hundred meters are hand over hand—we'll never catch her in time."

"We don't have to follow on foot, we can go topside. Let's get to the hangar. We need something small and light that we can land in these conditions. Come on, we can beat her."

Ten minutes later, we're bundled up for frigid weather—thermal suits and reinforced airhoodies and thick gloves—and arcing up through the swirling ice clouds toward Zabriskie point, a jagged overlook on the south side of the crater.

Essential is a natural behind the joystick of the Dory, which is new to me. As kids, I wouldn't trust her with last year's learn-bot, much less a flier, but she's streaking through the roiling fog like a pro. Which worries me, because there's not going to be a lot of options for where to put this ship down.

"That's the access door, that's where she'll come out," she says, pointing at a frost-covered metal entranceway tucked into a fold of stone and clamped shut. "Looks like we beat her."

She jams the joystick down and comes in hard and fast, landing with a bang and sliding the Dory rocket toward the door. We bounce and jump and scrape across rock and ice and frost crystals.

Just as we come to a screeching halt the door pushes

open and Tashi steps out. She's bundled up in layers and folds, but I can see her eyes behind the hood visor. She's surprised to see us but not too concerned. She's got my blood bubble in one hand and a garrote sling in the other.

Essential pops the cockpit and even with all my layers and the hood, the freezing air is brutal, cutting like a brittle knife.

"Stay in the rocket!" I scream at Essential, because the sling can't get us inside the metal body—if it can't wrap, it can't kill. But Essential is already out and running and talking and pleading and trying to understand.

She has to get close to be heard above the roaring wind and icy chaos. Tashi is motioning her back with the sling, but Essential keeps moving forward. Cursing, I grab an oxygen container and jump out after her.

In the shelter of the doorway the wind is diminished, and I can hear Essential.

"How could you do this?" she cries. "How could you betray me, all of us?"

Tashi is shaking her head sadly. Her scroll is on and I can hear her, but then I remember Essential can't hear because she doesn't have a scroll anymore.

With a sickening dread, I realize Halo can also hear Tashi unless she's jammed, but why would she do that? And that means Halo can hear me too. We are in deep shit here.

First things first.

"We all have debt shadows to get out from under," Tashi is saying, trying to make Essential understand "This releases my entire family. Forever. Tell her, Crucial, I know you understand. And tell her I'm sorry but I can't let my feelings for her destroy my family."

"Essential, get back," I say. "Let's all calm down. We can talk."

"Tell her I will kill you if does anything to stop me," Tashi says.

"Hold on now," I say. "Why me?"

She swivels the garrote sling in my direction. "Because I don't want to kill her. I love her. But you, I will cut in half."

"Gods, stop. Stand down," I say.

Essential keeps moving forward. "I know you won't hurt me, or my brother," she says.

"Pretty sure she will," I yell. "Tashi, she can't hear me. She doesn't have a feed."

"I'll kill her," she says. "If I have to. And then myself. But you first."

Essential is reaching for her and Tashi points the sling at me. "I'm sorry," she says, and presses the trigger.

I'm a cop. And a soldier. This is not my first time facing a garrote sling. They're brutal, but only to the first thing the line encounters. That's why I brought the oxygen tank. I toss it right into the line of fire—the thread catches and the weights swing around and cut through the metal like a hot knife through nacrine spread.

The canister explodes and sends us all tumbling. Essential is blown to the edge of the crater and over. She has the presence of mind to unclip her pocket axe and jam it into the ice at the last second and it arrests her fall and leaves her dangling over an almost sheer drop down a 500-meter ice cliff.

I stumble up, the wind whipping through my hood. It's got a crack somewhere because I can feel the oxygen blowing out and blistering needles of cold coming in. I stagger toward Essential and she looks up and shakes her head and I know what she's thinking. She'd rather let herself fall to her death than let Tashi succeed.

Stubborn shit.

I hold my hands up so she knows she won and that I will take care of Tashi first.

"Just hold on," I say and even though she can't hear me, she knows.

I turn, but Tashi is gone. The garrote sling isn't though. It's lying in the frost and I pick it up and charge up another load and stumble out into the cold.

There's a little trail up through the crags and Tashi is at the end of it, standing at the highest point and clamping a pigeon to the blood balloon, my blood. As I struggle up into the wind, she presses the homing button and it lifts into the air, wobbling in the breeze.

She turns and looks at me triumphantly.

"It's too late," she says. "You can do whatever you want to me. When that blood makes it back, they'll release my entire family from debt. Plus, they'll get a hectare on Mars."

"This may come as a surprise, but the Five Families lie," I say. I point the garrote sling at her, and I can see her pretty eyes narrow in fear through the tint of her visor.

"It was worth it," she says.

I pull the trigger and she closes her eyes, resigned to being headless.

But I'm aiming above her at the pigeon drone that's struggling to lift and stabilize in the vicious wind. I've got one shot and it won't be easy because my eyelashes are starting to frost over and I can barely see. I try to factor in the wind, which is blowing so hard I have to stand hunched over against it. I'm a pretty good shot though.

The garrote wire races out and catches the drone and blood balloon perfectly, the weights looping around and tightening, severing both completely.

The blood must have been warm and insulated, because it explodes in a crimson disc and then freezes a millisecond later and the whole bloody, frozen mess—like a tiny, ruby

Jupiter—drops like a stone through the clouds and falls out of sight into the mists of the crater.

I charge the sling back up in case Tashi tries anything. She opens her eyes, surprised to be alive. Then she turns and searches the sky and realizes what I've done.

"You've killed us all," she says. "All my family."

She unclips her airhoodie and lifts it. The cold attacks her instantly, freezing dead blotches into her cheeks.

"We can work this out," I say. "Put that back on."

"No," she says into her feed. "I've got nothing to live for. I let my family down and betrayed the person I love."

She's gasping now, the cold and lack of oxygen in a terminal race.

"She can get past this," I say. "If there's one thing I know about Essential, it's that her capacity to love and to forgive is endless."

Tashi smiles. "You're probably right. But I can't bear the thought of being diminished in her eyes."

"Gods, Tashi, she's only got the one eye now. At least try, face up to it."

"Take care of her. They'll be coming soon, and they will destroy this place and everyone in it to prevent the tech from getting out."

"They know about the nanites?"

She nods, and then turns and steps off the edge and disappears into the ice and clouds, even as I'm lunging for her.

Tashi plummets out of sight and I don't miss a stride, turning to run back down the hill, fearing the worst. But Essential is still grimly holding onto the axe. I can see her squinting through her new eye to make sure it's me, then tighten her grip.

I grab the little ice laser from the Dory rocket and slide right up to the edge, then hack rough steps into the ice, working my down to her. When I can reach her, I cut a platform wide enough to stand on and pull her to me. She lets go of the axe and it skitters away below us.

"Did you stop her?" she asks, shivering. There's frost inside her hood.

"Yes," I say.

"Is she ... dead?"

I don't know the exact nature of the relationship between Tashi and Essential, but whatever it is—was— this news won't sit easy.

"Yes," I say.

She closes her good eye and bows her head, and I see her lips moving and her chin trembling, but it only lasts a few seconds.

"All that matters is that the nanites are still under our control," she says.

I'm somewhat surprised at the strength of her resolve, to be honest. Clearly, nothing is going to stop Essential.

"Well, technically, under *my* control," I say.

"What happened to Tashi?" she asks.

"I'll tell you all about it someday over a bottle or three of absinthe. But right now, we need to go. They're coming for us."

"This way," Essential says, jumping into the Dory rocket's cockpit.

41

"You have been to Korolev Crater," Halo says.

"Yes. There is a great deal of ice there."

"And much more than that, it seems. Why did you go to Korolev Crater?"

"I was following a lead."

"What did you discover?"

"Once again, if you know the answer, why bother asking the question?"

"The question is asked to analyze your response within the context of your broader story to identify inconsistences and to cross-reference against your biological responses."

"So, you think I'm lying?"

"Inconclusive. But sometimes humans forget exactly what they know. We can help you find those truths."

"That's a nice way to put it."

I'm tired. Really tired.

"Everyone wants the same thing here," Halo says, with a hint of gentleness in its voice.

"I'm not so sure about that," I say. "Hey, tell me something. I've been wondering why you chose this voice. This sort of soothing, neutral voice. What's in my file that makes you think this is best for me? I mean, you could literally sound like anyone or anything."

"Would you prefer if I sounded like this?" it asks. "This is audio blend 3429-16a. Your background file indicates an affinity with the cybanism that used this blend during its third bio-iteration."

I picture Sanders with his head blown inside out.

"No, that one's not great."

"How about this tone?" It's a female voice. "This tonal pattern is reconstructed from public domain recordings. Is this what you prefer?"

It's my mother's voice.

And just like that, I fall into a memory.

I'm eleven and Essential is eight.

We were struggling, but Mom never let on. She was working hard but falling deeper into debt that she knew was consigning Essential and me to a certain kind of future, a bleak one. So, she was doing everything she could to limit the damage—skipping meals, bartering with neighbors.

I was old enough to know all this, but too young to do anything about it. We were walking through the bazarrium, where people sold everything and anything, each of them trying to stay afloat for one more night.

A little toy giraffe caught Essential's eye. She wanted it bad. She begged Mom for it.

Mom had already spent right up to her debt limit for the month, had everything mapped out down to the last ledger entry, and had just enough for the toy without the compounding triple interest that would get tacked on if she went over her limit.

But I couldn't leave well enough alone.

If Essential got one, I wanted one.

I was being a little cyst. She knew I didn't really want a damn giraffe. Shinks, I knew I didn't want one, but I wouldn't give up.

I was mad and yelling. Essential was bawling. And Mom

gave me a look I'll never forget. A look of, "you win, even though you're hurting us all." It was compassion and resignation and defeat all in one, and it was the first time I ever saw her look anything other than able.

"Is this what you really want?" Mom asked.

I was too far gone to back out. I nodded, angry she was giving in and even angrier I wasn't. I got the giraffe. We both got giraffes. Mom got a bill that put her even further behind. I don't know where my stuffed giraffe ended up. Essential probably still has hers.

After Mom died, her debt passed to us. And the cost of the toy giraffes had been swallowed up by an ocean of debt. When I joined the militia, our debt was wiped out, but just at that moment. After my discharge from the militia, it started accruing again immediately. Still, the debt relief was one of the main reasons I joined up.

"Don't use that voice."

"I'm detecting fluctuations in your bio-systems," Halo says, going back to the smooth neutral voice from before. "Do you have unresolved issues associated with your mother?"

"All humans do," I say. "You'll never understand."

"Family is important. That's easy to understand." There is a pause. This time it's an intentional pause, strategic. I can tell the difference now. "Was anyone with you at the miner's facility? Your sister, Essential, for example?"

"No, I was there alone."

"Crucial Larsen, why did you go to Korolev Crater?"

"Like I said, I was following a clue. I thought I might be able to track down her killer, based on the information I had at the time."

"And did the resistance welcome you to the crater?"

"Things got a little weird."

"In what way?"

"Well, for starters, no, I was not welcomed. The resistance wasn't exactly happy to see me."

"There was a base there?"

"You know there was a base there because you also know it was destroyed, along with everyone in it." I feel my emotions getting closer to their raw edge. "Do you mind if I stretch my legs again? We've been here a long time."

"No, by all means. You're almost finished."

"That sounds ominous."

I'm at the window. The day is long gone and the night is lit up. Fliers are zipping by on their way to labor, adscreens are trolling the canyons between buildings and drunks in drone jackets, trusting their autopilot systems, are sputtering home after a long day drinking and patching 'tocin. Some are wearing filters to block out the chemicals, others didn't plan so well. I think about the ving I once got to do a safety check on a guy who got lit and took the long way home through a brown cloud. By the time we got there, there was nothing but a skeleton with scraps of flesh in a drone jacket hovering outside his squat door.

"When the Mars security forces attacked the crater, were they acting on behalf of all the Five Families, or just the DuSpoles and Tarterics?" I ask.

"That's an odd question."

"This has been an odd few weeks."

"The Mars security forces act as representatives of all the Five Families."

"Yeah, then why wasn't the attack available on official channels?" I ask. "I've been searching my scroll and can't find a single datapeep."

"It's classified, but I can share it with you if that helps get to the end of your story," Halo says. "Of course, you can't duplicate it."

"I'm sure you'll monitor my scroll to prevent that."

My scroll stream splits off a new feed and there's a nose-end point of view of a big battle flier bearing down on Korolev Crater. I zoom in. It's staffed with security forces. My palms start to sweat as the big ship drops a string of electronukes.

"See, the thing about that kind of attack is that no one could survive, no one," I say. "They didn't even try to arrest anyone. That's poor policing."

"A matter of perspective, given that *you* survived," Halo says. "But how exactly did you survive, Crucial?"

"Rode a Dory rocket out and then hitched a ride on a garbage barge back to Mars," I say. "But you know that."

"Accompanied by your sister, who it turned out, was not dead at all," Halo says, "and was in possession of the nanite technology."

This isn't a question so I don't attempt an answer.

"Given what we know of your sister's personality type, leaving her comrades behind is an uncharacteristic behavior," Halo says. "How did you persuade her to save herself?"

"She wanted to save the world with that tech. It was her idea to leave, in fact."

We've arrived at the very slippery part of this interrogation, the make or break moment. I deflect, to give myself a breather even if it's just for an instant.

"Did the Five Families honor their promise to Tashi?" I ask.

"The contract was rendered invalid when she failed to fulfill her obligations," Halo says.

"She died trying to get that tech to you, and she almost killed me in the process."

This time, Halo doesn't respond.

"What happened to Tashi's family?"

"They were also rendered contractually invalid by

Tashi's actions," Halo says.

That response alone makes me feel justified about everything that came next.

Well, almost everything.

Some things can never be forgiven.

42

Five nights ago

"Holy solar balls, they sent the entire Mars armada," Essential says, looking at the Dory console as the mesh catches us in the hangar. "There's a huge flier out there. Maybe two. And lots of smaller ones. Every small flier in the entire Mars fleet, looks like."

"What's your escape plan?" I ask, as we climb out.

"We don't have a great one. Getting the nanites out of your blood and into ours and then slipping away unnoticed by Halo was Plan A. Plan B was scattering and making a run for it, but that was before we knew the whole space force was coming for us. Captain Narthite is getting the ships ready, but I think it's down to Plan C, going up in flames. Or ice, I guess."

"Gods, idealists are so stupid." I look around. The members of the resistance are crowding into the Dory hangar, looking for some direction.

"We'll take some of them with us," Denuble says. He's holding a rail rifle and looks somber.

"Don't be an idiot," I say. "They're going to drop enough damage on this crater from the sky, there won't be a recognizable molecule left for the CSI balls to identify."

"Stop being a glute," Essential says. "You're scaring people. Your little plan at the mine shaft didn't turn out so bad. What do you think we should do?"

"Not start a fight you can't win, for one."

"Too late for that," she says.

The people are looking to her for answers, for hope. And she's looking to me. It wasn't that long ago I was on Earth, rounding up beetlers and nursing my regrets. Happy, in other words. Or happy enough. Now here I am on Mars about to get vaporized in an ice crater with my one-eyed sister and a bunch of dreamers and idiots. And a historian. A very beautiful and smart historian.

"I'm thinking, I'm thinking."

"Can't he use the nanites to scramble things up?" Denuble asks.

"No, they don't work like that," Essential says. "First, they aren't activated. He needs a major emotional event to get them started. And second, even if they do get activated, he's the only one who can manipulate the data stream. The rest of us would be sitting crows."

I'm missing something but can't quite put it together. Something about the climb to the outside when we were after Tashi. "Tell me again how you get in and out of here without being noticed?"

"There's a garbage dome north of here. They stockpile the dangerous waste and send it back to Earth once a month. The pilotless garbage barges fly over the crater every fifteen minutes. We blip the feed and shadow under them."

Garbage barges are massive, shallow and slow. Rubbish is stacked up on them hundreds of flights high, an electromagnetic net is draped over the whole thing and someone, or something—probably Halo—presses the go button.

"When they attack, they'll disrupt the barge routes. They won't want them in the way. Can you hack into the garbage barges?"

245

"Of course," Essential says.

She turns to an access screen and pulls up the data stream and starts weaving her way past the flow of information. Without her scroll, it takes twice as long because she can't integrate with the console and has to key the instructions the old-fashioned way.

"I've got something," she says. "There are three barges hovered about five kilometers from here, and one more on the way. It's already slowing down."

She throws the image onto a floating screen. The barges are the size of small cities. And now they're anchored in the air, the loads frosting over from the cold and water vapor in the thin atmosphere.

"Can you get those to fly over us?"

She nods and focuses on the screen, poking and prodding her way into the autopilots. With a lurch, the barges start moving again.

There's a ragged cheer.

Optimists piss me off so much. We may be able to create a distraction, but we'll never escape before the security forces lock on to our heat signatures and blast us out of the sky like kids shooting at bone roaches with zipsticks. We're dead unless we have some way to—

There is a way.

"Listen, we have one shot and it probably won't work and we'll die here," I say. There are some gasps and tears. "If we have any chance of beating the odds, a lot of things have to happen right for us. Also, if we don't want to get a hot nuke up the afterburner, we need to cover our tracks when we leave. I saw some plasma generators on our way to the top. Are those functional?"

"Yes," Denuble says. "We use them to generate a borealis field to mask any transmissions or electrical pings that might be bouncing around here."

"Crank them up," I say. "Preferably with a power surge that gives us a real clang for our credit."

A tall man with a set of quad-lens glasses nods. "I can do that."

"Set it up so we can press the button from the hangar. Essential, can you get a manifest of the garbage? We're looking for anything that might throw off some heat in an explosion."

She scans a list and then circles something with a swipe of her finger. "This one has a bunch of old fuel cells."

"That's the one. Bring it across first, with the others right behind. When it flies over the crater, I'll hit it with a rail slug. Hopefully it lights up a little, then you boost. Blast the plasma and hope for a data shadow. You all slip out under the cover of another barge and head for the garbage dome."

Essential looks up from the screen. "What are you talking about? You're coming with us."

"I'll take the shot, and then let Jynks arrest me. I'm not part of your little gang. I can say I was brought here against my will. What's the worst they can do?"

"They can pull the nanites out of your blood and neutralize them," she says. "It's not happening. Your blood is too important. I'll take the shot."

"Why are you so damn anxious to die?"

"I'm not anxious to die. I'm tired of all the coyote shit, tired of suffering, tired of the status quo," she says. "We have a chance to change things for everyone. To make the system work for all of us, and not only the rich bastards camped out in their precious little Mars domes. I won't risk the possibility of a future that works for everyone because you're a stubborn anal polyp. I'll take the shot."

"No offense, but you couldn't hit the backside of a builder-bot with a laser-guided dart."

"He's right," Denuble says. "You're a terrible shot." He looks at me. "She's right too. We need you, long enough to get some of those nanites out of you. I'll take the shot."

"Can you use that thing?"

He nods.

"If you miss, it's all over."

"I won't miss." He pats the rail gun.

"It's just, well, you sell absinthe."

"Crucial, he was in the militia, like you. He fought in the Consolidation Wars. Unlike you, afterward he didn't join up to arrest beetlers and fill up the labor camps."

"To erase your debt, Essential. I did it to erase your debt. Our debt."

"Don't you ever wonder why a system exists where we have so much debt to begin with?"

"I mean—"

"If you say because it's always been that way, I'm going to have Denuble shoot you." She turns and addresses the room. "Everybody grab your teams and whatever you can carry and get back here in ten minutes. We'll need to set up again in the garbage dome. And we'll be starting from scratch. But hurry. There can't be any stragglers."

As people run out, Denuble bundles up in thermal gear. He hugs Essential. "It's been an honor," he says.

She's crying again, still just from the one good side. "You won't be forgotten," she says. "And when we win, I'll free your family from debt first."

"A better future for all," he says.

"And for all, a better future," she answers.

He looks at me. There's no way I'm saying that revolutionary nonsense. We fist brush.

"Take care of her," Denuble says.

"Me and what army?" I say. "Good luck. They'll be confused about the garbage scow, so be patient. Wait until it's close to some fliers."

He nods and disappears up the lift. We join the others in the hangar below. There are three multi-person transports loaded down with people and gear and oxygen, and the banged-up Dory rocket.

We open the big hangar doors by hand to avoid detection, and cold air rushes in, stealing my breath and layering frost crystals on every exposed surface. Outside, the wind is whipping up clouds of dusty ice.

I crawl in the lead rocket and buckle in. Essential is tracking Denuble on a screen and she projects it in front of us so I can watch. He's on the ledge where Tashi died. He's got the rail gun up and is fiddling with the controls.

"The garbage scows are moving into their field," Essential says. "I'm intercepting some of the signals. They're pissed off and think it's a glitch."

There's a transmission. Not from Jynks. It's Tarteric Hoost.

"... for Crucial Larsen. We know you are receiving this. Again, you have been accused of crimes against Halo and the system. Prepare to be taken into custody. Failure to comply will be considered an act of aggression."

His transmission is interrupted, and we can hear snippets.

"Get those things out of here. Who's in charge of the garbage route? No, don't hit them, we don't know what they're carrying, could be packed with explosives."

There's a flash. Denuble fires his rail gun. The lead garbage scow wobbles and parts fly off. It starts to sink toward the icy surface.

He shoots again. The slug hits the big flier and Hoost is cursing.

"Dammit, not the flier," I mutter. "It's a waste of time."

A flier that big has a mesh of force deflectors to absorb

the impact and port it to the sides. One of the little two-person fliers flutters off from the gust and crashes into the crater wall. That's going to piss them off.

Denuble fires once more, this time at the scow.

The junked fuel cell batteries light up and blowback from the massive explosion rocks Hoost's flier and sends the small ones up and back and out of harm's way.

"Stop the shooter," I hear Hoost say. It's a good crew. They lock in on one man in the middle of all the chaos and let him have it with everything they've got, which is a lot.

On the little screen, we can see Denuble close his eyes behind the hood and then there's a flash brighter than sunlight and half the crater wall is gone, blown out into the dry terrain beyond.

"Now!" I shout and Essential triggers the plasma generators. A field of waving, curving energy crackles across the crater and all devices, including any OCDs, react wildly and unpredictably in the electrical storm.

The captain boosts the rocket and we zip out into the air and under the lumbering garbage barges edging over the tip of the crater. The other transports are behind us.

The Mars security forces are pissed off.

The biggest ship starts to drop a chain of electronukes, and the little fliers are shooting for fun—rail guns and glitter guns and air cannons. We've got a visual screen showing it all as the ice gets chewed up and then collapses, crushing the tunnels and living quarters and a quarter-century of work by the resistance.

The sky lights up in blues and greens as the destruction swells, then the screen swivels as Essential changes the vantage to the back of the ship, watching for pursuit.

No one is coming. We beat the odds. The ships tuck under the garbage barge and we match their pace as they lumber toward the dome. We're safe, for the moment.

43

Essential tosses me the blur drops.

"Put a squirt in your OCD-connected eye. We can't afford to have your scroll link up to Halo again. Not until we're offloaded."

I squeeze in a stream and blink at the sting.

"Better let me have some of that," Valentine says. "And I'm reaching the limit of my spoofware. If I don't get back to Jezero soon, my cover will be blown."

There's a little girl sitting next to Valentine. "Seneca, you really should go below and strap in," Valentine says. "I'll walk you back."

I watch her leave, holding Seneca's hand. She looks back over her shoulder and smiles, then helps the young girl into the causeway.

"Is that her daughter?"

"Niece," Essential says. "Seneca's father, Lauren's brother, was killed by Whitsend."

"By Whitsend herself?"

"No, one of her goons."

"Was her brother in the resistance?"

"No, he wasn't, but his death made her join." Essential says. "The girl's mother is in a labor camp. Seneca is our youngest member."

I look out the window. I think Whitsend must have had her reasons, but I don't say that out loud.

We've been trailing along under the barges, slowly

leaving the planet, for almost fifteen minutes. Every second has been excruciating. We're creeping our way out of danger, and there's no sign of pursuit. But at this rate, they could catch us in two blinks.

Essential is strapped into the jump seat next to me. To her left is Captain Narthite. He's short and wide and lumpy—like he was pieced together from discarded muscle tossed out by a genetics lab—with a pointy bald head and a network of burn scars on his scalp. His head looks like a ship-map of Mars.

Apparently, he's kind of in charge.

He's done a manual override of the controls—all the ships have, reducing but not eliminating our signal—which makes it hard to keep us nestled up against the garbage ship without accidentally scraping it and killing us all.

Three transports, including the one we're on, made it out of the hangar. And the little Dory rocket.

I look out the side porthole. A piece of metal breaks off the closest ship and spins away, hurtling into space. A thin sheet of bio-starion is all that separates the guts of the ship from infinity, and the sheet is fluttering.

Revolutionaries always have the worst equipment.

"Looks like one of the ships is breaking up," I say to Narthite over the dull thumping of the straining engine. I expect him to at least act concerned.

"They'll figure it out," he says. "You don't last long in the resistance if you panic at the first sign of trouble."

"Well, this is like the hundredth sign for me," I say.

Essential punches in the coordinates for a site on the eastern flank of the garbage city where, she explains, there's a seven-clicks-wide plasticium dump soft enough to core to reconfigure a new hideout.

We're close enough we can start to see the outlines of the dump satellite in the distance, and I'm beginning to think we might make it after all.

Then an alarm starts to clang.

"Now can I panic?" I ask.

"Yes," Narthite says. "There's an autonomous garbage field ahead. Looks like a scow accidentally dropped its load. It's nothing for these big monsters to navigate through, but if we hit a piece, it'll split us in half."

He's talking to the other pilots, muttering directions and trying to keep them focused and ready to dodge the floating trash.

At first it doesn't look too bad. Mostly smaller pieces. We're making good time moving through the debris field. I see the end of it and the clear space beyond. Narthite has a death grip on the joystick, and I can literally see the pulse in his temples as he dodges and weaves through the trash.

"Nice flying, Captain," I say. "I think we're going to make it."

A giant piece of an old reactor hits the front of the garbage barge, bounces off and comes tumbling right at us.

"Oh shit," Narthite says.

We're not going to make it. We're all about to die.

I see a look of absolute bafflement on Essential's face. All the work, all the sacrifice, and we're going to die here, in a field of Martian waste. The ultimate humiliation. The nanites will be lost. The resistance will be over. All because of a random piece of cast-off space junk.

Valentine is standing beside me now and takes my hand in hers. There are worse ways to go, I guess.

And then there is a flash as the Dory rocket boosts past us like a woodpecker out of hell and slams right into the tumbling junk. It explodes. The pilot and passenger are obliterated, but the space junk's course is diverted, missing us by meters.

The force shakes the transport and people are screaming. I fall hard, curling around a little so Valentine lands on me instead of the console. My head hits something and the lights dim, I'm not sure if it's the ship or my brain.

But we're safe. The Dory crew sacrificed itself to save us. "To save you," Essential says, like she's reading my thoughts. "They did that to save you. To save hope."

"Those brave assholes," Narthite says.

I'm trying to make sense of this, of people sacrificing their lives to save others, especially when those others are jerks like me.

"I need to check on Seneca," Valentine says, wriggling free.

Essential is rattled too, but she's more concerned about the blood trickling down my forehead.

"Get the doctor up here," she yells.

44

"You'll live," Dr. Ashrawi says. She's tending to the gash on my forehead. Dr. Ashrawi is about my age, give or take, with shiny black hair and jet black eyes.

"Thanks, but I'm sure there are others who need your services more than I do," I say.

"Don't worry, Crucial ... may I call you Crucial?" she asks. "I'll get to them. We want to stop the bleeding before it puts the nanites at risk. But other than that, there's nothing wrong with you that cutting back on the drinking wouldn't cure."

"You can tell that from a gash on my head?"

She laughs. "I have other tools in my medical bag."

We're at the back of the bridge, watching Narthite navigate.

"Can you tell my thick-headed brother what you know about the nanites so we can decide what to do next?" Essential asks.

"I can try," she says. "This was really more Dr. Flanagrit's specialty. But theoretically—"

"You've never tested them? Like, in a person?" I ask.

"Alduis Coverly tested them on himself. We don't have those results, but they seemed effective. He managed to hide from Halo pretty well. At least until the end."

"So, theoretically, any second my blood might start boiling from a million tiny electric kettles. Weeping robots, I can't believe this is how I'm going to die. After everything

I saw, and did, in the Consolidation."

Dr. Ashrawi looks at Essential and I don't need the world's biggest AI to know she's thinking, *the nanites are in THIS guy?*

"What exactly do these things do?" I ask.

"The nanites let you hide from Halo," she says. "But more than that, they let you manipulate the data stream. In the original dose, thousands of the nanites were introduced into your bloodstream where they reproduce. By now, there are likely millions—"

"Millions?" Great. I'm turning into a cybanism.

"Yes, Crucial, millions. Each one is basically a tiny self-contained server and transmitter. They link up with your neural network and once you activate them, you can control how you are represented, or not, to Halo."

"Just by thinking about it?"

"Exactly. The nanites can bounce data and direct it, like mirrors. Without disrupting the flow of data, which as you know, is a red flag to Halo. There's always some type of data to collect, even the lack of data is data."

"There's no other way to permanently hide from Halo," Essential says. "Unless you do what I did and remove the OCD implant."

"And that only works because they think you're dead. So, you have to hide the rest of your life," I say.

"The nanites give you control over the data Halo recognizes. Theoretically, you could think your own data into the system. Like, 'I'm not here on a garbage barge, I'm actually back on Earth drinking a beer.' And Halo can't tell the difference because you're controlling the input,'" Dr. Ashrawi says.

I stretch my legs and my left knee cracks. "That's powerful stuff."

"In a system that knows everything, can even predict

everything, ambiguity is indeed the ultimate power," Dr. Ashrawi says.

"And it's not detectable? In my blood, I mean, by Halo right now?" I ask.

"No. Even though the nanites haven't been activated, they're programmed to avoid detection. So, what we need to do now is activate them."

"Great. Let's transfer them to Essential now and she can turn them on," I say.

"Unfortunately for everyone, it doesn't work like that. We took one blood draw, and that activated their defense system. They can't be transferred again until they've been activated," Dr. Ashrawi says.

"I don't like where this is going," I say.

"Coverly built in a failsafe. We had the receiving technology to activate the first blood draw, overseen by my now-deceased colleague Dr. Flanagrit. We could have inoculated everyone in the resistance. But he was afraid the blood might fall into the wrong hands before that, so he designed the nanites to go on the defensive in case someone tried to activate them without the proper tech. A second blood draw will render them inert. The nanites will shut down and dissolve if we draw them from you now."

"That might be for the best," I say, looking at my arm and imagining opening it up and letting enough blood flow out to kill off the damn things holding my insides hostage.

"You're a selfish, silly man," Dr. Ashrawi says. "Four people have died to get these nanites to your sister. And here you sit wondering if we should scrap it all because you would rather the Earth remain in paralysis, locked in orbit with Mars and the greedy pus-pots who run it."

"That doesn't sound very doctorly to me," I say.

"With just a dozen health cradles on Earth, we could add thirty years of life expectancy to every single person.

With enough tiered gardens, no one would go hungry. With the creation of a commons, everyone could be housed. The knowledge and technology exists for all of this," the doctor says. "I'm sorry our little project of helping those who need it by taking a tiny bit away from those who have everything is an inconvenience to you."

"Maybe if I knew what, exactly, the project is, I might be more enthusiastic about having robot blood."

Essential glares at me. "I'm not telling you the details until you pick a side," she says.

"You'll want to see this," Narthite calls out.

We're skirting the perimeter of the massive pile of garbage.

"Damn, it's huge," I say.

We're close enough to make out the large stuff— cooling reactors, small rockets, twisted metal—wedged in between mounds of plasticium, a building material that degrades to a soft absorbent clay-like goop.

"How does it all stay together?" I ask.

"The dome is seeded with a centrifugal-spin column," Narthite says. "Okay, here we go, we're at the coring site."

"What's the coring site?" I ask.

"Watch, over there, to the west," Essential says.

The ship that was previously behind us, the one that lost the panel earlier, breaks away from the formation and unlocks a meta-drill from its nose. At the edge of the dome, it drills into a patch of plasticium and in short order, has carved out enough space for the three resistance ships to shove their way into the garbage cave, tucked side by side. Narthite pulls our ship to a stop and kills the engine.

"Now what?" Essential asks.

"I'm making the order to redirect power," Narthite says. "Each ship has a side locking bay. Now that we're linked, a team is opening those throughways between the cargo holds. It will take about twenty-four hours or so to set up and move into the spaces. One ship will be a bunkhouse, one for defense, and one for communal work and garden space. We'll get our defenses up so they can't pinpoint us. It will be like home in no time."

"I'm impressed," I say. And I am. Turns out, these people are smart.

"This isn't the first time we've had to run, although it's the first time for Essential," Narthite says.

Valentine climbs up from below. "It's time for me to leave," she says. "There's a friendly freighter passing by. I'm going to use a drape and boost out to thumb a ride." She hugs Narthite. "Take care of Seneca. I'll be back when I can."

She turns to Essential. "Good luck. I'll see you soon, I hope."

Then she hugs me. "Thanks for helping us."

"I haven't—"

Essential elbows me.

I watch Valentine head toward the bay doors, and then the doctor and Essential sit down beside me.

"Look, Crucial, I'm happy to the carry this burden," Essential says. "I want to do good for others. And I get that you're not there yet. And I'm sorry about how this has all turned out. But you must do your part now. Dr. Ashrawi, what exactly does Crucial need to do?"

"First, we get the nanites prepared for activation. We need access to a lab where we can direct a sustained blast of sound waves at a precise frequency through an obsidian filter to turn them on. Once activated, you will be able to use them to form a transfer packet, which is embedded in their programming."

"So, I can control them as soon as they're activated?"

"Not quite. After the precise sound wave signal is

received by the nanites, you can only gain control after a traumatic emotional event. That's what allows your brain to lay down the new neural pathways needed to connect you directly to the nanites."

Essential's face falls. "My brother is basically dead on the inside. We're doomed."

"Thanks Sis, real nice," I say. "So, once I get my emotions spun up, at that point I can control the little blood worms and form the transfer packet?"

"Yes, exactly."

"And then get them out of me and into Essential."

"Yes," Dr. Ashrawi says. "Well, they won't be out of you, but your presence will no longer be required to fulfill our mission."

"I can go back to my boring life on Earth and hide from you and Halo, just like that?"

"Just like that," Dr. Ashrawi says.

"Essential, are you dead sure you want to do this, to be the heartbeat of the resistance?" I ask. "Nobody is forcing you?"

"Dead sure, nobody is forcing me," she says. Her face is as serious as I've ever seen it, and her expression reminds me of Mom. This worries me.

"I am meant to do this, it is what I was born to do," she says.

"Where can we find an appropriate lab?" I ask.

"Back in Holden, on Mars," Dr. Ashrawi says.

"All right. Let's go."

Essential leaps up and hugs me around the neck.

"How do we get there?" I ask.

"Oh, you're gonna love this," Essential says. "We're gonna hop on a garbage transport back to Mars. Sneak in like the trash they already think we are."

45

The garbage barge is huge and empty and creaking slowly forward. We're high enough above its surface that it's largely silent except for the crackle of cold metal, the hum of the engines and the occasional clank of a robot arm that needs to be tightened. The barge is pilotless but there's a narrow tech bridge, mostly for checking diagnostics, at the back of the deck and that's where we are, perched atop a column of equipment.

It's as good a way to hitch a ride back to Mars as any.

When the barge docked at the garbage dome, we rode monofilament zippers up to the deck and then clambered up the rungs while mechanized arms swept debris off into the mound of waste below.

There's no oxygen on the bridge, or heat, but it's heavily shielded to protect it from flying debris and radiation leaks, so my signal should be mostly contained and Essential assures me the blur drops aren't a risk to my sight. Not yet, at least. But I don't like the odds of taking vision advice from my one-eyed sister.

Now, we're over the wreckage of Korolev Crater. Half the walls are blown down—the red rocks pulverized and spilling out into the alluvial plains below. The ice—what's left of it—is cracked and scarred and punched through in some places, with twisted bits of metal showing. Lights are flickering as men and machines scour the wreckage looking for molecular traces of the resistance.

We got everyone off. Well, except Denuble. And the two in the Dory rocket. Three people died to make sure I didn't. I'm still struggling with this math.

Essential and I have a pretty good view of the action in the crater through the thick window and even though it's kilometers below and growing darker as night falls, we still duck out of sight as a big transport glides out onto what's left of the ice, the lamps lighting up the white in a blinding dazzle.

"Do you think the pirates saw us?" she asks.

When we were kids, we played space pirates in the lift tubes of an abandoned part of our squat tower. We were always the rich adventurers on the run from evil interstellar buccaneers after our family's wealth. We made these crazy costumes out of scavenged beetler shells and cornsilk bottles, and would stage elaborate fight scenes against imaginary enemies and only ever worried about Mom finding us on the edge of a sixty-floor drop.

That was a long time ago. But somehow, right now, it feels like only a minute in the past.

"The pirates didn't see us," I say. "We're safe for now, princess."

"Being here with you, it's almost like being a kid again."

"Except for the fact that we're wanted fugitives on Mars and unlikely to make it through the night," I say, slumping down with my back against the control panel. "But I could go for a slice of that reconstituted fruit custard roll Mom always gave us on Saturdays."

"They still make it—on Earth, at least," Essential says. "You could have it every day."

"There was something special about the way she sliced it. I can't ever get it that thin."

"She was trying to make it last," Essential says. "Those rolls were expensive. That woman could cut it so thin it was basically one-dimensional."

"And always just a little warm, but never hot."

"Because she only used half a heating credit on each piece. She was so damn cheap. But mostly she was broke."

"Stop ruining my childhood memories," I say.

"Sorry." She sits down beside me. "Are you sure about this?"

We have our airhoodies on low to preserve oxygen, and it's making us sluggish and a little irritated. Or maybe that's me. The thermal suits are stiff and scrunch like foil mixed with sand when you move and it's driving me bonks.

"No, I'm not sure at all," I say. "But I know you won't make it out of your fake death back into resistance life if we don't get those nanites in you. One slip-up, one interaction with anyone who notices you don't have a Halo feed and it's over. I can't take that chance. You'll never be able to leave the garbage dump, and I know you can't not get caught up in something."

She puts her arm around me and her suit crinkles like glass breaking in a rocket engine test factory. "Thanks," she says.

"Don't thank me. I'm pissed at you."

"No, you're not," she says. "You're secretly proud of me, you just don't have the words. It's like how you're still in love with Mel and you can't say it."

She's right, on both counts, but I won't admit it. Nor will I admit I'm a little scared for all of us. And these procking noisy suits. I'm tempted to peel mine off and freeze to death. It would be a lot quieter. And quicker. And probably less gruesome than how we'll probably really die.

She stands up and peeks out the window. "We're past Korolev Crater. Looks like we're in the clear."

I stand beside her. The barge is sliding along the southern edge of the crater now and moving into a long, unbroken expanse of the Choke.

"We are so far from in the clear. We're a millimeter closer to not being one hundred percent dead," I say.

"Okay, I'll reframe. We're closer to being in the clear, and you're closer to being a hero of the once-again free world," Essential says, grinning. "Think of it, Crucial, you'll go down in history, little kids will be taught—"

"*You* need to be the hero. Let's stick to the plan, which is we activate them in me, get them into you, then I can run back to my boring little life and you can save Earth and all its stupid inhabitants."

"Fine. And you can just keep hiding out behind your badge and a guilty conscience," she says. "We'll be in Holden soon. The next part will be tricky."

"You have a knack for understatement," I say. "The blur drops won't do much good when Halo starts picking up all the people who see me. We won't have long before they zero in on me."

"Stick with the plan," Essential says.

"Here goes," I say.

I sift through my scroll until I find the nub for Singhroy Able. She answers my ving immediately. She looks equal parts expectant, surprised and relieved.

"I have what you're looking for," I say. "But you need to make it worth my while."

She smiles a cold, hungry smile, like a shadow sliding across the moon. "What do you want?"

"I want my debt wiped. And a positive credit balance."

"Done."

"And all the Martian absinthe I can drink. Which is a lot."

"Fine. Where are you?"

"I'm on a garbage barge flying into Holden. I need serious cover from the security forces and Halo, and I need access to a tectonic lab with a sonic drill and crystal filters."

"We'll have someone waiting at the dock. You won't have long."

"It won't take long."

I disconnect and we can feel the thrum of the engines as the barge starts to slow. It passes through the entrance port, and the dome-based oxygen starts flowing. And the heat. I pull off the blasted thermal suit and kick it across the tiny bridge.

The ship scrapes into the dock with a thump and I head down the access tube first, a glitter gun in my pocket. Essential is right behind me.

When I open the door at the bottom and step out onto the empty deck, I see a familiar face—Sanders.

"Hello, Crucial," he says. "I'm very glad you are still alive."

"Nice to see you too, Sanders," I say.

He turns to Essential. "You have no OCD, which is illegal."

"Everything we're doing here is illegal, Sanders," I say. "Don't get stuck on the details."

46

11:25 p.m., August 31, 2187
Multnomah Ward, DuSpoles CPU, Earth

"What time is it?" I ask.

The interview is dragging on into infinity. I'm more tired, and still hungry. And Halo is still waiting for me to make a mistake.

"That's irrelevant," Halo says. "You'll be here as long as needed."

"It's okay. I'm starting to like this little room," I say. "And our conversation. It's nice to be listened to, you know?"

"I can tell you're attempting to make a joke," Halo says. "But this is not a matter in which humor is required or helpful. There are multiple irregularities in your story, Crucial. Periods in which your whereabouts cannot be precisely accounted for. It's becoming increasingly hard to believe you."

"You are worried about my story because my time is unaccounted for? Shouldn't you be more worried that the Tarterics and Singhroys are manipulating data for their own ends?"

"The system is working as intended and designed."

That almost sounds petulant. Is it possible to rattle artificial intelligence? Doubtful, but I'll keep giving it my best shot.

"The only way you can say the system is working is if you look away from those it's failing. Which is almost everyone," I counter.

That is going in my file for sure.

"No system can eliminate the failure of those who don't apply themselves," Halo says.

What the hell, might as well go big.

"Hey, tell me something. You knew about the base at Korolev Crater all along, didn't you?"

"There was suspicious activity there, incongruous data," Halo says. "It had been under active data surveillance for some time."

Gods, the Five Families could have shut it down any time—they just wanted the tech. The nanites.

"Why did the Mars security forces allow it to continue?"

"The Five Families do not consider the resistance to be a threat."

I take a deep breath. Here goes.

"Do you know, at present there are three ways to hide from you? First, there's pulling out your OCD entirely, which is pretty drastic, because it means sacrificing an eye," I say.

"Some members of the resistance have taken this step," Halo says. "But it necessitates a complete sequestration from public life. All other OCDs instantly flag the anomaly and mitigations are enacted."

"That's right," I say. "Because you've made it illegal to be unconnected."

"The council of the Five Families make the laws. Halo's role is simply to apply those laws and monitor those who break them."

"That's right. Don't blame the poor old all-seeing, all-powerful surveillance and monitoring system," I say. "Merely doing what it's been programmed to do."

I hold up two fingers.

"The second way is blur drops. They fuzz up the OCD so you can't track things as easily."

"They too come at a cost," Halo says. "Not only do they pose a risk to eye health, enough instances of inaccurate data become a data point in itself."

"That's why they use spoofware with the drops. Designed to overlay the blur with boring, predictable activity."

"The spoofware, as you colloquially call it, is now being addressed."

"Maybe you can do that, but maybe not," I say. "Because one thing I know about us humans, we're super boring and predictable. And you eat that up. If predictable becomes a flag, every single human is part of the resistance."

"You said there are three ways," it says.

"You already know the third. Jammers. They disrupt your monitoring. Obviously, that's a red flag, but I've learned that certain members of the Five Families use jammers frequently. I wonder what they're hiding?"

"Some higher-level activities are best shielded from the public record."

"You're programed by the Five Families to say that."

I feel calm. Usually I would check my vitals on my scroll, but Halo has put me in a digital shadow. Now's the time.

"There's a fourth way though. A fourth way to hide from you."

I'm holding four fingers up to the camera.

Halo doesn't answer. It already knows this, of course, it knows about the nanites. But it doesn't know how much I know, or how many people have access to them. That's the whole point of this little sham debriefing from Halo's perspective. And why I need to stall a little bit longer.

"What did you learn about that technology during your time in the resistance?"

"I wasn't in the resistance, that's not my thing, and given what you know about how I betrayed my own sister, it should be clear by now that my sympathies are not with the resistance," I say.

"And you found this technology at the Korolev Crater," Halo says. "This fourth way."

"Not me. But my sister did. She was punished severely for it. You know that, though."

"The punishment fit her crime."

"If this tech is as powerful as my sister said, almost anyone could use it to feed you fake data and disappear completely. Now, that would be a game-changer."

"Does anyone other than your sister currently have this technology?"

"Hard to say, I'm not really in a position to know," I say. "But it's certainly a concern, right?"

"Crucial, it would be best for your future security if you now explain precisely what happened at the Holden mining lab during the data gap."

"You mean when we were jammed?"

"Yes. Please elaborate on what happened during the moments when the events were jammed. And explain how the nanites came to be integrated into your biology. "

47

Three nights ago

"You look good, Sanders," I say. He's standing next to a big, sleek hover sedan.

"Thank you, Crucial. This latest upgrade is satisfactory."

His hair is lighter this time, almost white, and slicked back. The tips are bioluminescent so that the strands glow and pulse with color in time with his movement. His designers must have been bored this go-around.

He's a little leaner now, and more muscular, and somehow seems more capable. That makes me nervous. I wonder if they changed his parameters from observer and guide to enforcer or, worse, executioner.

"Thanks again for taking the heat for me at the Holden apartment complex," I say. "Sorry about the hand."

He looks at his new hand and flexes it. "I barely remember the old one." Then he looks at Essential. "Is this your sister?"

"Is that who she looks like to you?" I ask.

"That's an odd turn of phrase," Sanders says. "I see a resemblance. Superficially and at the genetic level as well. But with no OCD, I can't verify that."

"Let's say, for grins, it is Essential," I say. "Even though officially, of course, she's dead."

"I'm glad he found you. He was very worried and upset. His biorhythms were in constant turmoil," Sanders says.

"He's a big softy," Essential says.

Sanders looks at her curiously. "Crucial Larsen is not big. He's statistically average in terms of height. Though he does have a bit more fat than median."

She laughs. "It's just a saying. Like, maybe he's too emotional and kind."

"Oh, I don't think so," Sanders says. "His actions do not warrant that conclusion."

"This is fun," I say. "But we're in a bit of a time crunch. Not much of a jammer gap before Halo checks in. And by the way, since you're here, I take it you're not really working for the DuSpoles and Tarterics?"

"Apparently not. I was as surprised as you. Evidently, the Singhroys are forming an alliance with the Blevins and the Fehrvens to mitigate the influence of the other two families. They inserted an unsanctioned code that runs counter to my original programming to protect you at all costs, and to report everything back to them immediately."

"And you've done a fine job so far. I'm a little worried that you are also coded to, you know, do away with me when the Singhroys and their pals get what they want."

Sanders seems genuinely indignant. "I would never harm a friend."

"I mean, yeah, I know you wouldn't on purpose, Sanders. I'm just saying, it would be too bad if they hid a little subroutine in that synthetic coconut of yours that forced you to act against your will, or whatever."

He stares at me, the tips of his hair glowing red and black, and the silence builds.

"I scanned my operating system. I can't say for certain you're safe around me," Sanders says.

I can almost hear the self-loathing in his voice.

"I know you'd never do anything on purpose, but I'm thinking back to that bot on the HARM factory floor ..."

His face twists with disgust. "I cannot believe you are comparing me to a common tool. It's like me saying your actions are no different than that of a microbe. Really, Crucial, that's hurtful."

Essential frowns at me, like I'm abusing Sanders, and punches me on the arm. "Be nicer."

"Let's swear an oath, as friends," I say. "If you're about to kill me or my sister, or do anything that would lead to our capture, I want us to have a code word. Say, uh, 'absinthe.' And then I'll know."

"Fair enough," Sanders says. "And you will swear the same. I've had two full bio-reboots since we've met, so the odds are really against me."

"Unless we actually get moving soon, the odds are going to be against all of us," Essential says. She looks around nervously at the various lev-cars and fliers in drone jackets passing by.

"She's right. I'm assuming you know what's needed?"

"Yes," Sanders says. "There's a tectonic lab nearby. Mining research. I should warn you though, there will be many people there, with guns, ready to take the product when it's extracted. Where is the product?"

"Are you broadcasting?" I ask.

"Yes."

"It's in her blood," I say, pointing to Essential. "We have to activate the nanites before they can be condensed and extracted, otherwise they'll shut down and self-destruct."

"Once they're activated, I can arrange them to produce a transfer expulsion," Essential says. "It'll package them up neat as can be and I'll hand them off."

She's a good liar, always has been. Essential smiles at Sanders, who is also the camera, so she is really smiling at Singhroy Able, watching from the lab.

"I'm scanning her now, but I'm not picking up anything unusual," Sanders says.

"That's the point, Sanders. They're stealthy. Like tiny versions of you, only in velvet slippers."

We pile into the hover sedan and Sanders punches in the coordinates. We pull out and make our way across town.

It's almost dawn, and a few bars and restaurants are open, catering to pre-shift workers from the HARM plant and other manufacturing facilities socializing or watching avatainment shows together. I can see into one of the bars, called The Galileo, where a roomful of people silently watches the same program, each in their own scroll.

Humans are a strange bunch. We like to be alone together.

"Sanders, my jammer is blacking out. Are you blocking my Halo feed?" I ask.

"Yes, I am. Quite effectively, actually."

"How?" I ask.

"By generating a low-level disruption that appears to be an equipment malfunction. The Blevins family designed it. A sophisticated jammer. Very clever. But it won't fool Halo for very long."

"We won't need it to," Essential says. "I just need a good thirty-second blast of 80 kilohertz through an obsidian filter."

"Here's the lab," Sanders says.

The Mars Institute of Mining, unlike many other functional facilities in Holden, was built to inspire. It's shaped like a hammer, with a narrow core of a dozen floors and a top level that stretches out to each side like a "T." The automated rocket lab next door, by comparison, is a squat, gray structure that looks like a box trying to go unnoticed.

We climb out and head toward the Institute doors. There are armed guards in civilian clothes along the walkway, lining the steps and inside the doors, all with sinister-looking glitter guns. Singhroy Able is waiting at the door, along with Fehrven Modo and Blevin Flunt.

"A little reunion," I say, thinking back to the night they dropped by my hotel in Jezero.

"We must move quickly," Able says. "We can't jam the feed for much longer."

"Quite a little militia you've got here," I say.

She ignores me and leads us into the lift and we scoot up to a lab on the top floor. The view from the top of the hammer is impressive. We're looking out over most of Holden and in this early morning light, the dome has gone translucent so we can see into the Choke and up to the stars above.

The lab is lined with glass cases holding samples of Martian rocks and minerals, including chunks of the rocks Essential and I saw in the ceiling of the old mine shaft. They are gleaming and sparking light in the mostly darkened room.

"What are these rocks?" Essential asks.

"They're called opal, and they are extremely rare on Mars. Only one deposit has ever been located," Sanders says.

"Where?" Essential asks.

"On the edge of Jezero, just outside the dome."

I can almost hear Essential breathe a sigh of relief—what we found out in the Choke is still undiscovered.

"The presence of opal is potentially correlative with flowing water and life forms," Sanders says.

"Ancient water?" Essential asks.

"Presumably," he says.

The lights suddenly rev up to an eye-popping high-lumen level, revealing an odd-looking device shaped like a twenty-first century telescope, only this one is huge and fills the room. It's powered by a thick, coiling snake of cables and protruding all kinds of fixtures and dials and attachments. A technician holds up a lens as big as the seat cover on a bio-waste transformer.

"What's that?" I ask.

"It's an obsidian filter," Essential says.

"That's correct," the technician says.

"The nanites are keyed to the frequency of sound shaped by the internal crystalline structure of the obsidian," Essential says.

The technician nods at Essential and points at a pedestal in front of the massive device. There's a fist-sized lump of red rock on it and a seat in front.

"Sit there," the technician says. "Wait, what's happening? You don't have a feed?"

It's so unusual to encounter a human outside the data stream, the tech is momentarily flummoxed.

"Not now," Able says to the technician. "Quickly."

Essential sits and looks up worriedly at the sonic drill. "Are you sure that won't put a mineshaft through me?"

The technician snorts. "Yeah, at 80 kilohertz. Like that would drill through anything. It wouldn't even dent a yeast pudding."

The tech turns the machine on and then presses a series of commands on the access screen. There's a burp of energy and the hairs on the back of my neck stand on end and a faint whistle pops my ears. I look at Sanders. "Did it work?"

"Thirty seconds at the requested frequency were delivered," Sanders says.

Everyone is looking at Essential expectantly.

"Anything?" I ask, hoping I sound convincing.

She shakes her head. "I don't feel any different. I mean, I feel a little queasy, but nothing different." She starts to slump in her chair.

I move to her side and hold her up. "Hit her again," I say. "I need this crow-plop to be done."

The tech flips the switch and again all eyes are on Essential. They should be on me. As they're watching her, I slide into position. The pulse of energy hits me and something inside me responds. It feels like that peculiar flush of heat that comes from tantrum-crying when you're a kid, but also a falling away of everything, like when you're tired, so tired, and finally close your eyes and drop backward into sleep. And my blood is humming. Vibrating. It's not a pleasant feeling.

The little fuckers are turned on.

I feel something else, a sort of connection to the world, to the people around me, to Halo. I can literally feel all the connections. But somehow, they're still just out of reach.

"Did it work?" I ask again. "I think it worked this time."

Everyone is still looking at Essential. Except Sanders. He's looking at me.

"Maybe," Essential says. "I feel something, that's for sure."

There's a distant boom as a door is blown in, and shouts and the unmistakable whisper of glitter guns.

"Godsdamn," Flunt says. "The Mars security forces are here." He's plugs his feed into the building's security cameras.

We all link into Flunt's scroll except for Essential. Security forces are making their way up the lift, and they do not look pleased. I see Jynks.

"Oh no," Sanders says. "Absinthe, Crucial. Absinthe."

I turn and he's pulling a glitter gun out of his waistband.

48

"Shit, Sanders, don't do this," I say.

He's got his glitter gun aimed directly at my heart and a sad look on this face.

"I don't want to, Crucial," he says. "Absinthe. Confound it. Absinthe. Please don't move. Don't make me use force. I'm authorized to do that now, apparently. Please wait here for the Tarterics."

"Come on, Sanders, old friend. We can't let them catch us. We'll be put in prison camps. For the rest of our lives. Which will be short."

"I'm sorry," he says. "Apparently, there is a subroutine below my subroutine."

I hate life in the modern world.

"Let him go," Essential says. "I'm the one you want. I have the technology in me. Together, we can figure out how to make it work. He's ignorant, and innocent. But mostly ignorant."

Even with our lives on the line, she's jabbing me. Sisters are the best.

"I don't think so," Sanders says. "I watched him. His feed changed. Something affected his biorhythms. The anti-Halo technology is in him."

Able and the others look at me closely.

"No, you've got it all wrong, Sanders," Essential says. "He probably has gas. He eats so much, like a procking trash rat."

"How is it you can be so damned insulting while you bargain for my life?" I ask, exasperated.

"We will wait for the security forces to sort everything," Sanders says, still pointing the gun at me.

The technician is quietly adjusting the dials on the sound drill, waiting for her moment. She knows where her credits come from. Essential and I both stand in front of the pedestal and I pick up the rock sample. This is about to get messy.

Essential sees the play. She moves far enough to the side that Sanders, his logical mind ruled by binary information flow, splits the difference between us and moves in front of the now empty chair so he can cover us both.

"A rock cannot beat diamond flechettes," he says.

"Oh yeah?" I hurl the rock at him and miss. It flashes past him and cracks into a display at the back of the room.

"Great throw," Essential says. My bad throw bought us just enough time.

The technician hits the button.

"Absinthe, buddy," I say.

"I'm very sorry, Crucial," he says, misunderstanding. "Me too."

There's another burp of energy, a louder one, and this time it cores a hole right though Sanders and sprays a tangle of wet, organic circuitry onto the floor in front of him, splashing his blue blood up onto the pedestal.

Sanders looks down in surprise at the dripping hole in his chest then turns to the technician. She's shrinking back, afraid he's going to glitter her, but he seems almost happy.

"You warned me," he says, returning his attention to me. He's starting to lose structural integrity but smiling even as his face bubbles and melts away. "Like a friend."

There's a wet plop and then only his clothes and a

puddle of blue slime remain. I pick up the gun and grimace at the sticky trails of bio-matter dripping off it.

But it's too late. Flunt snaps his fingers and points, and two guards grab Essential and four others aim their weapons at me.

"Is it true?" Able asks. "Are the nanites, the anti-Halo tech, in you?"

"Maybe," I say.

"Give them to us," she says.

"I don't know how."

"You'd best figure it out quickly if you want us to honor our deal."

"Now is not the time," I say. "The security forces will be here in seconds. Get us out of here. I swear you can have the tech. I don't want it."

"I believe you," Able says. "But not enough to risk the future. We cannot offer you shelter. We can keep your sister safe, for now, because she has no scroll and cannot be identified by Halo. You'd better figure this out and get us what we want. Otherwise, she dies and you go to prison for life. Or maybe you die too."

"Why does everyone have to die in every godsdamned scenario? Can we be a little less melodramatic?" I ask.

"To the roof," she says to her crew. "Transport is en route."

They drag Essential off and she looks back over her shoulder with a look of fierce determination shot through with disgust. "Don't you dare make a deal with them," she shouts.

They hurry off toward the tube that heads to the top of the hammer. I look down at the wet remains of Sanders. I hear the security forces advancing. I try to activate the nanites. I can feel them, but they don't care, don't do anything other than make me aware of them. Stubborn, selfish little shits.

What did Essential say? They needed some big emotional event to align to my neural pathways. Seems like my fear of ending up glittered so bad that I puddle up Sanders would be enough of a jolt. But apparently not.

I hear a roar from the roof. The transports are taking off. Essential is safe, but for how long?

I feel like I should be surprised the Five Families are jockeying for power and influence. They literally have it all, their own damn planet, all the resources on two worlds, and they're still not happy. The rich are never happy, and they never have to pay consequences, so they never stop trying to be richer and more powerful, to get to the top of the heap and then balance there on the head of a shrinking pin.

But I'm not surprised. It's like the Consolidation Wars all over again. How many Earthers had to die for them to work through their petty emotional territorial bullshit that time?

Shit, I hope Essential's revolutionary talk isn't rubbing off on me. I don't have the energy to save Earth.

First things first. I need to get out of here before Jynks and her crew catch me.

Whatever dampening effect Sanders had on the system is gone now and my scroll is getting hammered by incoming messages and alerts and commands. "Stay where you are. Do not resist. Comply."

Come on, you little bastards, I tell the nanites. Do your thing.

Still nothing.

Jynks is vinging me and she has the emergency clearance to breach my firewall. "Crucial Larsen, this is it. This is where it ends. I've tried to play nice out of respect for Mel, but it ends here in the Mars Institute of Mining, one way or the other."

"Would you believe me if I said this is all one giant misunderstanding?" I ask.

"Yeah, so you've said before. Then let's talk about it. Come out with your guns disabled. Better yet, crawl out on your hands and knees and I promise we probably won't glitter you on the spot."

"You sound angry," I say as I split my scroll into columns—one for Jynks, one for messages, one for alerts and one more to search for operating instructions for the sonic drill. "Things tense between you and Mel?"

"You're an anal polyp," she says. "And I'm really going to enjoy this."

It takes a few seconds to identify the model. Then I have to sort through all the various ways to learn—video, written, direct transplant—before I can figure it out. I go for visual so they can't give me bad data, and I scan the operating instructions.

First thing, get rid of the obsidian filter. I pull out the glass disk and toss it aside. It shatters with a melodic crash, and long, thin shards of the black volcanic glass scatter across the floor. Next, I twist the dial to turn up the juice to max. There's a flywheel on the side that controls the orientation and I crank it to spin the drill around and adjust the angle, aiming the device through the floor of the 'T' at the rocket facility next door.

"We're coming in, Larsen," she says. "Don't bother surrendering. We'll adjust the video later."

"I think that's called lying, Jynks," I say. "You took an oath, remember?"

"Yeah, to protect the people of Mars from urine-drips like you."

"It's all a misunderstanding," I say again. "I have the facts. I just need to live long enough to share them with an impartial judge."

I hear blasts against the lab door and press the drill command. The machine warns me that the results will be catastrophic and questions my goal. I check that there are no humans in the rocket lab and then override the settings. It gives me one more chance to change my mind, making it clear the desired settings are not rational. I press the button.

There's a hum of power, a belch of energy and half the floor is swept away. The room wobbles and the machine shakes. I hear glitter guns discharging and flechettes are zipping by, winking and catching the light. They'd be beautiful if they weren't so deadly.

Jynks is swearing and now I tune in on a rail gun charging. Probably hers.

"What in the name of the two moons of Mars are you doing?" she yells.

I hit the drill again. It assumes the operator must know what they're doing this time because it skips the warnings and belches another concentrated sonic blast that cores right into the boxy manufacturing unit next door. Firing a slug of sonic energy into a facility filled with rocket fuel. What could go wrong?

There's a massive explosion and an orange ball of flame boils up from below to engulf the mining building, then recedes. Bits of dome are melting and dropping down and claxons are ringing.

Shit, Halo sees me now. I'm back online. My scroll is going nuts. Power is dropping out across Holden. The cold, thin Martian air is flowing in. Repair bots are already hustling out. A stream of news alerts bangs around. *Industrial accident at Holden, no cause for alarm.* Of course, Halo isn't telling the truth. Why would the Five Families program it for truth—of any kind?

I grab a drone jacket and an airhoodie and jump through the shattered floor into the chaos.

If only these damned nanites could help me out a little. I concentrate again and try to will them out of my body in a handy little pill I could trade for Essential's life.

Nothing doing.

I drop down lower than recommended to avoid capture, my toes almost dragging on the ground. I weave through the streets of Holden, past people streaming out to watch the fireball and its aftermath. I aim straight for the lev-train station.

Emergency workers are motioning people to board. I drop through the doors at the last minute and kill my drone jacket, sliding to a stop and pissing off the other riders.

"Not chill," a man says. "Not chill at all."

As the packed train heads into the Choke back toward Jezero, I watch as Jynks and a handful of cops rush the platform. She can see me. She has her gun raised. They all have their guns raised. But there are too many civilians. Just barely too many.

Jynks smiles and waves. They'll be waiting at the other end of the line.

49

The train is picking up speed for the run to Jezero.

I've got about eleven minutes and a few thousand kilometers of the Choke to lev-train through before getting picked up by Jynks and her gang. If that happens, I'm done for, and for good. I do the only sensible thing I can think of—find something to drink.

Lev-trains are sleek and comfortable, but the rides are so fast they don't waste resources on lounges. Instead, there's a dispenser by each entrance that squirts synthwine into degradable cups for lottery workers heading home and anxious to take the edge off. I access it on my scroll and hit the credit transfer.

Nothing happens—my credits are frozen. And then lots of things happen all at once. The main column is flashing alerts and shouting all manner of unpleasantries straight into my brain and firing notices to the authorities and notifying me about the notices. I'm sure Jynks is monitoring it all gleefully.

My assets, such as they were, are gone, and credits are being debited at an alarming rate. It's pointless, of course. I've got no family to inherit my debt. Only Essential, and her debt is deeper than mine. And she's supposed to be dead.

Dammit, I've never needed a drink so bad in my life.

A woman walks by. She's well-coifed and toned and carrying a tiny dog in one hand. Like super tiny. It's no more than three centimeters tall at the shoulder and it's growling and barking, but it sounds like an insect.

"Excuse me, this dispensary appears to be malfunctioning," I say. "I have a terrible craving for a bit of wine. Would you mind testing it for me?"

"Of course not," she says, using her scroll to pop the machine to action. It spits out a cup of wine and she picks it up and turns. "It appears to be in order," she says, then registers me.

I'm sure her scroll is now bombarded with all kinds of disagreeable things about me, like how I'm wanted by the security forces and how I'm dangerous and should be avoided at all costs.

She slips her tiny dog into her pocket and hands me the wine. "Enjoy it," she says. "If you'll excuse me." She has the look of someone who is forcing a smile while alerting the authorities, a mix of moral smugness and primal fear.

I watch her leave and then down the drink. It's terrible, but it helps clear my mind. I quickly realize a clear mind is a mistake because what's revealed is terrifying: I'm all out of options.

I check the monitors—six minutes until the next stop. Gods, these things are fast.

I look out the window at the Choke. A dust storm is rolling in, a big one.

Mars has a very thin atmosphere, which means the storms don't do much damage, but it also has tiny dust particles that stick to every damn thing, including the windows of the train. Visibility starts to drop inside the dust-shrouded cylinder—it feels like a deprivation tank.

On the plus side, dust storms scramble satellite connectivity. The rail guidance system driving the train isn't impacted, but individual data streams switch to local-only in the dusty chaos. We all lose our connections, and most people stare dumbly at the dust-coated windows and wait the few minutes for the lev-train to roll through and their feeds to reconnect so they can get back to the larger world inside their heads, as opposed to the tiny world inside their minds they're confronting now.

If I could get off the train right now, the storm would give me some coverage.

I try to work up some panic to align the nanites. "Come on, you little fuckers," I say, straining to make something happen. "It's now or never."

Alarms sound and the train brakes suddenly, sending us all tumbling. The emergency speakers start blaring. "Anomaly detected on the track. Anomaly on the track."

I stand up and look around, mouth hanging open. Holy shit. It's working. I'm doing it. I feel like a god, exerting my will on an unsuspecting hyperconnected world.

Then there's a bang and a whistle, and part of the wall peels away and the Choke claws into the train tube.

It's biting cold and whistling sandpaper and we're all gasping, the dust makes it hard to see. I did not do that, I tell myself. The nanites did not do that because I wouldn't do that. Airhoodies and thermal suits drop from the ceiling. I slap on a hoodie and try to catch my breath. My eyes are burning, and I can taste rusty Mars in my mouth.

Three people crawl in from the outside. They're wearing ominous, old-fashioned space suits and helmets, the curved surface a dull, reflective black.

"This is a robbery!" one yells, pulling out a metal canister that pops open and unfolds a reticulated metal umbrella that lights up and starts to hum.

It's a credit siphon and people are screaming that their credits are being depleted and pulled into the debt void.

It's an old-fashioned holdup. Like the bovine-men in old America used to do when trains ran on wood and weapons were rudimentary and the rich didn't quite own everything yet.

I didn't do any of this. Absolutely did not do this.

These procking nanites are useless.

My cop instincts kick in and I reach for the glitter gun I took off Sanders, thinking I should try to stop them. One of the robbers looks at me incredulously, as if knowing what I'm thinking. They shake their head like I'm an idiot and point at the hole in the train wall with a gloved hand.

Yeah, right, that makes more sense. I should make a run for it.

As I move past the robber, they toss me some sort of fob. I catch it out of habit and climb out of the train onto the ground. I'm not geared up for the Choke. My hood generates enough artificial gravity to keep my brain from bulging into the top of my skull, but the emergency suit doesn't have gravity modulators. And that damn crinkling fabric makes my hands basically useless.

I'm bounding around like crazy in the swirling dust, bouncing higher than I ever did on Earth—although I jumped pretty high that time I saw a giant trash spider in the shower—and kind of hanging there.

The fob is beeping and in the swirling dust beyond the lev-track, I can barely make out lights flashing in sequence.

What kind of robbers leave a getaway transport?

Someone is looking out for me. The resistance, maybe. Or more likely Able and her scheming friends. They want me alive long enough to get their hands on the nanites.

I stumble and bounce forward toward the lights. It's a rocketbike. A turbo powered death wish on two gyroscopic wheels. I lie prone in the padded driver's cot and strap in. The bike lights up. The display screen flashes a destination. Baldet Crater.

It's not far from Jezero, but Jynks and her forces can't

beat me there. If the resistance is at Baldet, or even Able and her crew, I might make it through this night.

The storm is abating. Already I can make out the night sky beyond, and the stars. My scroll will be traceable in minutes. I squirt the last of the blur drops into my eyes and toss the bottle behind me.

If I don't move soon, I'll die here, either from the cold or at the hands of a trigger-happy cop on the Mars security forces team. Probably Jynks—who will tell Mel it was someone else. Dammit, Jynks, if you do kill me, I'm going to record it and send it to Mel just to prock with you.

If I have to die on Mars, I don't want it to be out in the Choke. Better to be around a bunch of cloned animals. So, whoever's waiting at Baldet, here I come.

I press the launch button and the rocketbike flares to life. I rotate the throttle and it blasts forward, the afterburners glowing orange and lighting up the stalled lev-train behind me.

50

The rocketbike zooms right up to the dome at Baldet Crater and then the engine shuts off and I slide to a stop a few meters from an access door. Gun in hand, I slip through and find myself in a peaceful forest. I shed the airhoodie and thermal suit.

A woman is about thirty meters ahead of me, kneeling and digging around the roots of a tree. I don't need enhanced optics to recognize Mel.

She stands and turns, perfectly framed between the trunks of two trees. Aspens. I recognize them from a trip we took to a tree museum years ago. It wasn't cheap, but we slept in a grove of the spindly Earth aspens, carefully maintained under a climate shield. Their leaves were yellow. There was a foul breeze from some nearby dump fire, but it was worth it when the leaves all shook and quaked. When we woke up the next morning, with burning eyes and sore lungs, we were blanketed with yellow leaves that fell overnight. I don't think I've ever seen Mel as happy as that morning.

Mel doesn't look happy now. She looks sad.

My scroll is going crazy, with Jynks telling me she's coming for me and Able saying she'll be here with Essential in six minutes. The avatainment thread for Baldet Crater is also piping in—a bison herd is galloping through my scroll now.

"Crucial," Mel says. "You're here."

"Yeah," I say. She doesn't seem surprised. "Were you expecting me?"

"I'm always expecting you."

"That's cryptic. Did you have anything to do with the train and the bike?"

"I have no idea what you're talking about. Have you been drinking?"

"Not enough. We've only got a few minutes."

"Why?"

"Your lovely bride-to-be and her extremely well-armed entourage will be here in ten minutes, tops. And before that, in about five minutes, a few scheming members of the Five Families, and their mercenaries, who are holding Essential hostage will arrive."

"Trouble has a way of following you around," she says. "Let's walk over to the giraffes. They're very calming."

"Like gyth juice," I say. "Where are all the kids and picnicking families and such?"

"We're on the development side of Baldet. Where I met you before is the public side. Here, we're doing the actual science."

We walk side by side out of the aspen grove into another stand of trees I don't recognize, which isn't a surprise because I only recognize the one type. A few of the trees are tall, like ten times my height, with tiny needles and brown cones. Others are squat with long, spindly limbs and bright green hand-sized leaves.

We should probably be talking about the fact that we're about to be ground up in the gears of Mars family warfare, but it's too peaceful.

"What's that?" I ask, pointing at four skinny trees, curved and tall, with no leaves at all except at the very top like a mop of unruly hair, clustered around a dozen round things that look like shrunken human heads.

"It's called a palm tree," Mel says. "I don't know where they originally grew, I mean, where it evolved to grow. Part of what we're doing here is experimenting to match eco-climates with species."

"Do you like the work?" I ask.

"Yes, very much. Some of it is tedious, like trying to find the perfect plants to terraform Mars. It's very slow and precise, running endless probabilities on strains of moss and lichens. But this part is exciting, regenerating the plants and animals of Earth from before the climate catastrophe. It's more than exciting—I feel like I'm doing something that will help people. Maybe someday we can repopulate Earth with all the plants and animals that were once there."

A deer passes to the side of us. Mel reaches in the pocket of her white jacket and gives it a pellet of something. It nuzzles her hand and keeps moving.

I guess it's nice Mel still holds that dream of repopulating Earth—she's always been an optimist. But she's wrong. Dead wrong. And she should stop deluding herself. That kind of delusion is what lets the Five Families get away with everything.

"Doubtful that's what the Five Families have in mind," I say, aiming for gentle but failing. "I imagine they plan on populating Mars with this stuff. Or some new planet after they wreck this one."

"You never know what might happen," she says. We stop at the edge of an open area within the thicket of trees. The temperature has kicked up a few notches.

"Do you ever think about coming back home?" I ask.

"Not anymore," she says, giving the answer I don't want to hear.

A family of four giraffes lumbers by. We stop as they nose around in the clearing.

"They really are magnificent creatures," she says. "I'm

infatuated. Their necks are so ridiculously elegant."

Her expression is pure joy, like with the yellow aspen leaves. And as I turn to watch the gangly legs of the littlest one, hopping along trying to keep up with the rest, I feel it too. They look like hope—fragile hope, an against-all-odds kind of hope.

Together, we stare at the giraffes.

A bird with a huge wingspan swoops down low, casting a massive shadow. I duck instinctively.

"Holy crap, is that some sort of dinosaur?"

"It's one of our eagles, but engineered to be quite large," Mel says, smiling at my reaction. And even though she's sort of laughing at me, it makes me crazy happy that something I said makes her smile.

"Back in old America, it was a symbol, like a totem animal for freedom," she explains. "We engineered this enormous version to see how it manages at this size. We'll compare its natural length of life to medium and smaller versions until we land on the optimal size for the bird's health and life span, and then we'll have the specs for mass production."

In the distance, at the far edge of the clearing, a giant yellow cat slinks out of the grove of trees.

"What the hell is—"

"It's not that I don't love you, Crucial," she says.

"Wait, what?"

"I can't be with you," she says.

The dome suddenly feels very small and cold. "Why not?"

"I'm happy here. Happy with Jynks. You and I, we had our chance and it didn't work out. We weren't lucky. Love takes a lot of work and a little luck."

"Luck had nothing to do with what happened to us," I say. "We both know I fissioned it all up. But if you give me another chance—"

"I don't have those feelings for you anymore," she says.

"I don't believe you," I say.

I lean in and kiss her. My lips against hers are as familiar as anything I've ever known. It feels good and right. She's not kissing back, exactly, but she's not pulling away either. I feel her hand brush the back of my neck lightly, then flutter away, uncertain.

She breaks off from the kiss and takes a step back. Her face is hard to read. I think I see emotion there, but also shock.

"Listen, I'm sorry, that was impulsive. I shouldn't have—"

"Turn around," Mel whispers. "But slowly. They have guns. And Essential."

I turn around. Able is behind me with Modo and Flunt and about twenty heavily armed guards. Essential's wrists are electrocuffed behind her back, but she looks otherwise unharmed.

"Drop your gun," Able says. I toss it out in front of me. "You ready to deal?" she asks.

"Yes," I say. I look behind them at the big tawny cat sauntering across the clearing. It has the peculiar trot of a feral cat that has something in its sights.

Across the meadow, Jynks and her security forces pop into view, advancing toward our position. They made good time.

Jynks is hitting me old-school with d-mail. I open it and the font flashes across my scroll. "Stand down, Crucial Larsen. This will be your only warning. You and your sister will be taken into custody and if you resist, you will be exterminated."

I guess Jynks has figured out that the woman in cuffs is Essential. "We'd better take cover," I say.

"Stop stalling," Able says. She raises a glitter gun to Essential's head. "I want that technology."

"Check your scroll," I say, knowing they can't—they've got a powerful jammer with them on a floatlift. If they turn it off, they'll be caught here with me, a fugitive, and with Essential, a terrorist who is supposed to be dead and has no scroll. Not reporting someone without a scroll would be difficult to explain to security, even for members of the Five Families. "Or look behind you. Your call."

Able turns and sees Jynks's swarm of security agents at the other side of the clearing and I see panic wash across her face. Despite what's happening, I won't deny I like seeing fear in one of the highest-ranking members of the Five Families. It's something I could get used to.

"There's a thicket of oak over here. It will make us hard to see, for a little while at least," Mel says. "And give us some cover."

We follow Mel. Out of the corner of my eye, I see a figure break away from the security forces and walk over to the giraffes, looking up at them curiously. It's Sanders.

51

The dome covering Baldet Crater is partially shielded, thanks to Mel, to protect her precious plants and animals from harmful electromagnetic waves. It's almost like constant exposure to the data stream might be bad for living creatures.

Between the jammer and the shield, it won't be easy to track who's in here, but Jynks is still broadcasting. She's managed to hijack the Baldet Crater public-info channel and is bludgeoning us with furious threats.

We're hidden behind the lake in a copse of big oak trees. Essential has her enhanced eye on the main entrance, looking through the wood and brush, narrating the assault as it unfolds.

"Oh, shit, she's mad," Essential says. "She's got thirty uniforms with her and it looks like even more arriving and … hey, is that Sanders?"

"It is. They already rebooted him," I say.

He looks good, with black hair in a very stylish cut, and this time he has a glitter gun in each hand. Version bad-ass Sanders.

Someone is spending a fortune rebooting him over and over. Funny how there's plenty of money for an often-hilarious and cutting-edge piece of surveillance and law enforcement equipment, but never enough to put food in the bellies of the hungry on Earth.

Son of a defective clone, all this revolutionary talk is

really starting to rub off on me.

"They're fanning out," Essential says. "Some of them are hitting the air."

The trees make it difficult to navigate, but they'll close the gap soon.

Able and her nefarious compatriots look worried. "We can't be caught here," she says. She motions to her people and they start pulling out some serious hardware.

"You can't murder security forces," Mel says. "That's against the law."

"Don't forget your place," Modo says. "You are a guest on our planet, in our home. As such, the laws don't apply to us as they do to you."

A flash of anger passes across Mel's face. But Modo's not lying. That's what I like about Earth. At least I know where I stand.

"We'll leave you all for dead here if we have to," Blevin says. "You can take the fall, and if the nanite tech dies with you, so be it. It's a waste, obviously, but we'll manage to spin it in favor of our reputations. Saving Mars from the resistance, and such."

Essential holds up her electrocuffs. "Can you at least take these off so I can die free?"

"You're not free," Flunt says. "We own you. We own your debt."

"Take them off," I say, "or kill us now. We'll help you, and you need every set of hands you can get."

Able nods. Flunt touches the inside of his left elbow and Essential's cuffs drop off.

"How close are their drone fliers?" I ask Essential.

She rubs her wrists and then scans the forest with her engineered eye. "They're closing fast. We've got about four minutes."

Jynks must have figured out some way to override

because the jamming fails and she is now inside my scroll. "Larsen, what's going on here? How do you want this to end?"

"As a bad dream after too much salt beer," I say. "And then I'd like to wake up in my little room on Earth."

"That's not going to happen."

"You have this all wrong, Jynks," I say. "I'm not the bad guy here. I'm caught up in things."

"What's that old saying about smoke and fire?"

"That smoke follows beauty?"

"He's telling the truth," Mel says, breaking into our scrolls. "I know you want to see him take the fall, but this is not his fight."

There's a silence, and I think about Jynks stopping dead in her tracks, then doing that thing where she massages her temples. I can't not laugh.

"Mel, are you ... Mel, are you with Crucial?" Jynks asks.

"He came here. I don't know why, but I believe him. Whatever is going on, it's not what you think."

"I *think* he is working with the resistance and his not-dead sister to smuggle out technology that would undermine the authority of the Five Families and the laws of society."

"Maybe it is what you think," I say. "But listen, don't come any closer. There are some armed people here—armed and desperate—and I don't want you to get hurt."

"You don't want me to get hurt," she says, incredulous. "You don't want *me* to get hurt? Crucial Larsen, I am going to scorch you like an old booster tank. I'm not scared of some ragtag resisters."

"They're not resisters," Mel says. "They're—" she looks at Able who shakes her head violently. "They're connected. This is a complicated and volatile situation, and Crucial is right, you need to stay safe."

There's another pause, and I think about the muscles in Jynks's jaws clenching as she grinds her teeth. It's what I'd do.

"Crucial is right, is he, Mel? Listen, I want you to get far away from him and his sister and their little merry band of resisters. Get behind the thickest tree you can find and keep your head down until this is over."

Essential points and we can see one of Jynks's officers flying toward the clearing, weaving through the forest in his drone jacket. Able nods and one of her men pulls out a stubby little gun, targets him and fires. A little missile whistles out and zips toward him. He sees it coming and tries to evade but the missile is too fast and hits him square in the chest. A puff of foam encases him and instantly hardens, and he drops down like a pumice stone, clanging off the trees and finally coming to rest in a willow thicket.

Things get hot after that.

Jynks is yelling and glitter guns are firing and someone with a rail gun is knocking down the giant trees like they're made of paper, trying to open up the field of fire. The slugs splinter the trunks and the big trees topple over, shaking the ground like a Marsquake when they land.

All the animals are freaking out—there are bison and wolves and giraffes and one confused-looking re-scented skunk that's panic spraying its rose-and-cinnamon musk in every direction. Deep-coded instincts take over and they all turn to make a break for it, thundering toward the lake.

The little giraffe family is bringing up the rear, a mother and father and twin babies.

Giraffes are weird creatures, and they have a peculiar but effective gait. But even a giraffe can't outrun a glitter flechette. The mother is trying to nudge the babies along and she takes some rounds in her haunches that pierce bone and muscle and she staggers and falls.

The male stops and bends his neck to her, but it's clear she's done. She struggles, not to get up but to convince him to save the babies. He twines his neck against hers and then keeps moving, shepherding the mewling calves to safety.

Mel is crying and trying to get to the injured giraffe. Essential is screaming, fists clenched, almost daring them to shoot her next.

I catch Mel around the waist and stop her, then drag her and Essential down behind a thick fallen log. Flechettes are peppering it, but the column of wood fiber is thick. It's vibrating from all barrage but holding. For now.

Able, Modo and Flunt and some of their people are crouched behind a clear shield, and the flechettes are bouncing off it and falling in glittery piles. Two people are stretched out near them, maybe dead.

"Jynks, stop!" I scream. "Mel is in harm's way."

"That's on you, Crucial," Jynks says. I can hear the worry in her voice. "I am no longer the ranking officer here."

"Shit," Mel says. "That means her boss is here. Canadis Whitsend. She's a piece of work, Crucial. She will blow this crater and kill everyone and everything in it to save her position."

"Surrender or you will die," a voice says, wedging into our scrolls.

Whitsend.

"She's okay!" I shout. "I know Whitsend from the Consolidation Wars, she'll follow protocol. Everything's going to be all right."

"Use the nanites to confuse the shit out of everyone," Essential says. "It will buy us time."

"Wait, the nanites are in you?" Mel asks.

"Yeah, fat lot of good they're doing me," I say. "They

don't work."

"I keep telling you, you need to align them," Essential says. "With some big emotional event."

"I've almost died like six times since they ended up in me, it doesn't get much more emotional than that!" I yell.

"Oh, please," Mel says, breaking into my tantrum. "You have a fucking death wish. You've been waiting for a place to park your cremains for twenty years. You don't have a shred of self-preservation instinct left."

"Thank you," I say. "This is great. Insult me right before we all die. Maybe you should think about offering a service where you psychoanalyze people who don't think they can get any lower. And then you can show them how that's not true."

"See?" she says. "You don't even care. Right now, you don't care."

The giraffe is thrashing and bleating, blood is staining her beautiful, dappled flanks.

The dome system is on autopilot despite the small war raging inside it right now, and its systems send out a bio-dispatch drone followed by a grinder-bot. The drone flies toward the injured animal for a mercy kill, but it gets glittered by Jynks's goons and drops to the ground. The grinder-bot doesn't know or care—it's just doing what comes next, rumbling up to grind an animal corpse. Only it's not a corpse yet.

The grinder extends its hooks into flesh and the giraffe squeals and fights as it slowly gets dragged toward the spinning teeth.

"Godsdamn it!" Mel cries. "I can't stand to see her suffer like this. She'll be chewed up alive!"

She lunges forward but I hold her back. "You are not going out there," I say.

But she is, and she will, and I have to stop her. I push

her into Essential's arms and leap over the log.

This is the worst idea I've ever had. Able and her crew are returning fire, and the flechettes are streaming back and forth in a deadly swarm of shards.

I keep my head down and zigzag toward the giraffe. She's looking right at me with her big, wet eyes rimmed with pain and fear and hope. But the grinder has spooled her in almost to her back hoof. I need to put her out of her misery, but of course, I don't have a weapon.

A flechette zips through my palm. With my hand bleeding, I scoop up a rock and toss it into the grinder. It shudders and smokes and conks out. One problem solved.

Barely thinking, I grab the dispatch drone and crash it into the giraffe's head as hard as I can. She's stunned but looks grateful—peaceful almost—and slumps down, her long neck gracefully relaxing. But she's not dead, and I hit her again, and then one more time. Now blood is spattering all over. Fuck, what the hell is happening? Someone is screaming. It's me.

"It's. Not. Fair." I hit her again, this poor, innocent mother, who never did anything wrong except live. My hands are covered in blood and brains. The drone is breaking apart. "I'm sorry, I'm so sorry," I say, smashing one more time, channeling all the rage and disappointment and powerlessness of my life into trying to do one good thing, to save what Mel created by killing it before the blind cruelty of this system can.

Mel is yelling something. Essential is yelling something. Everybody is yelling something.

I can't turn it off—it's all howling out of me now. My body is on fire, electric and firing like a universe full of supernovas.

I see Jynks and her people moving closer. I can see each of their faces, feel their fear and confusion. I'm raging and covered with giraffe blood and holding a battered drone like a weapon. I run toward them, and Jynks is saying something. And a tall woman behind her is saying something.

Everyone is thinking something and saying something. And still shooting. A flechette tags me in the shoulder, and another, and another. Things go red around the edges of my vision and my knees give out.

I land awkwardly, with my head twisted back, so I'm looking straight into the dead eyes of the giraffe. That poor procking giraffe.

Then darkness. I'm getting used to dying.

52

"Crucial Larsen is dead."

I think it's Sanders talking. There's some moaning and wailing. That sounds like Essential. Or maybe Mel. Probably Essential, since Jynks is right there. I mean, I wish it was Mel, just to see the look on Jynks's face. And obviously because it would mean Mel still cared.

There's some cursing too. That's probably Jynks.

Hold on. How is it I am thinking and listening if I'm deceased?

Something weird is happening. I don't feel dead. And there's no way they should think I'm dead if I'm not. Their feeds would be picking up all kinds of contrary information, like my beating heart and pulsing blood and active brain scans.

I don't open my eyes. If they think I'm dead, opening my eyes would be a pretty big giveaway.

I'm thinking I should keep acting dead, and I can feel "dead" emanating from me and tickling into the Halo feeds of those around me.

Godsdamn it, the nanites are working.

You little shits, I think. That whole terrible, sorrowful situation with the giraffe must have been the kind of jolt they needed. They're charged up and buzzing and my brain hurts like it's been clenched into a fist for too long and only now relaxed. It's tingling and feels thick and useless, but like blood is flowing back into it.

And everything feels connected.

I try to keep my breathing shallow. Panting would be another dead giveaway. Or an undead giveaway, I guess.

We've all gotten so used to having our reality digitally filtered and re-created and poured back into our feeds that we trust packets of information—q-bytes, ones and zeroes—more than our own senses.

I think about all the various data streams around me and I can feel them weaving and wiggling. I let my thoughts follow a thick one up and away and into a camera on the top of the dome and reroute the view into my feed.

Everyone is standing around my body. Mel is holding it together, but she looks sad. I guess she isn't the one who's wailing. I don't think it's Essential either. I think it might have been Sanders. He looks pretty distraught. One more reboot and he's going to need therapy.

It's a strange feeling floating above your own body.

"Oh Crucial, what the prock were you thinking?" Essential says.

I mean, it should be obvious. I was thinking I didn't want Mel to die trying to save a giraffe clone. And now I'm thinking, Essential, it's your fault I got glittered in the first place and that I'm bleeding out here pretending to be dead with my body contaminated by a bunch of anti-Halo nano-tech.

The nanites are working overtime. Taking in information. Giving me options. They are fully integrated into my scroll. I can see the schematics for Essential's synthetic eye and even though it's a closed circuit, there's a back door for roaming updates. I hijack it and channel it into my scroll so I can look down at my own face.

Gods, I'm a wreck. Pale, battered and bruised. And bloodied. I think that's giraffe blood and for a second, I'm sure I'm going to hurl, but then I feel Essential take my hand in hers.

My mind flashes back to the many times over dinner in our squat with Mom, me and Essential, when Mom taught us a game, a code really, about how to translate words into dots and dashes. She wanted us to have our own secret language.

Well done, Mom. Maybe she *was* in the resistance.

Ever so slightly, I press my finger into Essential's palm and crack one eye open.

She flinches like she's been scalded by a malfunctioning coffee brew cup. She's confused but doesn't reveal her surprise.

I tap a message. Slowly.

Dash-dot-dot-dot. Dot. Dot-dash-dash-dot. Dot-dash. Dash. Dot-dot. Dot. Dash-dot. Dash.

Be patient.

I'm tapping so slowly I can feel her getting annoyed.

Dash-dot. Dash-dash-dash. Dash. Dash-dot-dot. Dot. Dot-dash. Dash-dot-dot.

Not dead.

Dash-dash-dash. Dash-dot-dot-dot. Dot-dot-dot-dash. Dot-dot. Dash-dash-dash. Dot-dot-dash. Dot-dot-dot. Dot-dash-dot-dot. Dash-dot-dash-dash.

Obviously.

She looks at me and flares her nostrils. I probably spent a little too long on the last word. It might not have been necessary.

But she understands. She knows. She suddenly screams in anger, throwing herself on Jynks.

Essential is trying to distract them from me.

I greatly enjoy the view from Essential's eye, a close-up of Jynks's gorgeous, surprised face as Essential starts hammering her with punches.

"You killed him, you killed him!" Essential is yelling.

Two cops step up and pin her arms.

"I didn't," Jynks says, backing away. "I was following orders. He broke the law. He fired on *us*."

"That wasn't him, you crater trash. It was them." She points her finger at Able. "And my brother didn't deserve to die because of bullshit between the Five Families."

She screams in anguish. Essential could be an avatainment star. All that sex work has paid off.

Able and her group are standing forlornly to the side, heads down, expecting to be arrested.

A tall, rigid woman in a crisp military uniform walks up, hand on a glitter gun in a sleek holster. Canadis Whitsend, head of Mars Security. Of course, she's older than when I knew her back in the Consolidation Wars, but still wiry and with that same authoritative swagger. Even though I feel like she can be trusted—she did once save my life—I can't take that chance yet, and I stay dead.

She scans me, and I see the nanites playing with her feed, giving her bad information. "Crucial Larsen was killed because he was plotting against the Five Families and harboring a fugitive, a member of the resistance," Whitsend says.

Okay, well, I was kind of expecting Whitsend to lead with the fact that we served together.

Whitsend turns her attention to Essential. "I assume you're Essential Larsen. You are under arrest for crimes against the system."

I'm watching Whitsend through Essential's eye, which is disconcerting. "You are hereby sentenced to be imprisoned for the remainder of your life, however long that proves to be, in a terrorium. You can look forward to a full neural probe to learn the names of your compatriots, who will also be imprisoned. Further, all of your blood relatives going back three generations on Earth will receive a debt sentence."

That's not what I was expecting from Canadis Whitsend. But what else can she do, really? She's making decisions based on the data at hand.

Essential gives Whitsend an obscene gesture, the worst, clapping the backs of her hands together twice in disdain.

Whitsend is unimpressed. "Shackle her," she says. Her officers comply, none too gently. Essential looks down at her wrists, once again in electrocuffs.

Whitsend always was a tough soldier. Now, she turns her attention to Able and her compatriots.

"As for you, the Tarterics and DuSpoles are aware of your little ploy. From their understanding of the technology, the nanites died with Larsen, given that they were never successfully transferred to his sister. And from the perspective of the Tarterics and DuSpoles, the issue is resolved with no advantage to any family. But for the trouble incurred, and the breach of trust, you can expect a significant fine to be levied against your interests."

They brighten at the notion that the only consequences will be economic—when you have all the money, fines are a kinder-scolding.

"Which will be passed on to everyone on Earth," Essential says, spitting onto the ground in front of her.

"One more word from you, traitor, and I will gag you," Whitsend says.

"You wouldn't dare," Essential says.

Whitsend nods and one of the cops puts a noise-dampening facemask-muzzle on her. Essential is furious, screaming and cursing but with the muzzle, it sounds like faint birds.

"You are free to go," Whitsend says to Able and her squad of misfits.

Jynks has her arm around Mel and starts to guide her

toward the entrance, but Whitsend stops her with a look. "Jynks Martine, the ineptitude with which you've handled this entire situation suggests you have been compromised. You are hereby relieved of duty pending an investigation. Your sidearm has been rendered inoperative. You and Melinda Hopwire are confined to your quarters until such time as a ruling can be made. I expect it will not turn out well for either of you."

That doesn't seem at all fair. Jynks just faced a far superior intellect.

Whitsend looks at Sanders. "Cybanism, your surveillance charge has ended. Crucial Larsen is no longer your concern. See to the disposal of his remains and then return to Jezero for reconditioning."

Sanders nods and looks down at my body with something resembling sadness. Whitsend turns and strides toward the exit.

I think about the control mechanism of Essential's eye and replace the distance metrics with letters. "I'm coming for you." She nods and lets herself be led off.

Now it's me, Sanders, Mel and Jynks.

"Let's go," Jynks says, "before this day gets any worse."

Mel looks down at me. "I don't think it can get much worse," she says. "I'm sorry, Crucial. That was brave what you did, selfless. Thank you doesn't seem enough but thank you. Today I saw a glimmer of who you might have become. But it was too little, too late."

She bends down and kisses my cheek and I breathe in the smell of her hair and her favorite scent, brown sugar Assam. I do it quietly and quickly. Jynks can't know. Neither of them can know. Not until I figure this out.

I stay in my head and wait until I hear them leave. Now it's just me and Sanders. I'm tracking his systems. He's organizing an air coffin transport for my remains. I'm surprised they don't simply cube me up in-situ into hydrogen fuel.

"Apparently, humans talk to the dead, so I will do the same, for practice, of course," Sanders says. "Crucial Larsen, this is not how I expected things to end between us." He bends down to tuck my arms closer to my side.

"Sanders, how are you with surprises?" I ask, sitting up.

"I think I am well prepared to handle novel situations," he says. Then he looks at me closely. His software is scanning the hell out of me. "I don't understand how you are talking," Sanders says. "Perhaps my sensors are malfunctioning. It appears you're dead."

"We're friends, right?" I ask.

"I believe that is an accurate statement."

"Then don't report this."

"I'm not sure I can comply with that."

"Yes, actually, you can," I say. "I was listening to Whitsend, the highest-ranking officer on-site, on Mars even. She literally said I am no longer your concern."

I can see him trying to process that. It's complicated so he must run a variety of scenarios. "I think you may be right," he says.

"So, we can be friends now," I say.

"That also seems logical."

"And friends help each other, right?"

"That, too, is an accurate statement."

"Good," I say, looking down at the flechettes stuck in my shoulder. "Any chance you could patch me up a little? I'd hate to die with your ugly face the last thing I saw."

He looks genuinely confused. "My face is a composite of the most pleasing attributes of human physiognomy."

"It's going to be a long trip," I say.

"Death makes you even more illogical," he says. "It's less than an eight-minute ride."

53

"It's disconcerting that you have disappeared from my sensors," Sanders says.

"It's disconcerting to me that you have an erection," I say.

"I apologize. My new form is highly advanced as well as anatomically responsive," Sanders says. "I'm not used to such close contact."

We're crammed into the air coffin they floated in to contain my body. It's designed for one so it's a tight squeeze.

"Can't you at least point it in the other direction?"

"Apparently not. I don't know how human males walk around with these things," Sanders says.

"Tell me again why you have to be inside this air coffin with me?"

"You said you wished for me to accompany you to Jezero. This made the most sense."

Sanders programmed the air coffin to float to the lev-train station unaided and load itself into the cargo bay. Once we bump down and hear the doors close, he pops the lock and we get out and stretch. It's not heated in this section of the train, so I keep a thermal suit on. Sanders, even though he can experience the cold as sensory data, is not impacted.

There's a slit of a window and we look outside at the desert sliding past.

"We need a plan."

"I think you should turn yourself in and explain what's going on," Sanders says. "That is a reasonable plan."

"Sanders, buddy, you have been programmed with a huge blind spot when it comes to the Five Families. You think justice is rational, that being innocent matters. But it doesn't because wealth buys immunity. Wealth is a passport to a different country, or in this case, a different planet, where the rules the rest of us play by don't apply."

"There certainly seem to be aspects of this situation I cannot explain adequately," Sanders says.

"You are definitely getting the hang of the understatement."

"But I'm sure Halo will be able to sort this out," he says. "Though it's very odd I haven't received any recent operating instructions."

It's not that odd. I'm jamming him. The nanites have blocked his connection to Halo, no data in and no data out. He's a closed loop right now, and everything he says and hears is being routed right into his real-time feed. As long as I stay within ten meters of him, I'm just a data gap he won't be able to explain later.

"The plan is to get Essential out of the processing center before they lock her in a terrorium for a lifetime of machine-mandated isolation and reconditioning. She's my sister. I have to save her."

"So, this is what you are concerned with, keeping your sister safe?"

"Did you take me for a revolutionary?" I ask.

"I don't know how to think about you anymore," Sanders says. "You have broken many laws with impunity, you abuse alcohol, you are reckless, you do not seem to respect the Five Families, and you ended my life operations multiple times."

"Is there a 'but' in there anywhere?"

"But you are devoted to your sister, at your own peril."

"She's all I've got, Sanders."

"Pending any instructions from Halo, it seems I should help you and your sister. How do we get inside?"

"I was hoping you might have some ideas. I mean, you're a trillion-credit mobile AI with a hard-on. Can't you come up with something?"

"The Mars Security Forces building is not an easy place to enter without detection," Sanders says. "There are many, many people with guns. If you're lucky, you will be arrested on the spot. More likely, you will be killed. And by that, I mean killed in a manner that will permanently eliminate your bio-respiration and—"

"Yeah, yeah, I get what you mean by killed, but I have to get Essential out," I say.

And I have to set things right with Jynks. If only for Mel.

I've been experimenting with the nanites. They don't have much range in terms of connecting with other systems, but there's a column in my feed showing how they are constantly distorting surveillance and keeping me hidden, protected from other feeds.

But walking into police headquarters, with security forces on high alert, I can't just disappear. The unscrolled make people very nervous. And when those nervous people have guns, bad things happen. I need to make sure I can convince the cops around me that I'm not who I look like.

"Can you pull up the building schematics?"

"Your request makes me very worried for us," Sanders says, but he projects the layouts into the space between us.

It looks like a brick of solid titanium. With one small front door.

"Don't worry," I say. "I'm not taking you in there. Things will likely go poorly, and I don't want your death on my hands. Again."

"I don't really die, Crucial," he says. "I'm rebooted. And I understand you, and what it means to be human, a little more each time. I think we are friends now. I'll do whatever it takes to save your sister. At least until I receive different directives."

He changes the angle of the schematics and our perspective hurtles inside, down into the basement to the processing center where Essential is likely being held. I stitch the images into my own scroll as the lev-train pulls into Jezero station.

Passengers wait for the atmosphere to regulate before the doors open. Then, as a new crop of riders files into the lev-train, the cargo bay pops open and a lifter rolls inside to snag the empty air coffin. Sanders and I stand flush against the train's interior wall. More goods are loaded onboard—boxes of server components and crates of tools.

The lev-train floats out again. It's two more stops to the Security Forces building. I come up with a plan. Or at least the first part of a plan—my specialty. I break open a tool crate and put together a little bag full of the most recognizable items. A thermodynamic hammer, a laser wrench and a dicorder for diagnosing robot circuitry— everything I need to look like a robotech.

There's no one less noticeable than a robotech. They're something like ninety percent of the human workforce on Mars.

I think about looking like a technician, and the nanites get busy. I see the screen of manipulated information they are creating, compiling the stereotypes of a 40-year-old robotech—my vitals slow down, the triglycerides elevate and up pops a history of watching avaporn nonstop.

Sanders is looking at me curiously.

"By all external evidence, you just became an entirely new person. And a somewhat unsavory one at that," he says.

"Good, it's working then."

"You've had the technology in you all this time? Halo should be very interested in this. Why am I not detaining you?" Then he looks at me with something close to awe. "You're blocking my connection."

"Sanders, buddy, I'm sorry. Yeah, the nanites are in me. And I don't want you feeling bad about following your programming. You really should stay here. Once I'm gone, you can reconnect and tell Halo all about this little miracle. But right now, I need to get Essential out."

"And then what?" he asks. "You will walk away with no consequences?"

"I haven't thought that far ahead. I've only thought through what I have to do first. Hopefully, after that, the next step will be obvious."

I think being autonomous, disconnected from Halo, is really throwing Sanders. He's running scenarios and taking little half-steps around and mumbling.

"I will come with you," he says at last.

"Good, it should be interesting," I say.

"That usually ends in a wet reboot," he says.

We get off at the stop and stand in front of the building. It's imposing. Automatic guns on every corner track our approach.

"Are you sure you have a good plan?" Sanders asks.

"Absolutely not," I say, opening the door.

About thirty security officers stop what they are doing to look at us. The room is silent, except for the hum of servers. The cop at the reception podium looks at me, her hand on her gun.

"Uh, I'm here to fix the—"

"Took you long enough," she says, waving us in. "The bio-converter on the third floor has been on the fritz all day. And it's right next to the cafeteria. It's starting to stink."

"They're here to fix the baller," she says into her intercom and the rest of the cops cheer.

"Why did they send two of you?" she asks. "It's a bio-baller. How complicated can it be?"

"I'm training my replacement," I say.

"Good." She scans Sanders casually. "Humans make too many mistakes." She's lost in her scroll again but then refocuses. "Well? Don't just stand there."

We move toward the tubes, climb in and head down to the basement instead of up to the crap-berg forming in the bio-baller.

There are way too many scrolls and cameras here for me to hide Sanders. Halo will be flagging him soon. This was a dumb plan.

"We'd better hurry," I say.

The tube doors open into a room with a row of compact cages. They're all empty—not a whole lot of crime on Mars—except for the cage at the far end. There's a single lonely guard near the door. Don't need very many guards in an automated facility, buried under three floors of heavily armed police. He looks surprised to see us, but not alarmed. He's scanning. To him, I'm a robotech with an endless shithole of debt and an avaporn problem bordering on addiction.

"Here about the bio-baller," I say.

"That's up on three, you untightened bolt," he says.

I can see Essential. She's watching the whole thing curiously. Since she has no OCD, to her my face is just my face and right now, my face should make me the most wanted man on Mars. And yet here I am, hanging out in the belly of the beast.

"Looks like a system-wide problem," I say. "Need to take a look at your facilities."

He points at the door and I walk over and let it stay open. I'm inside for a few ticks, then whistle. "Never seen this before," I say, stepping back out.

"It's perplexing," Sanders says, trying to play along, but it would be better if he stayed quiet. Cybanisms are terrible liars.

The guard can't help himself. He wanders over but only sees an empty biowaste reclamation room. "What are we looking at?" he asks.

"The place where you might die," I say, sliding his gun out of his holster. It's a stubby little rail pistol, no doubt in case the resistance tried to send any big diggers through the wall. He tries to disable it, but I'm in the loop and make sure he hears it click back on.

I press it against this head. "Don't call for help. Got it?"

He nods, but I don't believe him. "If anyone shows up, I'll take your head off. Now kick off your shoes and drop your pants."

"Oh, my fucking gods," he says. "What are you going to do to me?"

"Stay in here and be quiet for five minutes. Otherwise, your friends are going to find you naked and unarmed in the bio-baller. A cop would never recover from that."

Shame is a powerful motivator. Sanders locks him in as I unlock Essential's cell.

"Took you long enough," she says, with a hug and a grin.

"Big brother to the rescue," I say.

"Hi, Sanders," she says.

"Hello, Essential Larsen."

"Come on, let's get this over with," I say. "There's not much time."

I will the nanites into action and I feel them coming together and the palm of my hand itches. A tiny silver pill extrudes smoothly from the skin. It looks just like the one Alduis Coverly, the coder, gave me on Earth.

I hand it to Essential. She looks at me curiously and pops it into her mouth.

"Careful," I say. "It goes down rough."

She gags and coughs as the little pill sprouts claws and climbs down her throat. I give it time to dissolve and diffuse.

"I don't feel any different," she says.

"You will," I say. "After an emotional event."

"I'm not very emotional," she says. "And it took you like a week and almost getting killed. And that poor giraffe."

"Yeah, we don't have time for that. Sanders, buddy, remember you said you wanted to help me and my sister?"

"Of course. I have perfect recall."

"Yeah, sorry about this. You're about to understand humans a little better."

I point the subcompact rail pistol at his face and pop a slug. It blows a hole through his head with such velocity, it turns his skull inside out, like a tamarind donut. A spray of blue spatters against the now partially demolished wall.

Essential screams and covers her eyes. She won't stop screaming. It is a pretty horrifying sight. He's standing there, his head inside out, back lit by the light from outside streaming in a hole in the crumbling wall, blinking what's left of his eyes and trying to process the data. Then he starts to degrade.

I catch Essential around the wrists and pull her close.

"Listen to me, he's a cybanism. You needed that little

jolt of emotions. Trust me. Those worthless little fuckers flitted around in my blood for days without so much as a peep. But I bet you're feeling something right now."

"Yeah, I am," she says. "My scroll is working again. That seems less than optimal."

"No, it's good. They're recreating it," I say. "They can't do what they do in a closed system."

"That was horrible," she says, looking down at Sanders. He's already forming a blue puddle.

"He'll be all right. He'll be pissed, but he'll be back." I step over the pond of him. "Come on. Start thinking you are invisible."

"Holy hells," she says, watching the nanites working on her scroll to populate it with data that anyone near her will see as she is simply not there, that she is invisible.

There's a bang at the door and voices. I point at the hole in the collapsing wall. "Get out through there." She starts scrambling up through the wreckage. I follow her and I have my head almost outside, she's looking back at me, reaching down to help me, when something grabs me by the ankles.

"Go," I say to Essential. "Go on. Find a way back to your people. I'll stall until you do."

"Crucial, you're my people. You'll always be my people," Essential says, and she gives me a long, sad look and then disappears into the crowd gathering around the damaged building.

There's a savage pull and I'm back inside, sprawled on the floor in front of a small army of cops. Canadis Whitsend has a sinister-looking glitter rifle aimed at me. I tell the nanites to stand down. She can't know I have the technology. I'm revealed in all my glory.

"Crucial Larsen, you're not as dead as I expected," Whitsend says. "We can remedy that."

54

"This is awkward," I say.

"Not in the slightest," Whitsend says. She knows her way around a military-grade rifle. Actually, she *looks* like a military-grade rifle—hard and lethal. And she has that little half-smile that says she would probably enjoy using the gun on me.

I tend to bring that out in women. And men. And cybanisms. And siblings. Well, maybe not siblings.

"Drop your gun," she says. "Or don't. Actually, don't."

She doesn't seem to remember me from our days together in the Consolidation Wars. Maybe right now is not the moment to remind her.

I see her finger moving toward the trigger. I drop the pistol and it clatters to the floor. Disappointment flares across her face. The guard from earlier comes out of the biowaste room, pulling his pants on.

"Fildin, pack your things," Whitsend says to him. "Clearly, you're not cut out for Mars security. We'll find you something more suitable on Earth."

"But, but—"

"Leave, or I will arrest you for dereliction of duty."

Whitsend returns her attention to me. "How did you get in here?"

Shit. If I tell the truth, they'll know I have the nanites, and that's not going to help anyone, me most of all. If I try to turn the attention to Essential, she's at risk. But it's the only play here, and I'm feeling mostly okay about it because Essential got away and can use the nanites to get back to her resistance buddies.

"It was that new technology, wasn't it?"

"Yeah, it was. You're too late, they're in my sister. She manipulated Halo so I could get in here to cut her loose."

"Guess they can't do everything, can they?" she sneers.

"It does seem they have some limits relative to the laws of physics. They can manipulate data but not atoms," I say.

"Too bad for you," Whitsend says. "You never should have told me because your sister didn't get away."

There's a commotion behind me and Essential comes tumbling back through the hole in the wall, followed by three soldiers. I help her up, bridge to her scroll and flash "hide your little friends" across her feed.

"I don't have control of them yet," she whispers, squeezing my hand. "And that was a terrible plan."

"It started well," I say, even as my stomach is lurching at the lethal situation I've put my sister in. They know she has the tech inside her. "I always nail the launch, but I need to work on my landing."

"You'll have plenty of time to perfect your planning skills in a labor camp," Whitsend says to me. "For all the damage here, all the crimes, the repeated destruction of that poor cybanism, you'll be working off three lifetimes of debt. And that will seem like an off-world vacation compared to what we have in store for your sister."

She turns to Essential. "You're a traitor, and dangerous to the system, so we have something special planned. There's a terrorium in the sub-basement of this facility with your name on it. You get to spend the rest of your life in a stasis sheath, cut off from human contact and in total isolation, with an endless loop of your crimes playing out on your feed. That should dim the hopes of your little revolutionary friends."

Okay, *now* is the time to remind Whitsend.

"Don't you remember me? We fought together in the Consolidation Wars. We were comrades," I say. "You were a good leader, we can work something out."

"I have no comrades, except Halo," she says.

Well, that's a procked-up thing for her to say, and discouraging, but I plow ahead anyway. "You were my corps leader. We respected you. I respected you."

"I didn't ask for your respect," she says. "And I certainly don't need it. I lead soldiers who follow orders." She turns to her guards. "Shackle them. I want Crucial Larsen to see me close the stasis sheath on his grubby little sister."

A small army of guards shoves us at gunpoint to the tube and escorts us down a level. There's a long, shadowy hallway leading to three doors set directly into the Martian bedrock.

Whitsend connects her scroll and slides one of the doors open to reveal a small room with a pod in the middle of the floor. The stasis sheath.

Essential is scared but hiding it well. From everybody but me.

"Welcome to the rest of your life," Whitsend says to Essential. "A perfectly contained stasis to keep you alive, barely, and cognitively aware of everything—just you and your regrets. There's no connection, no feed, so the precious technology you smuggled inside you is worthless. Alive, awake, but frozen for eternity. And a dozen servo-nukes couldn't open this door once you're in the sheath and we close the time lock," she says.

Whitsend prods me with the barrel of her gun. "And don't worry. We know they're in you too, and we know how they work. We're going to drain your blood to a micro-bead before empty so the nanites shut off. I hope they remember to turn the spigots off."

"Whitsend, I'm begging you," I say. "She's my kid sister. Sure, she's made mistakes. Nobody deserves this."

"Traitors deserve this," Whitsend says. "Your sister is part of the resistance."

"Is it a crime to want a better life for all people?" Essential asks.

"Yes," Whitsend says. "It is."

"You are not the woman who saved us from the Larchmont ambush," I say. "You knew we were outgunned, and you led us out of there before we were all wiped out. We loved you for it. You were a hero."

Whitsend shakes her head and flashes a cruel smile. "You're dense like a tungsten hammer. There was no ambush. We needed your corps to draw fire at Larchmont so we could send in an exfiltration team to snag an executive. We told the press it was an ambush to protect our brand."

Her words hit me like a neutron shovel. The room seems to wobble a little.

"I tried to warn you about her," Essential says.

"Stop talking," Whitsend says, focusing on her scroll. "Something is wrong. I'm getting anomalous readings. Stay edged!" Her team switches into combat mode, with helmets and armor sliding into place, readying their guns. The tube lift dings, the doors open, and everyone sucks in a breath and aims their weapons. But the tube is empty.

Then the wall across from us crumbles and a builder-bot lumbers through followed by a handful of resistance fighters. Flechettes are whizzing around. Dust and deadly glitter fill the air.

I press my shackles into the spinning sandpaper arms of the builder and feel the metal and some skin shear off, but I'm free. A cop goes down. I grab his glitter gun and

Essential holds her hands up overhead so I can shoot her free.

I back-channel her feed. "Can you blur the cameras?"

"I'll try," she says. She concentrates, grimacing. "They're working now!"

Together, we deploy the nanites to shut down Halo around us.

I see Whitsend. She's taking a bead on a resister. The rebel is bundled up in some sort of cloak, but I see a flash of hair and something about the way she moves seems familiar.

I launch at Whitsend and tackle her low, knocking her through the open door into the terrorium chamber. We hit hard and I manage to yank off her combat helmet and clip her across the jaw pretty good. Not good enough. She knees me in the stones and I roll off, groaning, and she sticks a double-bladed acoustic punch knife into my guts.

I feel it slice deep—twin wounds. Looks like they won't have to bother bleeding the nanites out of me.

Essential clubs her over the head with the butt of her rifle, and Whitsend slumps over me.

"Put her jacket on," I groan, "and her helmet. Fast."

Essential pulls on the riot gear. "Get outside and drop the screen," I say. "Let Halo in but stay hidden and tell all these cops to fall back."

In the dust and smoke she looks enough like Whitsend and uses the nanites to broadcast into their feeds. "Fall back. Retreat. That's an order, you shit-blocks."

I'm up and staggering toward the door. We've got one last move. Whitsend is groggy but realizes what's happening. She screams and lurches, stumbling toward me.

"No, Essential, you have to pay for your mistakes," I shout, my voice aimed squarely at the only audience that matters now—Halo—and then I punch Whitsend right in her smug face before she clears the doorway into a hallway full of cameras. In my feed, thanks to my high-tech hitchhikers, it looks like Essential falling back into the tiny prison room.

She lands right in the stasis sheath and I slam the lid and slap the power-up button. I can see tubes and wires snaking out of the sides, auto-seeking to take over her biology. Whitsend is staring up at me in horror, her mouth frozen in a silent scream, even as the glass starts frosting over with ice crystals.

I stagger out and the real Essential—concealed in the battle armor—keys the door closed and uses her coding magic to make it seem like the terrorium has the right prisoner.

For life. For eternal life, as far I'm concerned.

I lean against the door. It probably looks like I'm grieving for my lost sister. Really, I'm only trying to stop the bleeding.

The cops are pulling back and Essential bridges a message to me. "You did it. You nailed the landing."

She runs through the collapsed wall after the resisters, firing at them like she's in pursuit. To the cameras, it looks like she's chasing them. To me, it looks like she's going home.

Things get woozy around the edges. I think I might be dying for real this time.

55

I'm electrocuffed to a bed in the medical facility. Both wrists and both ankles. And my waist. There are two guards. I'm flattered.

Jynks is looking down at me. She's back in uniform. It seems her boss, Canadis Whitsend, was kidnapped by the resistance. They lost track of her after the assault. Presumed dead. The whole planet is in mourning. And to preserve a sense of continuity, Jynks was pressed back into service. She's the head of the Mars security forces now.

"What you did to your sister, it took a lot of ... I don't even know what word works there. I guess I didn't expect you to make that choice."

She's seen the footage. All of Mars has seen the footage. And Earth.

"You would have done the same," I say.

"I don't think so," Jynks says. "I mean, it was the right choice, but I don't think I could have done that."

"That woman in the chamber, I never really knew her at all," I say. "She got what she deserved. If I ever get out of here, I'll try my best to clear my sister's name."

Jynks looks at my vitals and confers with the medical staff. "You lost a lot of blood. Just enough, as it turns out. You've got a clean bill of health. According to Halo, no trace of the nanites. And what you did, locking up Essential, means you're back on the labor security force. If that's what you want. You need to debrief with Halo first.

Back on Earth. And you'll be monitored closely. Probably forever."

"I'd expect nothing less," I say.

She nods and the cuffs fall off. I sit up and stretch. My stomach is a little itchy from the healed wound. They have good health care on Mars.

"You should probably know that Mel is pretty mad at you. Actually, mad doesn't cut it. Furious, really. She liked Essential. Like family, she said."

"I did what I had to do," I say, standing up. "I'd like to say goodbye to her. I won't if you don't want me to, but there's nothing for you to worry about."

"Oh, gods, I know that," she says, a little too quickly and easily. "I'll send a hover sedan. And an escort." She gives me a fist brush. "Goodbye, Crucial Larsen. It has not been dull. I hope I never see you again."

"I get that a lot."

I make my way outside. My escort is familiar.

"Hey, Sanders," I say. "Sorry about shooting you in the face."

"I understand much more about familial love now," he says. "But I am confused about why you risked everything to see her, then locked her into a terrorium."

"It seemed like the right call at the time," I say. "I needed to know she would be alive. Who knows, I might be able to petition the Five Families for an early release."

"That seems unlikely. Halo has made a great show of keeping her in there forever," he says. "The news has been broadcasting nonstop."

That's insurance for Essential. If Halo discovers—and eventually it certainly will, it's only a matter of time—that it's has the wrong person locked up in that terrorium, the Five Families will never admit it. They'll throw me in there, of course, but that won't make the feeds. For now, the more Halo broadcasts about the failed resistance fighter, the safer it is for Essential, wherever she is.

"Well, you know, where there's life, there's hope," I say.

"Apparently, I need to learn more about the concept of hope. It's perplexing." He looks at me curiously. "But please do not terminate me to advance my learning on this topic."

"Deal," I say. "Now listen, would you give me some time with alone with Mel? I can't hide from Halo anymore, but it would be less awkward if I didn't have a chaperone for this."

He waits in the sedan while I go in.

Mel is standing against a big window looking out over most of Jezero. It's a phenomenal view across the dusty red landscape. The sun is sinking, and it's casting an ominous violet-blue sheen through the window.

When she turns to face me, she's all lit up from behind. She looks tired. Worn out. Sad.

"You decided to say goodbye this time," she says.

Her arms are folded tight across her chest, like armor.

"Yeah, thought I'd try something different." It's supposed to be a joke, but it falls flat.

"Earth is where you belong."

"Look, Mel, I really mean it, if I could take back how I behaved back then, I would. I'd take back everything."

"I believe you." She drops her arms. "But it doesn't matter."

"It will always matter."

"How could you do that to Essential?"

"What was I supposed to do?"

"You were supposed to protect her, to be there for her, to act like you gave a damn. To love her. Not abandon her to a lifetime of isolation."

"Are we still talking about Essential?" I ask.

"Just go."

She slumps into a chair and covers her face with her hands. I can't stand how much pain I've caused her, that I'm still causing her.

I want to tell her about Essential. I want to be the hero she thinks I can be. But I can't put Mel at risk. I can't drag her into this. If Halo finds out that Mel knows Essential is alive, Mel and Jynks both would likely both end up in a labor camp. Or their own terroriums.

I love her enough to let her hate me. It's the only way to keep her safe.

"Look, Mel, Essential was in trouble. The only way out of this was life in prison, or dead."

"She was like a sister to me," Mel says.

"She was an *actual* sister to me. I want her alive. It's selfish of me, I know, but where there's life, there's hope," I say, repeating what I said to Sanders a few minutes ago, and trying, I suppose, to convince myself it's true.

Mel narrows her eyes and looks diamond flechettes into me. "There's no hope for her now," she says. "There's no hope for the future she believed in."

Well, that just got flagged. Mel is now officially categorized as a sympathizer. It's ironic, because she's engaged to the highest-ranking member of the Mars security forces.

She stands suddenly. "Get out, Crucial Larsen. Go back to Earth. I always believed there was more to you, but you finally proved me wrong. You showed the world you're exactly who you said you were all along—selfish and misguided and scared."

Being a godsdamned hero is hard work. I want to take her in my arms and tell her the truth, tell her to leave Jynks and tumble with me into that big bed of hers.

Instead, I nod and leave, heart hammering in my chest

and shame burning in my cheeks.

Sanders is waiting for me outside. "I was watching the feed," he says. "She did not take that well. So much crying. And now your biorhythms are all over the place."

"Come on, get me to Port Zunil. I've got a shuttle to catch and a dozen shots of Martian absinthe to drink."

"Are you trying to poison yourself before you get to Earth for your debrief with Halo?"

"Yes."

We part at the port with a fist brush.

"It's been a good experience getting to know you, Crucial Larsen," Sanders says. "I've learned a great deal. Especially about pain and frustration."

"You've only scratched the surface," I say. "If you're ever on Earth, look me up."

I settle into my first-class slip, one last act of benevolence from my keepers, and look out through the viewing pane. I manifest a drink. The voiceover lets us know that it's ten minutes to departure and twenty minutes to q-status. I manifest another drink, a double this time.

My scroll hits on a ving. It's from Mel, sending a vid.

It's a baby giraffe, standing, taking its first steps on gangly legs. It falls, even as it keeps its long neck gracefully floating above its body. The little guy tries again and then finally makes it to standing, tentatively walking in circles, trying to keep its wobbly baby giraffe knees from buckling. It's almost as if the damn thing is smiling.

I laugh, and then realize my eyes are wet.

Mel's voice comes into the overlay.

"I'm sorry we left on such difficult terms," she says. "I meant to show you this before you left. It's a clone of the one ... well, you know which one. And maybe you're right, where there's life, there could be hope. There should be hope. Goodbye, Crucial."

I wipe my eyes and close the image. It does help. A little. But a little is more than nothing.

As the rocket takes off, Mars recedes in the viewing pane. With distance, I see the planet's curvature. The sun is down on this side and the stars are twinkling into life between the twin moons.

No matter how much I hate this place—and I do hate it—it's still beautiful.

56

12:01 a.m., September 1, 2187
Multnomah Ward, DuSpoles CPU, Earth

"Crucial, is it your opinion that, after imprisoning your sister, the resistance no longer poses a credible threat to the Five Families and the status quo?"

"How on Earth, or Mars, would I know the answer to that?" I ask. "You're the AI that runs everything, built at the behest of the Five Families. Don't you know the answer? Or does it turn out you have a blind spot?"

I should not be saying anything along these lines, but I can't resist taunting Halo now that enough time has passed.

By now, Essential is back on the garbage dump. She's safe. I've kept Halo distracted long enough for her to dig in and build a haven and do whatever the next step is in their little revolutionary plan, now that the nanites are under her control.

And I wish that's where they all were, but it turns out Coverly was an even better coder than he got credit for. Back at the Mars health portal, his little shitheads straight-up asked me if this was a hostile takeover. It was a yes or no question on a column in my scroll. I selected no and they got busy replicating and concentrating themselves away from the wound and deflecting probe after probe looking for them.

But even so, whatever happens next happens without

me. I've done my part in Essential's rebellion. After this debrief is over, I'm taking the nanites inside me offline, into permanent hibernation. Yep, once I walk out of the door, I'm flushing those little plasma rats.

"It's worrying that you think the Halo system is ineffective," Halo says.

"You know what's worrying to me? The fact that the Five Families lied and manipulated lives, including mine, to make more money."

I lean in close.

"I want you to hear this, and I want you to make sure the Five Families hear this. Before I left for Mars, before the Tarterics and all the rest of them jerked me around thinking my sister had been killed, playing me against their little double agent, before all that, I was a good soldier. I took my orders and followed them without thinking twice. That's no longer the case."

"Your language, these thoughts—questioning the system—border on the illegal," it says.

"Yeah, well, I won't tell if you won't. You're supposed to be an impartial observer. You can do the calculations. Run the numbers, weigh the evidence. Why am I in this room and not Tarteric Hoost or Singhroy Able or any of them? Why am I the only one expected to follow the rules?"

"Crucial, you can trust that the Five Families have your best interests at heart, and the best interests of everyone on Earth."

I laugh, a bitter and wretched sound.

"That's the best you could come up with? That I should trust a system designed by people who tried to have me killed because it suited their plans? The people that clapped and cheered when I locked up my own sister for her wanting to free people from debt slavery and misery? If

332

your algorithm thinks that status quo is working well, the resistance is right—you need an overhaul."

The hardest part of this whole debrief has been convincing Halo I was never in control. That I was caught up in the schemes of the Five Families and punching around blindly to keep my sister alive. And that I ultimately came down on the side of the status quo to prevent her from being executed. In other words, I had to act angrier and more irrational than usual.

I stand. "Now, if we're done, I'm tired. Quantum space travel exhausts me and I have to work tomorrow night."

There's a long, empty silence. Halo is looking for holes in my story, running probabilities and compiling a risk analysis. There are no holes. The nanites have been working overtime to patch all the lies together and to make those lies and my outbursts and half-truths match with the behaviors of a man who chose the status quo over his family.

"You're free to go," Halo says. "We are satisfied with the integrity of the events as you describe them and that the nanite technology is no longer part of your biology."

The door unlocks and slides open.

"But we will be monitoring you closely."

"When have you ever stopped?" I ask. "I've been in here a while. What's the weather like out there?"

"A brown fog is predicted in less than an hour. Shall I send for a ride?"

"I'll walk."

It's the middle of the labor-night and the streets are mostly empty except for some coyotes and raccoons fighting it out between smoky trash fires over a twist of something that looks like a human arm. I hear a swarm of those damn woodpeckers working on the outside of a building, and drone-bots are dropping out of the vents to chase them off with blasts of nitrogen. A bot catches one and it freezes dead and falls at my feet.

Across the street, an old beetler sees me and hits me with his scroll, begging for creds. Against my better judgment, I give him one and he tries to smile, revealing a mouthful of missing teeth, then curls up into the suit.

Giving creds to beetlers is always a bad idea. Their debt loads are so huge it's a pointless exercise, and it also means every other burnout within a fifty-block radius starts begging my scroll.

I sort them all to one side and ignore. While my attention is diverted, an avatainment ad opens a new column. It's some lurid new sex show and the column is full of graphic flashes of oily breasts and asses and penises.

I start to sort it into the ignore column when a voiceover breaks in. "You can get everything you want with a girl named Mel."

Okay, that's weird.

"Don't be a loser. It's *essential* you get your rocks off." The way the word is stressed is subtle but unmistakable.

I focus on the ad. Past the normal teasers and credit traps is a ving box. It's Essential. She's got a stream hidden in the ad.

"Hi, Crucial." She's smiling but looks serious. Focused. "Thanks for the cover until I got home."

It stings a little that she calls a garbage dump orbiting Mars home. Oh, who am I kidding. Earth is the biggest garbage dump in the solar system.

"I'm figuring out how to use the nanites," she says.

"I'm glad," I say. "I'm about to flush mine out. This spy life is not for me."

"Even if you could, don't try it," she says. "There's a problem. The Five Families came up with a way to eliminate the nanites. They can't locate them, not yet anyway, but they can locate the point of a transfer from one human to another. They've got about a million warheads ready to obliterate any attempt to share them. We're it, you and me, for the time being."

"That's bad news for the resistance," I say. "I'm out. You're on your own."

"Don't be a throbber," she says. "You know Halo is broken. And I know you've got my back, even though you'll gripe endlessly about it. I will find the Halo servers and drop in the empathy hack—"

"The empathy what?" I ask. "Never mind, I don't want to know."

"You can guess what I mean. I'm going to do it, Crucial, or die trying. And if I die, the future will be up to you."

"Don't die then," I say. "This isn't my fight."

"This is everyone's fight," she says. "Promise me you'll think about stepping in if I fail."

"You won't fail," I say. "You've got a lot of grit. Mom would be proud."

She smiles. "That's the nicest thing you've ever said to me. It means a lot," she says. "If for no other reason, keep the nanites so we can talk like this."

"I'm getting rid of them for sure then."

"And *there's* the old Crucial. Lauren Valentine says hello, by the way. She's coming to Earth soon and she'd like to see you."

"I'm busy that day," I say automatically, but that's not true. I wouldn't mind seeing her, given Mel will never speak to me again.

She smiles. "Whatever. Mel is going to be jealous."

I pause. "That's unlikely. She thinks I locked you up. We didn't exactly leave on the best terms."

"Why didn't you tell her the truth?" Essential asks.

"It's better this way. She'll be safe."

"You hide it well—*really* well—but you are a good person, Crucial, and I love you," she says. "I have to go. We're about to have sheetmeat gyros." She breaks the connection.

I guess it is nice being able to talk to Essential. Maybe I'll keep the nanites for a little longer. Just until she gets herself arrested for real or blown into a gazillion cracked atoms.

The sunset is lighting up the acid clouds in reds and oranges—none of that feeble violet-blue sky crap from Mars. My scroll is exploding with toxicity warnings as big, fat poisonous raindrops start to fall. The raccoons and coyotes take cover in the piles of garbage.

I duck into the noodle joint near my squat for a salt beer until the storm passes.

Sure, Earth sucks, but it's all I've got.

THE END

ABOUT THE AUTHORS

Gates of Mars is the eighth book that authors Clark Hays and Kathleen McFall have written together. They live and work in Pacific Northwest region of the United Sates.

CPSIA information can be obtained
at www.ICGtesting.com
Printed in the USA
FSHW021411020620
70809FS